"SHE NEEDED HIM"

He wanted to oblige her. Damn, did he want to oblige her.

Casually, Stan moved closer to her until he invaded her space, and her alarm thumped louder with every beat of her heart. He left himself wide open to her, relishing each tingle she felt, absorbing each small shiver of excitement—and letting it excite him in return.

Reaching out, he brushed the side of his thumb along her jawline, up and over her downy cheek, tickling the dangling earrings that suddenly seemed damn sexy. "Maybe you need the iced tea," he murmured, his attention dipping to her naked mouth. Jenna never wore lipstick, and he liked the look of her soft, full lips glistening from the glide of her tongue. Oh, yeah, he liked that a lot. "You feel . . . warm, Jenna."

Her breaths came fast and uneven. "I've been . . . working."

And fantasizing. About him.

Delicious

LORI FOSTER
LUCY MONROE
SARAH TITLE

KENSINGTON PUBLISHING CORP.
http://www.kensingtonbooks.com

KENSINGTON BOOKS are published by

Kensington Publishing Corp.
119 West 40th Street
New York, NY 10018

All Kensington Titles, Imprints, and Distributed Lines are available at special quantity discounts for bulk purchases for sales promotion, premiums, fund-raising, and educational or institutional use. Special book excerpts or customized printings can also be created to fit specific needs. For details, write or phone the office of the Kensington special sales manager: Kensington Publishing Corp., 119 West 40th Street, New York, NY 10018, attn: Special Sales Department, Phone: 1-800-221-2647.

Kensington and the K logo Reg. U.S. Pat. & TM Off.

ISBN-13: 978-0-7582-9525-5
ISBN-10: 0-7582-9525-1
First Kensinton Mass Market Edition: December 2013

eISBN-13: 978-0-7582-9526-2
eISBN-10: 0-7582-9526-X
First Kensington Electronic Edition: December 2013

10 9 8 7 6 5 4 3 2 1

Printed in the United States of America

ONCE IN A
BLUE MOON

Lori Foster

One

Lunacy, that's what they'd call it. Pure, plain, lock-em-up-and-throw-away-the-key lunacy. And all because of a stupid moon—the second *full* moon in July. If anyone knew, they'd label him crazy for sure. Not that he planned to tell anyone. He'd tried that once as a kid, and everyone had had a freakin' shit fit, so no more.

But damn it, why now, when he had a full week of landscaping work, a book deadline, and a newspaper interview to get through?

As Stan Tucker walked down the clean sidewalk of Delicious, Ohio, enjoying the fresh air and bright sunshine of July, he did his best to block the voices. Not much of a problem there since most people's thoughts were boring as hell. Grocery lists, appointments, and work woes vied with guilt, jealousy, and self-pity. It amazed him that mankind didn't have more important things to think about.

He ran a hand through his hair, mussing it worse than half a day's work and uneasy breezes had already done. Dirt and noticeable sweat stains covered his shirt, and dried mud clung to his boots. But despite his occasional celebrity status, he still worked hard, and if the

interviewer didn't like it, he could take a hike. His pub-
licist would snarl and groan, but Stan just plain didn't
care.

As he passed people on the sidewalk, more voices
battered his already fractured senses. Stan narrowed
his eyes, again tuning them out. It didn't take much effort to put their private thoughts, their personal conversations, on hold, but it bugged him that he had to bother.
He'd hoped that moving to Delicious, away from the
crowds and human congestion, would help. But thanks
to the approach of the full moon, the second in this
month, he'd become privy to the introspection of all who
got close to him, and not a one of them had a thought
worth hearing.

Disgusted, he shoved open the fancy, etched-glass
double doors of the small bookstore, The Book Nook,
owned by Jenna Rowan. The bookstore was across
Jonathan Avenue and up one building from his garden
center. Stan owned several acres that backed up to
Golden Lake, with his home next door to the garden
center. A short jaunt would take him to the town square
and the fancy fountain erected by the citizens long before he'd moved in.

Thanks to the apple trees growing wild around the
lake, the town's structures had some whimsical names,
including the Garden of Eden Salon, Johnny Appleseed
Museum, and Granny Smith's Apothecary. Old Orchard
Inn, a charming but outdated B&B and restaurant,
used the apple trees on their lot for daily fare offered to
the guests. In the afternoon you could smell the scents
of cooking applesauce, apple pie, and apple cider.

Stan appreciated the novelty of Delicious as much
as the laid-back, easy pace.

The second he entered The Book Nook, chilled, condi-
tioned air hit his heated face and the scent of fresh cinnamon got pulled deep into his lungs. Stan liked The

Book Nook, every tidy shelf, polished tabletop, the scents, the colors . . . and the proprietor. Yeah, he especially liked her.

As usual, his gaze sought out Jenna, and he found her toward the back aisle, stocking new books on a shelf. Today she wore her honey blond hair twisted into a sloppy loop, clipped at the back of her head with a large gold barrette.

He soaked in the sight of her, making note of her long floral dress and flat leather sandals. He'd known Jenna about six months now, ever since he'd moved to Delicious to escape the chaos of Chicago. Thanks to him, her bookstore had become a tourist attraction, not that she gave him any special attention for it.

Jenna treated everyone, young and old, male and female, with a sort of maternal consideration that never failed to frustrate him. He wanted her, but she saw him only as a friend.

In nature and appearance, Jenna was the sweetest thing he'd ever met, caring and protective of one and all. He liked the fact that she was near his age, close to forty. She'd been widowed about three years now, yet she never dated, never gave any guy—especially not him—more than a friendly smile and platonic attention. With just the smallest encouragement from her, he'd make a move.

But she never encouraged him.

When he released the door, the bell chimed, and Jenna glanced up. Dangly earrings moved against her cheek, drawing attention to a dimple that formed when her mouth kicked up on one side. "Hello, Stan. All ready for your interview?"

She straightened, and the dress pulled taut over her sumptuous behind and thighs. Unlike younger women he knew, Jenna had a full figure meant to attract men. Feeling strangely intense, Stan strode toward her and for a moment, only a single moment, he forgot to bar the thoughts bombarding his brain.

Like a clap of thunder, Jenna's nervousness struck him, but at the same time, giddy excitement rippled . . . and clear as a bell, he saw what she saw: him naked, sweaty, fucking—

Staggered, Stan drew up short. Her thoughts were so incredibly vivid that his jaw clenched and his stomach bottomed out on a rage of sexual desire.

Watching him, Jenna licked her lips and smoothed her skirt with visible uneasiness. "Stan? Are you all right?"

Incredible. She looked innocently concerned when Stan knew good and well what she'd been thinking. About *him*.

Why had she never let on?

As he continued to stand there, staring hard, absorbing her wanton musings, she laughed. "What is it? What's wrong?"

Her thoughts were so evident to him, he saw them with the same color and clarity of a moving picture. *Her stomach was quivering, deep inside her, down low* . . . Jesus. Out of self-preservation and to prevent a boner, Stan attempted to block her thoughts. Muscles tight, he took a step back, distancing himself physically as well as mentally.

It didn't help. Sensation continued to roll over him with the effect of a tactile stroke. "Nothing's wrong." Except that he was suddenly turned on and they were in a public place and he had an interview to do any second now.

Her smile faltered. Her gaze skimmed down his body, over his crotch, then jerked upward again. "It's probably the heat, then."

He hadn't suffered an unwanted erection since his teen years!

As casual and natural as ever, pretending she hadn't noticed the bulge in his jeans, she breezed out of the aisle and strode past him. Buttons marched up the front of her dress, from the hem to a scooped neck, and she'd left several undone all the way to her knees. With her long stride, the dress fanned out around her, showing smooth, shapely calves and a sexy ankle bracelet. "Would you like something to drink? I've just made lemonade. Or we have tea, of course."

Lemonade? No, he wanted her. Right now. Maybe on the counter or up against one of the book aisles. Watching the sensual sway of that sweet behind, he almost missed her panicked thought. *Oh, God. Did he see me looking at him?*

He soaked in her response to him—and knew that he'd have to have her. Soon. Tonight if he could manage it. Hell, if she'd shown even the slightest interest, they'd already be intimately involved. But she hadn't. She kept her attraction to him private, so private that if it weren't for the blue moon, the second full moon this hot July, he still wouldn't have a clue.

She glanced over her shoulder, innocence personified. "Stan?"

Oh, she was good. "Tea." He drew a calming breath and said belatedly, "Thanks."

How should he proceed? They weren't teenagers. Hell, at forty, it had been a long time since he'd done any serious flirting. Before leaving Chicago, he'd known several women who wanted no more than he did—a good time with someone safe, and no commitments.

When they wanted him, they let him know. Or vice versa. There was no mind reading, no guessing, no need to use his rather rusty skills at wooing.

But that was before he'd moved to Delicious. Before he'd met Jenna. Before he'd even really known what he wanted.

Now he knew.

Jenna was different from other women, certainly different from the women he'd been with in the past. She was the commitment type. She'd been married, and by what he'd heard from the gossiping denizens of Delicious, her marriage had been a very happy one.

Watching while she poured tea into a tall glass of ice, Stan cautiously approached. Jenna always kept fresh drinks and cookies for the neighbors who visited her store. Book shopping at The Nook was more like visiting a favored relative, one who pampered you and made you feel special.

Everyone spoke to her, spilling out ailments and troubles or sharing news good or bad. And when Jenna listened, you got the feeling she really cared. When she said, "How are you?" she meant it.

Did she care about him?

If he kept listening to her very sexual thoughts, he'd end up climbing over the counter to show her just how hot the reality would be. Knowing she wouldn't like that, he tried distracting himself. "Where's the reporter?"

Jenna drew a deep breath, and no way in hell could he not notice that. Even nearing the big Four-Oh, she still had one of the best racks he'd ever seen. Her breasts were heavy, but suited her sturdy frame. She wasn't a frail woman, but rather one with meat on her bones. Shapely in the extreme, sexy as hell. . . . His gaze zeroed in on her chest and got stuck there.

"He, ah, ran to the drugstore to buy new batteries. He should be here in just a few minutes."

Stan's gaze lifted and locked with hers. Sensation crackled between them. His awareness of her as a sexual woman ratcheted up another notch. Even without hearing her thoughts, what she wanted from him, with him, would be obvious to any red-blooded male. Heat blazed in her eyes and flushed her cheeks. A pulse fluttered in her pale throat. Her lips parted . . .

Amazing. A mom of two, a quiet bookworm, a woman who remained circumspect in every aspect of her life—and she lusted after him with all this wanton creativity.

Not since the skill had first come to him when he was a kid of twelve, twenty-eight years ago, had Stan so appreciated the strange effect the blue moon had on him. It started with the waxing Gibbous, then expanded and increased as the moon became full, and began to abate with the waning Gibbous. But at midnight, when the moon was most full, the ability was so clean, so acute, that it used to scare him.

His parents didn't know. The one time he'd tried to tell them they'd freaked out, thinking he was mental or miserable or having some kind of psychosis. He'd retrenched and never mentioned it to them again.

When he was twenty and away at college, he signed up for a course on parapsychology. One classmate who specialized in the effects of the moon gave him an explanation that made sense. At least in part.

According to his friend, wavelengths of light came from a full moon and that affected his inner pathogens. With further studies, Stan had learned that different colors of lights caused varying emotional reactions in people. It made sense that the light of a full moon, twice in the same month, could cause effects.

In him, it heightened his sixth sense to the level that he could hear other people's tedious inner musings.

Now he could hear, *feel,* Jenna's most private yearnings, and for once he appreciated his gift. Nothing tedious in being wanted sexually. Especially when the level of want bordered on desperate.

She needed a good lay. She needed him.

He wanted to oblige her. Damn, did he want to oblige her.

Casually, Stan moved closer to her until he invaded her space, and her alarm thumped louder with every beat of her heart. He left himself wide open to her, relishing each tingle she felt, absorbing each small shiver of excitement—and letting it excite him in return. He no longer cared that he had a near-lethal erection.

Reaching out, he brushed the side of his thumb along her jawline, up and over her downy cheek, tickling the dangling earrings that suddenly seemed damn sexy. "Maybe you need the iced tea," he murmured, his attention dipping to her naked mouth. Jenna never wore lipstick, and he liked the look of her soft, full lips glistening from the glide of her tongue. Oh, yeah, he liked that a lot. "You feel . . . warm, Jenna."

Her breaths came fast and uneven. "I've been . . . working."

And fantasizing. About him.

Lazily, Stan continued to touch her. "Me, too. Out in the sun all day. It's so damn humid, I know I'm sweaty." His thumb stroked lower, near the corner of her mouth. "But I didn't have time to change."

Her eyelids got heavy, drooping over her green eyes. Shakily, she lifted a hand and closed it over his wrist—but she didn't push him away. "You look . . . fine." *Downright edible.* She cleared her throat. "No reason to change."

Stan's slow smile alarmed her further. "You don't mind my jeans and clumpy boots?" He used both hands now to cup her face, relishing the velvet texture of her skin. "They're such a contrast to you, all soft and pretty and fresh."

Her eyes widened, dark with confusion and curbed excitement, searching his. He leaned forward, wanting her mouth, needing to know her taste—

The bell over the door chimed.

Jenna jerked away so quickly, she left Stan holding air. Face hot, she ducked to the back of the store and into the storage room, closing the door softly behind her.

Well, hell. He'd probably rushed things, Stan realized, aware of her exaggerated embarrassment. But holding back had been impossible. Especially with her desire so clear to him—giving permission to his desire, leaving the way wide open for some mutual satisfaction.

With her in another room and the reporter looming, Stan's focus on Jenna was diluted. He caught the garbled mental intrusion from the reporter and blocked it.

Teeming with frustration, he readjusted himself within the confines of his stiff jeans and then faced the reporter, who luckily had his attention on his recorder as he snapped in batteries. "Sorry I'm late," he called out without looking up. "Batteries died."

The sooner he got the interview over, the sooner he could get back to Jenna. Stan strode forward. "No problem, but let's make it quick, if you don't mind. I have a lot to do today."

From behind her counter, Jenna Rowan watched Stan on the pretense of listening to the interview. Stan might be a renowned landscaper, author of several best-selling gardening books, and an expert businessman now featured on the local radio station every Saturday morning, but it was his colorful past that made him a favorite among the media.

For years, Stan Tucker had wavered in and out of trouble. As a much younger man, he'd narrowly missed spending time in jail. He'd been married and divorced, a celebrated playboy, and now . . . he planted flowers.

Jenna sighed softly. She had no doubt Stan could retire comfortably, but his extreme energy level forced him to always do something, to be active, in the sun, sweating, working his muscles . . .

Oh, she knew what he could do with her—if only he were interested. How he'd use that energy in bed teased at her senses every time he got near. To call Stan handsome would be very misleading. He was far too raw, too rough, to be termed anything so pretty. He could appear cruel—wow. Like he did now, glancing at her with those fierce eyes as if he knew her thoughts and didn't like them one bit.

Hands shaking, Jenna pretended to straighten the paperwork behind her counter. In truth, she couldn't seem to keep him off her mind. Maybe the idea of turning forty next month had caused her hormones to go on a rampage. Or maybe three years of celibacy was three years too long. Whatever the cause, she wanted sex. Hot, gritty, sweaty sex.

With Stan.

She craved it, aching with the need at night in her lonely bed, unable to sleep. Whenever she daydreamed, which lately seemed to be all the time, it was Stan Tucker she saw. In his prime, he had thick but natural muscles and undeniable strength. His light brown eyes looked almost golden at times. Working in the harsh sunshine had streaked his brown hair that was usually unkempt and so sexy she wanted to touch it.

She wanted to touch him.

All over. Both of them buck naked . . .

With a clatter, Stan suddenly shoved back his chair. Pulled out of her current fantasy, Jenna jumped.

Stan stared at her, all that severe attention startling her while the reporter simply waited in stunned silence.

Stalking toward her, Stan leaned in, close enough that she could feel his breath and smell the rich musky sweat of his skin. God, he was *so* male . . .

Voice rough edged, almost desperate, he whispered, "Jenna, honey, do you think you could find something to do in the back? Or better yet, go take your lunch break."

He wanted rid of her?

Cursing low, Stan ran a big, darkly tanned hand over the back of his neck. His eyes lifted, his gaze boring into her. "I'm going to sound dumb as shit, but you're making me nervous."

"Why?"

"You're listening in."

"Oh." She licked her lips, trying to understand—and got distracted by the way he stared at her mouth. "I . . . I always listen."

"This time it's bothering me." His gaze caught hers again. His voice lowered to a ferocious growl. His eyes narrowed. "I keep thinking of you instead of what I'm saying."

"You do?"

"Yeah." He glanced over her from head to toe. "You look great in that dress."

The reporter cleared his throat. "Is everything okay?"

He likes my dress? Flustered, Jenna pushed off her stool and tried an uncertain smile. "I understand. It's all right. I was getting hungry anyway." She glanced at her watch. "Half an hour okay?"

Stan hesitated, appearing angry, then annoyed. Taking her totally off guard, he caught her around the neck and pulled her forward over the counter while he leaned in. Then, as if he had the right, as if he'd done it a million times, he put his mouth to hers, firm and warm, lingering, one heartbeat, two . . . and he lifted away. "Thanks." No smile, no softness.

Jenna touched her lips, tingling from her mouth to her breasts and down into her womb. "Oh, uh . . ."

Face hard, expression harder, Stan went back to the reporter. "Now, where were we?"

The reporter said, "You were telling me about . . ."

In Jenna's mind, the words trailed off. Who cared what they said? Stan had just kissed her. A brief, almost nonsexual kiss, except that she wanted to melt on the spot.

Knowing she needed a breath of fresh air and a few minutes to figure out what had just happened, she grabbed her purse and made a hasty retreat, pausing only long enough to put her CLOSED sign in the door so Stan and the reporter wouldn't be interrupted.

At a fast clip, she went down the walkway to the Mom and Pop diner next door, on the corner of Jonathan Ave. and Winesap Lane. She darted inside. There were a few customers present, the normal lunch crowd, but no one paid her any attention. And thank God, because she just knew she breathed too fast and looked the fool.

Hand pressed to her heart, Jenna glanced around and located an empty booth in the very back, away from windows and other patrons. Normally reserved for the few smokers who came into the diner, it stayed almost abandoned, and so that's where Jenna headed. She needed the privacy, and the lack of prying eyes would help her get collected.

Legs shaking, she hurried over to the plastic seat and slid in. Her mind in a riot of mayhem, she covered her mouth.

Just *what* had happened? One minute, Stan was merely a friend, then in the next, he'd kissed her. Or had he meant it as a friendly gesture and she, being a widow with desperate clichéd lust, read more into it than she should have? Whatever it meant, wow, what a hot smooch. She'd always known it'd be that way, that with Stan, every sense would be magnified and a simple kiss could never be simple. No two ways about it, the man turned her on, always had.

But being a mother took priority over everything

else, making an affair taboo. No matter what she felt for Stan, all she could indulge were fantasies. Now, if Stan was the type who wanted to settle down and enjoy domestic bliss . . . but he wasn't. She might be half in love already, but Stan Tucker didn't feel the same way.

She'd do well to remember that one small fact.

Ten minutes later, the waitress noticed Jenna buried in the corner and, full of good spirit and sunshine, hustled over to take her order. Jenna finally shook off her daze. She didn't want anyone else to read the carnal hunger on her face. For crying out loud, at her age, with her family responsibilities, she had to be very discreet about her shameful hankering for one very hot landscape and gardening expert.

"Hey, Jenna." Marylou Jasper, an eighteen-year-old working toward college funds, pulled out her white pad and a pen. Because the owner of the diner liked to experiment with new things, they didn't offer a regular menu. On any given day, it was anyone's guess what would be served.

Trying to appear normal, rather than ravaged with lust, Jenna smiled and said, "What do we have today, Marylou?"

"I just made a pot of coffee, the peach pie is still hot, croissants are fresh from the oven, and we have some really awesome chicken salad to go with them. There's also chili, hamburgers, and lunchmeat sandwiches. So what can I getcha today?"

Maybe food would help settle the churning in her stomach. Jenna smiled. "The chicken salad on a croissant, a pickle slice or two, please, and a diet cola."

Marylou rolled her eyes. "Why you always wanna drink that nasty diet stuff, I'll never understand."

Of course she couldn't understand. Being a typical eighteen-year-old with a slender body and not an ounce of fat, Marylou could eat anything she fancied. Her brown hair shone with natural highlights, and her blue eyes were always smiling. Jenna had no doubt the girl could have her pick of beaus. "That's because you're young and shapely, but I'm old and—"

"Very shapely."

Ohmigod. At the sound of that rough male voice, Jenna stiffened. Eyes wide, heart hammering madly, she swiveled around to see Stan stepping past Marylou. Without an invitation, he joined her at the booth, placing his perfect body on the opposite bench, directly in front of her.

Sexual tension, thick as soup, suddenly hung in the air. Marylou just stood there, her mouth gaping, her eyes going back and forth with a ping-pong effect.

Unconcerned, Stan glanced up at her and said, "I'll have whatever Jenna ordered—but make my cola nondiet."

"Oh." Marylou shook herself. "Right." Then with a big fat smile, "I'll get right on the order." And whistling, she took herself off with telling haste, no doubt on her way to the kitchen to relay a whole lot more than a simple order.

Confused, excited, giddy with expectation, Jenna soaked in the sight of Stan. She savored the wild beating of her heart, the dryness in her mouth, and the curl of excitement deep inside her. It had been so long since she'd felt such wonderful things.

Stan smiled with shrewd calculation. "The interview finished early."

Jenna wondered if he'd rushed through it. She cleared her throat. "After that unexpected compliment . . ." She hesitated. What if he hadn't meant it as such? What if instead, he'd been remarking on her weight? She could stand to lose a few pounds—

"A compliment you deserve," Stan interjected, his gaze intent on her face. "Your figure is spectacular."

"Oh." A blush of happiness warmed her from the inside out. "Well, thank you. But you realize Marylou is going to start some ripe gossip."

Reaching across the booth, Stan took her trembling hand, holding her firm. "Gossip implies rumor or hearsay." His rough fingers moved over her palm. "But if what she says is true, how can it be gossip?"

TWO

Damn, he liked the way Jenna's cheeks warmed and how her fast breathing shimmied her breasts. And that tiny pulse fluttering in her throat gave everything away, even if he didn't have access to her every emotion and sensation.

Stan brushed his fingertips over her palm again, felt the undulating wave of growing response that rolled through her, and he pushed up from his seat.

At the same time, Jenna pressed her shoulders back in the booth, not out of disinterest, but from utter surprise. That didn't deter Stan at all, not when he knew she wanted him, that her longing was so strong it scared her a little.

Holding her hand so she couldn't completely retreat, he leaned over her, hesitated with his mouth a breath away from hers, building the anticipation, then gave in to the urge.

Jenna made a small sound as his mouth covered hers, and this time he made damn sure she wouldn't mistake his claim as some forward form of friendship. As he deepened the kiss, her mouth softened, her lips parting, and Stan used just the tip of his tongue to taste her, just inside her lips, over her teeth, touching against her own tongue—and retreating.

Jesus. Heart thumping hard, thighs tense, Stan pulled back. He'd meant to tease her, to make her understand what he wanted from her. But while Jenna did look more heated than ever, Stan felt ready to self-combust. Hell, at his age he'd done his fair share of necking. It shouldn't have been any big deal.

But not once could he remember enjoying the feel and taste of a woman's mouth quite so much. He wasn't a sweaty-palmed, hair-triggered kid anymore, not by a long shot, but damn if he didn't want to drag Jenna out of the booth and rush her to the nearest form of privacy they could find.

A simple kiss had him primed, and he knew it was the woman responsible, not the kiss itself.

As he settled back in his seat, a little disconcerted by her effect on him, Jenna touched her lips. Voice faint, gaze searching, she whispered, "What was that?"

Stan made a sound of disgust. Her confusion mirrored his but probably for different reasons. "I thought it was a kiss."

Her gaze dropped, and she looked around the table-top, at her hands, at his. "Yes." Her green eyes lifted. "A kiss, but . . ."

Stan flattened his mouth. "I know. A punch in the gut, huh? Kissing is nice, but kissing you flattens me. It makes me think of a hell of a lot more than mouth on mouth, that's for damn sure."

Her hand went to her stomach, and she nodded. "I don't understand, Stan. What are we doing?"

Marylou reappeared, her expression filled with titillated nosiness. "Got your sandwiches and stuff." Wide-eyed, she looked between the two of them, plopping down the plates and glasses without the attention necessary to the task.

Stan scooted his plate back a little so it didn't end up in his lap. "Thanks."

Jenna wouldn't look at Marylou, and that bothered him.

Marylou lingered, and that bothered him even more.

"That's all we need for now, Marylou. But save me a piece of pie, okay?"

"Oh."

At least the girl knew a dismissal when she heard one.

Wearing a smile, she nodded. "Yeah, 'kay, sure. No problem, Stan." With a lot of reluctance, she eased herself out of hearing range.

Jenna moaned and put her face in her hands. "It's starting already."

It had started the moment he stepped into her shop and knew she pictured him naked. Over her. With her naked, under him, anxious and ready to come.

It was Stan's turn to groan. "When do you get off today?"

Her head shot up. "Why?"

Rolling his eyes, Stan said, "Honey, something's happening between us. You know that as much as I do. I want to see you. I damn sure intend to kiss you again." He shifted his booted feet under the table until they caged her smaller feet in. "So tell me, when do you get off?"

Her regret bombarded him before she answered. "At five, but I have to get home to Ryan because Rachelle has a date."

Her son Ryan was a rambunctious ten-year-old, and her daughter Rachelle was a beautiful eighteen-year-old young lady. Stan had met them both several times now. Jenna sometimes kept Ryan at the bookstore with her, and with the town so small, you eventually ran into everyone at one time or another. He'd seen them in the grocery, at the fountain in front of the town square, and at the diner.

She had nice kids, polite and happy and healthy.

A family get-together wasn't quite what Stan had in mind, but he knew he'd go nuts wondering about things if he went home alone. "Why don't you let me take you both out on the boat?"

Turbulent puzzlement warred with buoyant desire. Stan's heart wanted to melt. How long had it been since a guy asked her out? Had the fact of her kids been a deterrent? Hell, as a divorced bachelor with no close family, the idea of her children pleased him. He liked kids—always had.

Jenna was a terrific mom, and that appealed to him as much as everything else. It emphasized her loving nature, her sense of responsibility, and the loyalty she had for those she loved. Important qualities. More important than her sexy good looks—which he appreciated, too.

Filled with wariness, she licked her lips and said, "Ryan would love that, I'm sure."

Stan leaned one elbow on the table and cupped her face with his right hand. "I'm glad. But what about you?"

"What about me?"

"You enjoy boating?" His fingertips brushed over her cheek, down to her throat and across the very top of her chest. "You're so fair. You don't get out in the sun much, do you?"

Her eyes sank closed. "Stan, you have to stop touching me."

"But I don't want to stop." And if she'd be truthful, she wanted more touches, not less.

She drew an unsteady breath. "I don't really want you to stop."

Stan stared in amazement.

"But I can't think when you touch me."

Her honesty astounded him. And left him shaken. He thought of his ex-wife, of the lies he'd learned during a blue moon—no, forget that. He'd gotten over her and her deceptions ages ago, and he wouldn't mar his time with Jenna by thinking of that.

"All right." Stan dropped his hand, but said, "I like it that you tell me what you're feeling."

Horrified, she gave a shaky laugh. "Oh, no, never that. Well, maybe some of what I'm thinking, but not all."

A predator's delight curled through him. *Too late, sweetheart,* he could have told her, but she wasn't ready to hear about his whacky relationship with the moon. He didn't want to send her running from him with truths she couldn't handle.

"Why not?" he asked, just to tease her. "What is it you're thinking, Jenna?"

"I'm thinking that this is happening awfully fast."

"We've known each other six months."

"I know. So . . . Why now?"

Deliberately dragging things along, Stan took a bite of his croissant and contemplated her while chewing. Flustered, Jenna nibbled on her own sandwich while she waited.

"Tomorrow night, there'll be a full moon," Stan finally told her, deciding it might be best to ease her into the idea of his lunar-inspired intuition.

"And so you're going to change into a lycanthrope?"

"A werewolf?" He hated that stupid legend. Whenever he researched the moon, he invariably ran into the myths.

She grinned. "I remember the whole wolf transformation really ramped up Jack Nicholson's libido in the movie." She toyed with her sandwich. "Are you telling me you're the same? Should I expect you to sprout hair on your back and start howling at the moon?"

Stan gave her a long look. "I might howl, strictly out of sexual frustration, you understand. But I won't actually turn into an animal." He ran a hand through his shaggy hair. "Hell, I'm hairy enough as it is. Any more would be overkill."

Her gaze went to his chest, then his forearms. Her voice again grew quiet, a sure sign of her mood. "You're just hairy enough. It's sexy. Very manly." Then she shook her head. "So tell me, what does a full moon have to do with you kissing me twice, when in six months, you've never given me a second look?"

Disbelief left him speechless, but he could tell by her expression—as well as her thoughts—that she believed what she said.

"Jenna, honey, there's not a man alive who doesn't give you second looks. And third and fourth looks, for that matter."

"Right," she said in exaggerated tolerance. "I'm almost forty. I've had two kids. I'm hardly a sex symbol."

"Wrong. You're incredibly sexy. Warm, friendly . . . and sweet enough to eat."

He tacked that last on just to prod her, and sure enough, she caught her breath—then got exactly the visual he wanted. Watching her, seeing what she saw, made him feel it almost as if he had her spread out on his bed, completely naked, twisting with pleasure while he showed her his favorite way to make a woman come.

"Damn." He rubbed his face, then gulped down half his coke. He had to stop tormenting himself.

"Stan?" His name emerged as a thread of sound, filled with longing.

Nodding, jaw tight, Stan said, "You see?" He struggled to keep the harshness, the savage need, from his tone. "The moon affects us all, Jenna, did you know that? It's called the Lunar Effect and can be responsible for everything from mental disorders to heightened awareness."

She didn't dispute him, but then, her mind was still on other, more carnal matters, making him nuts.

Stan took her hand again. "Listen to me, Jenna. Studies have proven that more crimes, more births, more conceptions, more animal bites, and more unintentional poisonings all occur during a full moon. The earth and sun and moon are all lined up, causing higher tides, and you have to believe if the moon can do that, it can damn sure work on our glands, our organs, and our moods."

She blinked hard. "So . . . you're interested in me because of the moon?"

"No way." He'd been hooked from the first day he saw her, he just hadn't realized that the feeling was mutual. "Didn't you hear what I said about you being sexy? I've wanted you since day one. Make no mistakes about that. And the more I get to know you, the more I want you. But maybe it's the moon that's bringing us together, that's helping us to admit it."

Stan waited, but she didn't deny wanting him, and something strangely close to anxiety uncoiled and relaxed in his chest.

Yet her lack of a denial wasn't enough. He squeezed her fingers. "Tell me you want me, Jenna," he commanded. "Say it."

Marylou chose that inauspicious moment to come bebopping back to the table. "You guys ready for your pie?" She eyed Jenna's uneaten food and raised an eyebrow. "You don't like the chicken salad?"

"Oh, uh . . ." Flushed, Jenna picked up her croissant. "It's wonderful, I've just . . ."

Swallowing his curse, Stan said, "Give us ten more minutes, Marylou, then bring two slices of pie and two coffees."

Jenna protested. "I'll need to get back to the store soon."

"I locked up." Stan pulled her keys from his pocket and slid them across the table. "The reporter's long gone. The bookstore is safe." He pressed his feet farther under the booth, letting his calves brush hers. "Stay for pie."

Marylou giggled. "Yeah, Jenna. Live a little. Stay for pie."

Giggling got on Stan's nerves, but the girl was a good sort and a hard worker, so Stan winked at her and said, "Maybe seeing it will convince her."

"Right." Again, Marylou hurried off.

Glancing at her watch, Jenna said, "I suppose I can stay a little longer. I haven't even been gone a half hour."

Stan just waited.

With slender fingers, Jenna smoothed her hair, glanced at him and away, and finally drew a deep breath. He could feel her working up her nerve, and it was both endearing and a gigantic turn-on.

"Yes, I want you." Before Stan could recover from that awesome declaration, she added with earnest sincerity and an appalling lack of deception, "I have since the first day I met you."

"You never let on."

"I didn't think there was any reason to." In explanation, she said, "If you think I'm attractive . . . well, it's nothing compared to what I think about you. It's probably safe to say you're the sexiest man I've ever laid eyes on. Of course, every woman in town thinks so, so I'm sure you're used to hearing that."

"No," Stan growled, floored with how her announcement affected him. "I'm damn well not used to it at all. But it wouldn't matter anyway, because you're not every other woman in town. You're special—to me, and to everyone who meets you."

Shrugging that off, she sipped at her drink and nibbled on her sandwich. Again Stan waited, sensing her efforts to sort things out, to decipher both his feelings and her own. Picking up a pickle slice, she whispered, "Are we going to have an affair, Stan?"

For some reason, he didn't like her wording. An affair indicated a noncommittal relationship, and damn it, Jenna was the type of woman a man settled down with. She was every man's fantasy, proper on the outside, torrid on the inside. He wanted to know both sides better.

"I'm going to take you and your son out on the boat tonight. If Ryan wants, he can do some tubing. Or just swim in the cove. We'll talk. Maybe grab dinner somewhere. And later, when Ryan gets ready for bed, I'm going to kiss you again—probably do more than kiss you."

Alarm skittered through her. "Oh, but—"

"Jenna," he said, cutting off her objection, "I understand your privacy is limited. Your kids are a big part of your life, and that's how it should be. Know that I'd never make things awkward with them."

Jenna watched him with longing on her face as well as in her heart. She craved the special bond between a man and a woman, but her kids came first, and Stan appreciated that. Even if he hadn't read it in her head, he'd have said and done the same things. He was sure of it.

How hard would it be for a woman with children to develop any sort of intimacy with a man? Was that why she'd never dated, because it was just too complicated? Well, he wasn't a bastard who'd ever make her choose or pressure her into an uncomfortable situation.

"Later," Stan added, wanting her to have no misunderstandings on his intentions, "when we can find some private time so you can relax and enjoy every single second, I intend to make love to you."

The pickle slice slipped from her lax fingers and landed half on the plate, half on the tabletop.

"You'll like what I do to you, Jenna. I'll make sure of it."

Her head moved in a dazed nod of acknowledgment. "I believe you." But the images in her head weren't of him touching her. Just the opposite.

Her sexual imagination played for him like a porn video, and he was the recipient of every hot, wet kiss, every lick and gentle suck and firm stroke. Jesus, the woman had a great knack for covering the details.

On the ragged edge, glad the booth hid his arousal, Stan leaned forward again. "I'm not a kid, Jenna, after a quick tumble and instant gratification. Should I tell you what I want?"

The word, *"Yes,"* floated out on a breath from between her parted lips.

"I want a woman who isn't shy in the sack. A woman who'll let me make her feel good without hiding under the sheets or turning out the lights." And then, pushing her, he said, "I want a woman who wants me the same way. Who enjoys getting naked and sweaty, fucking, sucking, with no taboos as long as we both enjoy it."

Oh, yeah, Jenna was that woman. Just hearing him say it had her primed and ready and squirming in her seat.

"I want a woman," Stan added, knowing how his words would hit her, "who insists on a screaming orgasm every time."

Out of the corner of his eye, Stan saw Marylou approaching. The girl's timing couldn't be worse, what with Jenna flushed, soft in all the right places, her eyes heavy, her nipples taut against her dress.

"Blow your nose," Stan told her, quickly handing her his paper napkin.

Some of the sensual haze faded from her darkened eyes. "Excuse me?"

"Marylou's on her way, and honey, she'll take one look at you and think I've been getting you off under the table. Take the napkin, lower your face, and blow."

Jenna fumbled to do just that, her hands shaking, her breath coming too fast. She turned awkwardly away and lowered her face just as Marylou set the plates of peach pie on the table.

"You want me to take some of these dishes?" she asked, hoping for a reason to hang around.

"That's all right," Stan told her. "We'll be done shortly, and then you can get it all." He handed her a twenty, which more than covered the bill, and said, "Keep the change."

Stan knew she was saving for college, so he always gave her a huge tip. Marylou saw nothing amiss. "Thanks, Stan. See ya later, Jenna." And off she went.

Jenna's forehead hit the table. "Oh, God," she said, her voice muffled through the napkin still covering her face. "I'll never be able to come in here again."

Stan couldn't resist touching her hair. He glided his fingers over the warm silk, thinking of it loose and drifting over his body—his chest, his abdomen. His thighs.

He lifted her face. "So you're a hot woman with a sexual appetite? It's nobody's business—but mine." He brushed her lips with his thumb. "I'll keep our secret."

Jenna looked at her uneaten croissant and then at the piece of pie. She shook her head. "I can't eat."

"Yes, you can." Stan picked up her sandwich and handed it to her. "I'll help. For the rest of our meal, I'll make sure we talk about something else."

Jenna still struggled to get her breathing in order. "Like what?"

There were times when the nonglamorous job of

gardening came in handy. "A new low-maintenance rose shrub that'd look great in that bare spot at the side of The Nook. It's going to be a big seller, so you need to order it now."

Bemused, Jenna listened as he detailed the finer points of the flower, and within minutes, she'd consumed her lunch. Lust, Stan knew, worked up an appetite, so he enjoyed watching Jenna eat.

After he gave her an evening of mind-blowing sex, he'd feed her a four-course meal. She'd forget about her diet colas and aversion to pie and learn to appreciate her curves as much as he did.

But for now, he had to get back to work before he forgot his good intentions. He walked Jenna back to the bookstore, gave her a brief kiss on her delicious mouth, and told her he'd see her at five-thirty, at her house.

Hopefully the lake water would be cold. Because he had a feeling Jenna's more sumptuous thoughts were going to be hell on his libido, and on his control. Out on the boat, at least he'd be able to dunk himself in the water as necessary.

Three

When Jenna got home, rushing so she'd have time to refresh her hair and make-up before Stan showed up, she discovered her daughter still in the bathroom, primping for her date.

When she knocked, Rachelle said, "I'll be out in a few minutes."

Jenna sighed. "Hello to you, too, honey."

The door opened. "Hey, Mom. I thought you were Ryan."

They exchanged a quick hug, and Jenna asked, "Where is your brother?"

Wrinkling her nose, Rachelle said, "Out back, digging up worms in the hopes you'll take him fishing."

Because Rachelle still had hot rollers in her long blond hair and only half her make-up on, Jenna knew she'd be busy longer than the predicated "few minutes." Sharing one bathroom with an eighteen-year-old daughter wasn't easy.

But at the same time, Jenna knew she was going to miss her something awful when college started. "I'll let him know I'm home." Then she hesitated. "Where are you going tonight?"

"To the movies, and then the Old Orchard Inn for dinner."

Jenna frowned. The theater was located just outside of town, and that was bad enough, but the Old Orchard Inn was also a B&B—meaning there were beds right upstairs. At eighteen, Rachelle was on the verge of being a woman, but she was still Jenna's little girl. She didn't want to be smothering, but neither could she be cavalier. "You're going to be late?"

Rachelle shrugged. "Maybe midnight or so. Is that okay?"

"I suppose so." But as usual, Jenna felt the need to lecture. "Please just remember that as nice as Terrance seems, it's *you* I trust, not him. If he tries to buy you alcohol or if anything happens—"

Rachelle rolled her eyes and headed back into the bathroom. "I know, I know. I'll call a cab, or call you, or I'll hit him over the head. Don't worry, Mom. It's just dinner and a movie. I promise."

Don't worry? Dear God, Jenna well remembered the raging hormones of youth, how she and her husband had found plenty of inconspicuous places to explore their sexuality. They'd married young and had a wonderful marriage that had lasted until his death three years ago.

But Jenna wanted so much more for her daughter. . . .

"Mom!" Ryan came thundering into the house with all the delicacy of a herd of elephants. His untied, dirty sneakers brought him to a skidding halt on the hardwood floor right in front of Jenna. "I've dug up a bunch of night crawlers." He lifted a paper cup filled with dirt and wiggling worms. "Let's go fishing."

Hiding her revulsion, Jenna peered into the cup. "Wow, you do have a bunch. And they're so . . ." She swallowed hard. "Big."

"They're juicy," Ryan said. "The fish'll love 'em."

Jenna mentally prepared herself and said a quick prayer that her son would be happy with the change of plans. "I'm sure there'll be time for some fishing, but guess what? Stan Tucker offered to take us out on his boat."

Ryan's eyes widened. A heartbeat later, the bathroom door opened and Rachelle stuck her head out, her eyebrows raised in comical wonder.

Dear God, Jenna thought, she'd rendered both kids mute.

Forging on, she cleared her throat and tried to be casual when she felt nearly frantic instead. "I don't know what type of boat he has, but he said you could go tubing or swim in the cove. We can take the fishing gear along. Stan might like to fish, too."

Still, both children just stared at her. A deep breath, then another, and a bright smile. "You remember Stan, don't you?"

They each nodded. Ryan fought a grin. "For real? He'll take me tubing?"

"That's what he said."

Rachelle sent Jenna a sly look—and began teasing. In a soft, singsong voice, she said, "Mom's got a boyfriend, Mom's got a boyfriend . . ."

"Rachelle! Of course I don't. Stan is a—"

"Stud," Rachelle said. "And if he's not a boyfriend, then why are you turning bright red?" Laughing, Rachelle threw her arms around Jenna and squeezed. "I think it's cool."

"Me, too." Ryan was suddenly beside himself, jiggling, hopping, and antsy with anticipation. "When's he gettin' here?"

Jenna glanced at her watch and gulped. Time slipped by far too fast. "In about ten minutes."

"*Mom.*" Rachelle pulled her into the bathroom. "For heaven's sake. Why didn't you say something! It's all yours. I'll finish up in my room." Hands flying, she un-plugged her rollers, grabbed no less than three hair-brushes and her assortment of make-up, and said, "Don't just stand there, Mom. Do something with yourself. Change into your bathing suit and that really cute cover-up you have. And let your hair loose. The wind from the boat will tear it out of the clip anyway."

Rachelle closed the door before Jenna could think of a single thing to say, but she heard her daughter give rapid orders to Ryan. "Now, behave yourself, squirt. Don't be a toad, okay? Show Mr. Tucker your best side. Don't embarrass Mom—"

Their voices faded as Rachelle dragged Ryan and his worms down the hall, listing off all the things he shouldn't do.

Jenna stared at herself in the mirror. Oh, God, she was still red-faced. But not for the reason Rachelle assumed. She didn't suffer embarrassment so much as unbridled eagerness. She'd turn forty soon. She was a middle-aged widow, a mother of two children, one a grown daughter. She owned her own business.

But at the moment, she felt like a giddy teenager on her first date.

Jenna put her hands to her warm cheeks and sur-veyed her appearance. Yes, definitely a mess. No way would she wear a bathing suit—the very idea of show-ing so much skin to Stan left her mortified. The years, and two births, had not been kind to her body. Any man who hadn't seen her before she lost her figure sure wasn't going to see her now, at least, not so soon.

If, as Stan said, they eventually made love . . . yes. She craved his description of unrestrained, bold love-making. Jenna sighed. Then, and only then, she'd let him look all he wanted. After all, if he was looking, she'd get to look, too. And Stan Tucker was a definite feast for the eyes.

*   *   *

Stan arrived five minutes early. The hazy sun and low ninety-degree temps had him wearing reflective sunglasses and casual khaki shorts with a mostly unbuttoned white cotton shirt. He'd showered, shaved, slapped on a spicy fragrance, brushed his teeth, combed his hair—and generally spiffed up as much as a gardener in the midst of a small town during a heat wave could.

He parked his sporty red SUV in Jenna's drive and got out, peering at her tidy ranch-style home with a critical eye. Updated landscaping would improve the looks of the house a lot, not to mention the trim could use a fresh coat of paint.

He was considering that when he saw the small, compact body bounce off the porch swing and stand at the top step, hands on hips, eyes squinted from the sunshine. He seemed to be restraining himself with great effort.

Stan couldn't quite tell if Jenna's son wanted to challenge him or welcome him with berserk joy.

Joy won out. He leaped off the steps and came dashing across the lawn, bubbling over with enthusiasm. "Mom said you were coming."

Stan smiled, amused at the boundless energy vibrating from the boy. He opened his mind to him and then wished he hadn't. Ryan still missed his father terribly, and a giant void existed inside him. He was so hungry for a father figure that Stan put a hand to his chest, rubbing at the ache of a broken heart.

"That's right," Stan said. "Boating alone is no fun, so I'm hoping you're game."

"You bet I am!" Ryan leaned around him to see his SUV. "Where's yer boat?"

"I keep it docked at the lake."

"We used to have a boat. But Mom sold it." His face scrunched up. "Cuz of my dad dying and everything."

"You haven't been boating since?"

Skinny shoulders lifted in a shrug. "I go with friends sometimes. But Mom likes to worry, and sometimes she doesn't let me go."

A smile tugged at Stan's mouth. He touched the boy's head and started him toward the house. "It's a mother's sacred job to worry, and I bet your mother is good at anything she does—including worrying."

"Yeah, she's real good at it."

His long face got Stan to chuckling. "Speaking of your mom, is she ready?"

"I dunno. She was runnin' around, grabbin' clothes and changin' clothes and complainin' about her hair and—"

"*Ryan.*" That stern admonishment came from a younger version of Jenna poised in the doorway. Rachelle pasted on a friendly smile. "Hello, Mr. Tucker."

Stan looked her over and knew poor Jenna must do most of her worrying about her daughter. The girl was a real looker and, from what he remembered, smart to boot. The little dress she wore would make any lad with hormones go nuts. It was stylish, but it also accented her figure a bit more than any protective, father-aged man would like.

"Rachelle." If she were his daughter, he'd dress her in a potato sack—but he hid that thought with a cordial smile. "Call me Stan."

"All right, Stan." Her return smile was pretty and welcoming and made Stan want to protect her from the world. "Mom's almost ready. You want to come in for iced tea? I just made it fresh."

"Hey! I was gonna show him where I dug up most of my worms," Ryan protested.

Rachelle's face tightened. "Stan might not want to look at worms, Ryan." She bestowed another beatific smile on Stan. "Come on in out of that heat. It's much cooler inside."

It didn't require a mind reader to know that Rachelle wanted to make a good impression. She sensed that her mother wasn't completely happy on her own and maybe saw him as a step in the right direction. Yet it was so much more than that. Both Rachelle's and Ryan's neediness clawed at him, destroying his composure. The love they felt for Jenna was overpowering, but with that love was an almost desperate craving for a return of things lost—a happy home with two parents, a more flexible budget, family vacations.

Jenna tried to fill the gap in their lives, but she could only do so much. Ryan missed the male camaraderie that only another guy could supply. And Rachelle missed her father's teasing protectiveness and the smell of his aftershave, the way he lifted her off her feet when he hugged her. She missed knowing her daddy was there, the backbone to their home, ready and able to defend them all.

Stan tried prodding her thoughts a little, to see if there were particular concerns on money, but he wasn't skilled enough to separate the many emotions swirling between the two kids. And truthfully, his own emotions were getting in the way now, because he cared—about both of them, and about their mom.

Wanting to please both kids, he pulled off his sunglasses and gave his most charming smile to Rachelle. "If you could pour me the tea—with plenty of ice, please—both Ryan and I'll be right in. Just give me two minutes to see this worm farm he's discovered. Okay?"

Rachelle shot her brother a look of disgust, but accepted the compromise. "I'll be in the kitchen. Just come in the back door."

Ryan grabbed Stan's hand and tugged. "It's this way. C'mon. I found about a gazillion of them under one rock. My cup wasn't big enough for them all, so I left some so that next time I fish, I can get 'em. Mom said you might let me fish off your boat. Can I bring my rod and reel?"

Ryan didn't wait for an answer. He didn't even draw a breath.

"It's one my dad bought me and it's really cool, like for an expert fisherman or something. Dad said I had all the makings of a professional. But that was three years ago, so I'm rusty now. Me and Dad used to fish in the mornin's, when the fish were really bitin' and you could fill the boat up with enough bass for dinner."

The rambling monologue brought them through the backyard and all the way to the perimeter where the woods bordered. Jenna had a spacious lot with plenty of room for kids to play. He liked it.

"Of course you can fish," Stan told Ryan. "We'll go back in the cove where the big ones hang out."

"Seriously?"

Stan laughed. "You haven't fished in three years?"

"Sure I have. Mom takes me sometimes when she doesn't have to work. But she works lots, and she doesn't know much about fishing anyway, so she doesn't like for me to cast the rod." In a stage whisper, Ryan said, "I got a lure caught in her hair once. So now we just take reg'lar poles. She'll hand me worms, but she won't put them on a hook or nothing like that. I can tell she don't really like fishing too much."

"You're obviously an astute young man."

"What's astute?"

"It means you're already good at reading women. Trust me, it'll come in handy someday." Stan crouched down with interest when Ryan used all his meager strength to lift a heavy rock.

"You see 'em?" Ryan asked, his voice strained as he struggled with the stone.

"I sure do. You were smart to leave some here. They'll probably just get bigger, so next time you fish, imagine what they'll look like."

"Wow." Ryan dropped the rock to the side, leaving the worms exposed. "I hadn't thought of that."

"They'll have nothing to do but eat and grow."

"They don't have mouths. How can they eat?"

Stan turned to Ryan. "You're kidding, right? Of course they have mouths. Look at this one. He's grinning at you."

Ryan chuckled. "Is not."

Stan lifted one long, squirming worm and explained. "These first few segments hold the brain, hearts, and breathing organs. Did you know that a worm has five pairs of hearts?"

"Wow."

Stan nodded. "The rest of the inside of an earthworm is filled with the intestines, which digest its food."

"So all of that is belly?"

"Close enough. Earthworms eat soil and the organic material in it—like insect parts and bacteria."

"Gross."

"Right here's the mouth, but it's covered by a flap called the prostomium, which helps the earthworm sense light and vibrations, so it can find its way around. Tiny bristles, called setae, are on most of the earthworm's body."

Ryan gave him a skeptical look. "How do you know that's the mouth end and not the butt end?"

"Simple. This is the end he led with when he was crawling. Now, wouldn't you crawl head first, instead of butt first?"

Ryan grinned. "Yeah, I would."

"All these worms mean you have good earth here.

They aerate it and make the soil richer with their castings."

"What are castings?"

Grinning, thoroughly enjoying himself, Stan said in a whisper, "Poo."

Ryan started laughing—and suddenly Stan felt it, simple happiness, gratitude, and overwhelming tenderness. So much tenderness he felt wrapped in it, lending him a peace he hadn't experienced in years. He turned his head and smiled at Jenna, standing behind him.

She wore a beige tank top and matching capris, with an oversized mesh tunic over the top. A floppy-brimmed straw hat shielded her face from the sun. Her long hair hung free to her shoulders. She looked . . . fabulous. Comfortable. Casual. *Sexy.*

And she had her heart in her eyes.

Stan narrowed his gaze on her face. "Have you been eavesdropping on our worm lessons?"

Her mouth curled, and more tenderness blanketed around Stan. "Fascinating stuff," she teased. "How could I resist?"

Stan's heart wanted to crumble. Witnessing her son's happiness had given her great joy and had shifted her emotions for him from purely sexual to so much more.

Such a simple thing—sharing laughter with her son. And now she was soft and emotional, even tearful.

He stood, stepped closer to her, and whispered, "Hi," then kissed her on the cheek.

Ryan stared wide-eyed.

So she'd understand, he said, "Ryan was entertaining me while you finished getting ready." Without really thinking about it, he sought out the little boy, his palm to the top of Ryan's sun-warmed hair. "If it's okay with you, I'd like to ask Ryan to go fishing with me some morning. He tells me that's how it's done, and being he's an expert, I'm sure I could learn a thing or two."

With Ryan's loud squeal of excitement, Jenna's lips quivered. "He'd love that," she whispered with tearful gratitude that cut Stan like a sharp knife.

Damn, he wanted this woman to be happy, all the time, every second of the day. She deserved that, and by God, he'd see to it. Somehow.

He brushed her cheek with his thumb. "Me, too."

Blinking away the tears, she said, "Ryan, let's go get washed up and let Stan drink his tea, so we can get to the lake before it gets any later."

Stan put his right arm around Jenna's waist and his left hand on Ryan's bony shoulder. Together, like a family, they crossed the grassy lawn to the back door of her house.

Rachelle waited in the doorway, watching them all with a sort of earnest serenity. Stan wanted to close them all out, just to regain his balance, but he couldn't. It seemed intrusive, knowing what was in their hearts, but at the same time, he felt compelled to know even more, to understand them so he could get a toehold into their lives.

A flicker of concern struck him, and he found himself asking Rachelle about her plans for college as they entered the kitchen. Tea waited on the table, but he and Ryan washed their hands first. Over his shoulder, Stan glanced at Rachelle.

She didn't quite meet his gaze. "I'm going to a state school here."

The way she said that told him volumes. "What do you want to study?" He took a seat next to Jenna and sipped his tea. "This is good, Rachelle, thanks."

"You're welcome." She laced her fingers together over her middle. "Don't laugh, but I'll be an art major."

"Now, why would I laugh at that?" Her self-conscious shrug prompted him to dig further. "What type of art?"

"Graphic design. I want to do ad layouts."

Ryan said, "Like on cereal boxes."

Rolling her eyes, Rachelle said, "Maybe some cereal boxes."

Stan settled back in his seat. He had a feeling he already knew the answer, but he asked it anyway. "You doing the state school because you want to be close to home, or did you decide it was the best choice?"

Rachelle darted a glance at her mother. "I want to be close to home."

Jenna reached for Rachelle's hand and gave it a squeeze. "Actually, since she was fourteen, she's had her heart set on SCAD—Savannah College of Art and Design. Now, we just can't afford it."

"And she don't wanna leave me," Ryan boasted.

Half laughing, Rachelle mussed his hair. "You would be missed, rat."

True enough, Stan realized. Rachelle wanted to be close at hand to help her mother out with Ryan. A little awed, he acknowledged what an amazing young lady she was. "I have a feeling that whatever college you choose, you'll do great." But in his heart, Stan wanted her to have the college of her choice, not be limited by funds and responsibilities.

He wondered if he could manage that somehow. God knew he had more money than his simple lifestyle required. One look at Jenna, and he knew she was far too proud to take a handout.

Ryan guzzled his tea, fed up with idle chitchat when swimming, boating and fishing awaited. Nothing more was said on colleges. Stan assured Jenna he had everything on the boat that they'd need—life preservers, a tube and ski rope, sunscreen and towels.

Rachelle's date showed up the same time they were ready to leave. Stan took one look at the young man and wanted to forbid the date. Dumb. But damn it, he knew exactly what both kids were planning, and he felt like a peeping Tom. Quickly, he blocked the intimate thoughts, but he couldn't remove the warning scowl from his face when he looked at Terrance.

Before they drove off, Jenna again cautioned her daughter to be careful and made her promise she'd call if she was later than midnight.

On the way to the lake, Jenna was quiet, but then Ryan talked nonstop, leaving little room for adult conversation. Stan didn't mind. He enjoyed Ryan's chatter, and he sensed the peacefulness of Jenna's mood. She simply enjoyed the ride and her son's giddiness.

Ryan loved Stan's SUV and asked permission to touch every single button and knob. Stan figured if he liked the car, he'd go bonkers over his Stingray 220DR deck boat that looked a lot like a pontoon on steroids. When Ryan spotted the boat, Stan wasn't disappointed with his reaction.

He'd nearly run to the dock when Jenna caught him and hauled him back. Her rules required a life preserver before Ryan got anywhere near the murky lake water.

Golden Lake had one small station to gas up your boat and a goodie shack that sold everything from ice cream to beer to bait. Stan loaded up on snacks, premade sandwiches, and bought plenty of colas to stow in the ice chest beneath the fresh water sink in the cabin.

The rest of the evening went by in a blur for Stan. He'd never dated a woman with kids, and his ex-wife hadn't wanted any. Ryan on water was a revelation. He went tubing for what seemed like forever, never tiring, loving the big waves and the sun and the cold spray of water from the boat. Since Jenna enjoyed it, too, and he enjoyed watching her, Stan had no complaints.

Afterward, he dropped anchor in the mossy cove. Jenna and Ryan had put on sunscreen earlier, but they needed a fresh application. When she finished with her son, Stan took the bottle from her hands.

"Let me."

She glanced at Ryan, who sat on the back of the boat, his feet braced on the ladder, his rod cast out near the shore. When her gaze came back to Stan, it was hotter than the evening sun. "All right."

She had already removed her tunic, and Stan eyed her golden shoulders and collarbone, and the way the tank top hugged her breasts. Unless he missed his guess, she wasn't wearing a bra. With the summer heat, it made sense to wear as little as possible, but he'd never seen her without a bra. His palms itched to hold her, to feel the shape and weight of her breasts, to explore her nipples . . .

Swallowing a groan, he poured a small amount of sunscreen into his palms and said, "Lift your hair."

She did so slowly, and it was such a provocative pose that Stan couldn't help but think of sexual things. As he smoothed the sunscreen onto her neck, shoulders, and upper chest, she dropped her hair, and her eyes closed.

If her son weren't sitting a few feet away, singing off key to the Beach Boys in the CD player, he'd show Jenna just how close to reality her imagination had gotten.

But her son was near, and that meant Stan had to behave himself, no matter how hard behaving might be.

Hard being the operative word.

With an apologetic smile, Stan kissed the tip of her nose and went over the side of the boat into the icy water.

The splash drew Ryan's attention, and he quickly reeled in his line so he could swim, too. The water cooled Stan's ardor, but nothing could appease the growing ache in his heart—except having Jenna for his own.

Permanently.

Four

After a long swim, Ryan took turns eating and fishing, which meant Jenna had her work cut out for her trying to keep worm slime off his hands and out of the pretzel bag. The sink got more use in one day than it ever had in the rest of the time Stan had owned the boat. Ryan claimed they had everything they needed, so they never had to go back.

Jenna told him they at least had to be home when Rachelle returned from her date. She kept her cell phone out and available so she wouldn't miss a call, and Stan wondered if she wasn't maybe more aware of Terrance's intentions than he'd first assumed.

After catching several fish that he threw back for being too small, Stan put away his rod and folded out the backseats. When opened, they supplied the space equivalent to a bed. Shirtless, wearing only his still damp shorts, he settled into the corner with an icy cola and stretched out his legs to watch Jenna play mom.

By the time Ryan began to wind down, the sun had sunk low in the sky, turning everything around it crimson red. Wearing trunks, a life preserver, and a towel, Ryan half lounged in the bow seats, his hair tangled from sun, wind, and water, his hands limp on the fishing rod.

The CD player sent music over the surface of the lake. Somewhere off in the distance, a cow lowed. Along the shore, frogs croaked. Back in the cove, away from the power boats and jet skis, it was peaceful. And . . . comforting.

As Ryan nodded off, Jenna slid the pole from his hand and reeled it in. She rolled up a towel to use for a pillow and eased Ryan to his side. He didn't awaken.

"Amazing." Stan watched the boy sleep and shook his head. The rocking of the boat lulled him, too, but he couldn't remember a time when he'd ever, not even as a kid, fallen asleep so easily.

"He sleeps like a baby," Jenna told him, taking the seat facing Stan, her bare feet curled under her, her hair dancing in the breeze. She closed her eyes and sighed. "Thank you, Stan. This has been wonderful. I'd forgotten just how relaxing the water can be, how all your worries just seem to disappear."

His gaze trained on her serene features, Stan asked, "What worries do you have, Jenna?"

"The same as any other mother, I suppose." Her eyes stayed closed, and her voice whispered past her smiling mouth. "Luckily, I've been blessed with really terrific kids."

Stan figured that had more to do with her than anything else. "You're a terrific mom."

"I try." The smile faded and she sighed again. "I only want them to be happy. It's not always easy. But Stan?" Her lashes lifted and she looked directly at him, inadvertently sharing with him everything she felt, everything that was near and dear in her heart. "Thank you for today. It's the most fun Ryan's had in ages."

A lump the size of a grapefruit lodged in Stan's throat. "For me, too."

She didn't believe him. She thought he wanted to get laid and was doing what he thought necessary to make it happen. Not a nice opinion of him, but given his colorful past and even his more current public lifestyle, Stan couldn't really blame her.

But he could convince her otherwise. Stan patted the seat beside him. "Come here, woman, and let me kiss you."

Rather than refuse him, she glanced at Ryan. "He's still sleeping."

Stan nodded. "Yeah, I know."

Her bottom lip got caught in her teeth. Feeling guilty, then determined, she glanced again at Ryan before sliding out of the seat and over next to Stan. He put his arm around her and tugged her into his side. Even with the setting sun, the temperatures still hung in the upper eighties, but a soft breeze stirred the air.

Eyes searching, Jenna peered up into his face—and Stan was lost.

He cupped her cheek and gently touched his mouth to hers. Her dewy skin held the fragrance of the wind and the lake—and woman, an aphrodisiac so powerful that Stan had to struggle to keep himself in check. He wanted to absorb her, to nuzzle into all her dark, damp places and fill himself with the luscious scent of her.

Instead, he contented himself with tasting her mouth, keeping things easy and gentle, when inside, his blood raged and his heart thundered. He wanted her, more than he'd ever wanted any other woman.

Maybe more than he'd ever wanted anything else in his life.

He had to start sharing some truths.

Against her lips, he murmured, "Even two days from a full moon, the moon can be ninety-seven percent illuminated. Did you know that?"

Confused, laughing a little, Jenna pulled back. "No, I

had no idea." She leaned into him again, trying to deepen the kiss.

Stan accepted the invitation of her parted lips, dipping his tongue inside, still gentle, exploring with a leisureliness that belied the bulge in his shorts and the tightness of his muscles.

When her breath grew choppy and her hands clutched at him, Stan ended the kiss and glanced at Ryan. The boy snored, affording him more opportunity to ease her into the idea of his gift.

With his fingertips exploring the delicate texture of her cheekbone, Stan whispered, "Although Full Moon happens every month at a specific date and time, it seems full for several nights in a row. If the sky's clear, the effect can be the same."

"What effect?"

He touched his mouth to her bottom lip, licked, sucked carefully. "Any that might occur," he explained. "Some people feel unsettled, some get heightened emotions. There are suicides and, on the opposite scale, a lot of lovemaking."

"I hope you're thinking more of the latter."

Smiling, Stan continued to educate her. The more she knew, the easier it'd be for her to accept when he told her everything. And he would tell her. She had a right to know that he could read her thoughts. It was the worst invasion of privacy, but it was also something he couldn't always control.

His ex-wife had hated it, but then, she'd had secrets better left concealed. He already knew Jenna would never cheat. She was as loyal, as moral, as any person he'd ever met. If she took a vow, she'd mean it—till death do us part.

The thought excited him more, because he wanted her as his own, now and forever. He wanted more days like today, with better nights to follow. He wanted it all.

"The percentage of the moon's disk that's illuminated changes slowly around the time of Full Moon, so most people won't notice the difference. Even two days from Full Moon, people can still be suffering the Lunar Effect."

Her small hand came up to his jaw, her brow drawn in a slight frown. "Stan, I don't know what you're talking about."

"You've been thinking about me a lot lately. Sexually explicit thoughts."

She ducked her face and touched her fingertips to his chest hair. "Yes."

"Have you always?"

One shoulder lifted. "I've always been aware of you. I've always been attracted to you. And, yes, I've thought of you that way plenty of times."

He felt her thoughts skittering this way and that, and said, "But?"

"But lately, I don't know. It's been different. Stronger. Even . . . powerful. I thought maybe it was because I'm turning forty soon." Her smile went crooked, creating that small dimple he adored. "Maybe old age is catching up with me, turning me into a lech."

The admission made her uneasy, leaving her embarrassed and uncertain. Stan didn't want her to ever be ashamed of her sexuality. He slid his hand under her hair, kneading her nape, turning her face up to his. "There's nothing wrong with wanting me, Jenna." And with grave sincerity, "For a night, or for more than a night."

He posed it as a statement—but waited to see how she'd react, where her personal thoughts would take her.

His chest expanded on a deep breath, and relief filled him. Yeah, Jenna wanted him forever, never mind that she considered that a farfetched fantasy. He could get around that, but he didn't want to pressure her for things she didn't want.

She wanted him, and he'd show her just how possible that could be.

To better his odds of winning her over, Stan absorbed every nuance of her feelings for him. Her logical mind shied away from the idea of pinning him down, because she didn't think he could be satisfied with one woman. She'd had fidelity and loyalty and commitment from her first husband, and that's what she wanted again.

She would never settle for less—but then, neither would he.

Stan didn't like it that she saw him as a playboy, a mature man with too much money, too much recognition, and too many women at his disposal. True, he'd spent a few years wallowing in the celebrity status of his newfound popularity. And women had come easy over the years. But that didn't mean he wanted to remain a bachelor forever.

His healthy bank account could be an asset to her, a way to send Rachelle to the college of her choice, enough money to reinstate the missed family vacations, the boat, the comfort of financial security.

But Jenna wouldn't care about the benefits he could bring if she thought she couldn't trust him. Stan cursed softly, making Jenna press back in puzzlement. "What is it?" she asked.

"Can we talk seriously for a few minutes?"

She stared at him, looked at her hand on his chest, then at his mouth. She blinked. "Sure, Stan. Talking is just what I had in mind."

Laughing, he pulled her closer so that her cheek nestled on his shoulder. It felt good to hold her. Almost as nice as kissing her. "Don't be a tease, woman. You know damn good and well you weren't going to do anything with Ryan so close."

"Of course I wouldn't. But a few more kisses would have been nice."

His hand opened on her waist, and he squeezed. She was rounded in all the right places, full of curves and soft like a woman should be. He couldn't wait to feel her under him, all that softness cushioning his harder frame.

Stan swallowed a growl, knowing he had to keep on track. "I'll kiss you silly tonight," he promised in a raw, dark whisper, "after you tuck Ryan into bed."

Her thoughts were too naked, too vulnerable and anxious, and Stan felt like a bastard for being privy to them. But he had to make her understand that he wasn't a cheat, that ten easy women meant nothing compared to a woman he could love.

Nothing meant more to him than Jenna did.

She was close, wanting him, confused by her feelings but determined to do what was right for her children and for herself. She didn't want her kids hurt, and she feared that involving him in their lives, only to say goodbye when he grew bored and left, would leave her kids unhappy.

Stan listened to the knocking of his heart, but that became a primal beat, urging him on, heightening his awareness of her as a gentle woman, sexy as hell and damp in all the right places. Her thoughts veered, picturing him naked, her hands all over him, her mouth following . . .

Abruptly, Stan pushed away from her. Bending forward, his elbows on his knees, he tapped his fisted hands against his chin. She tortured him without even knowing it.

Not looking at Jenna, determined to get her mind off sex so he could think straight, he asked, "How much do you know about my past?"

Her confusion warred with her instinctive need to offer comfort. "I know what the press has shared." Her hand touched his back, resting on his shoulder blade. "I know that you got in trouble a few times when you were younger."

Feeling dangerous, Stan twisted to face her. "I've been convicted of assault and battery."

Her fingers stilled. "You beat someone up?"

"The creep was going to jump a guy we worked with. He and his girlfriend had broken up, and she'd chosen this other guy . . ." Stan ran a hand through his hair. "He was going to wait for him by his car one night and use a tire iron on him. So I stopped him."

Her comforting fingers again drifted over his back. "And they convicted you for that?"

Stan could understand her astonishment. Under normal circumstances, he'd be considered a hero.

Only there was nothing normal about the way he got his information.

"I got a year's suspended sentence."

"But . . ."

"No one knew what he intended, Jenna, and I couldn't prove it." Stan turned completely to face her until their knees touched. He clasped her wrist. "My wife cheated on me. That's why I divorced her."

His jump in topic left her floundering, but her concern and caring remained a live thing, drowning out her puzzlement at his current mood. "Stan, I'm so sorry. I didn't know that."

"I wanted what you had, Jenna. Trust, love, fidelity. That's not what I got. Within a month, she'd gone bed hopping."

Her heart was soft and open to him, and that left her exposed. But she was the type of woman who always cared deeply about others, too much to protect herself. "How did you find out?"

She thought he'd walked in on the sordid scene and she hurt for him. The truth was worse. Stan pulled away from her and looked up at the sky. This was harder than he'd ever imagined. "The moon will be out soon."

More confusion, then impatience. "I don't understand this fixation you have about the moon. It's like you're trying to tell me something—or maybe several things—but you're not being clear."

"I know." He felt like a damn coward but decided to take her home before telling her. Ryan could awaken any minute, interrupting them. But once she had him tucked into bed, Stan would be in a better position.

If his truths shocked her too much, he could always take advantage of her sexual attraction to bring her back to him. No, he wouldn't make love to her with her kids in range, but he could kiss her silly, heat her up with a touch, make whispered, sensual promises that would leave her desperate to accept him, on any level.

"It's getting late. We should be heading back."

Her pride kept her from pushing him. Back going straight, chin lifting, Jenna said, "All right. Fine. If that's what you want."

He'd hurt her, when that was the last thing he wanted to do. But he'd make it up to her. After he talked her around her disbelief, he'd prove to her that he could be everything she wanted in a man, and more.

Turning on the boat lights both stern and aft lent a mellow glow to the cabin. The sun had long since sunk behind the hills, leaving the sky dark with shades of deep lavender and gray. A few stars appeared, surrounding the moon that hung like a fat crystal ball, taunting him.

Jenna remained oblivious to it all as she struggled to understand what had happened. Stan finished lifting the anchor, then glanced at her and cursed softly. She thought he'd led her on. She thought he'd changed his mind about wanting her.

He pulled her resisting body close, until her breasts were against his chest and their heartbeats mingled.

"Jenna," he said, and pressed a kiss to her forehead, to her chin, and finally on her pursed mouth. "It's a lot to ask, but do you think you could trust me just a little longer?"

"What does trust have to do with it?"

He kneaded her shoulders and put his forehead to hers. "Everything. It has everything to do with it. We'll talk when you've got Ryan in bed. Okay?"

"I won't sleep with you at my house."

She sounded so prudish, Stan smiled. "I already know that, but for the record, I wouldn't ask you to." He smoothed his thumb over her chin. "I have scruples, too, you know. And I like your kids. I wouldn't do anything to upset them."

She only half believed him. "Well . . . all right, then."

"Good." Half was better than not at all. "Let's get home." The sooner he got this over with, the sooner he could have her in his bed. He glanced at Ryan. "Want me to move him back here?"

Curled on the padded bow seats, Ryan looked comfortable and down for the count. He didn't awaken even when the engine roared to life.

"I'll keep an eye on him." Jenna pulled on her overtunic, settled in the passenger seat beside Stan, and looked over the calm surface of the lake. "Rachelle was always a light sleeper, like me. But Ryan is like his dad. A herd of stampeding buffalo wouldn't wake him. He'll probably sleep straight through the night."

And with a little luck, Stan thought, Jenna would accept his odd relationship with the moon. Because one way or another, she'd have to accept him. Now that he knew so much about her, he knew she was meant to be his.

Convincing her would be the trick.

Five

Rachelle pulled up about the same time that Stan parked his SUV in the drive. Dividing her attention between Stan's strange behavior, her sleeping son, and the fact that her daughter just left Terrance's car with the slamming of his car door and without a farewell kiss, Jenna automatically prioritized.

She opened her car door and stepped out. The full moon filled the yard with light, making the porch lamp unnecessary. "Rachelle? Is everything okay?"

Already on her way toward them, Rachelle ignored how Terrance sped away. "I'm great," she said, with the false brightness Jenna recognized as anger. "Fine, perfect, peachy-keen."

Jenna had a very bad feeling about this. "What happened?"

Suddenly Stan was beside her. His hands landed on her shoulders and he pulled her back into his chest. "Nothing that Rachelle couldn't handle, isn't that right, Rachelle?"

Jenna saw her daughter's mouth twist in a wry smile. "If you call bashing the little weasel over the head handling it, then yeah, I handled it." Rachelle lifted her wrist and checked out the illuminated face of her watch. "Hey, it's only ten-thirty. I thought you guys would hang out longer."

An obvious attempt to change the subject, but Jenna wasn't ready to let it go. "Rachelle . . ."

Again, Stan squeezed her shoulders, almost as if to convince her to put off her questions. She didn't want to, but perhaps Stan felt uncomfortable being privy to their family business.

He leaned down and whispered in her ear, "She'll talk when she's ready, honey. Give her a little time."

Indeed, Rachelle seemed determined to change the subject. She peered at the SUV and grinned. "The squirt's asleep?"

Stan said, "He snores like a trucker."

Laughing, Rachelle hefted her purse strap up to her shoulder and headed for the vehicle. "I'll take him in so you two can . . . visit more." After a wink to Stan that had Jenna blushing, Rachelle got Ryan on his feet, but his eyes remained closed.

"Want me to carry him in?" Stan offered.

"Thanks, but I've got it covered." Ryan was more a sleepwalker than a willing participant as Rachelle guided him up the porch and inside.

After one more quick smile and a suspiciously scheming look, she closed the door and the porch light went out. A little embarrassed, Jenna shook her head. Her daughter could use an ounce or so of subtlety.

"Don't worry about it," Stan said. "She's just showing that she likes me."

Of course she did, Jenna thought. Everything about Stan was likable, from his easy nature to his charming smile. But she sensed it was more than that for Rachelle, almost as if she felt something had been missing from their lives, and Stan could fix that.

It made her feel like a bad mother, as if she hadn't done the best she could for her kids.

In her own grief, had she neglected a portion of her children's needs? The last three years hadn't been easy for any of them, but she'd thought her kids were now happy and well adjusted. As a single parent, there were too many times when she couldn't be somewhere, couldn't do something . . .

"You're tense," Stan said. "Let's sit on the porch swing and talk."

Jenna nodded agreement, but at the same time, she worried over how quickly her kids had accepted Stan. What would they do when Stan stopped coming over? They'd be hurt for sure. Maybe she'd be smarter to end things now, before she slept with him . . .

"Come on." His tone grim, Stan slid his arm around her waist and urged her along the walkway.

Absently, her thoughts still jumbled, Jenna told him, "Today was wonderful, Stan. I haven't seen Ryan so excited in a very long time. Thank you."

"No thanks necessary. I enjoyed myself."

They reached the porch swing, and Jenna shook off her odd distraction. "I'm sorry. Maybe I should go in." If she sat down, he'd kiss her, and she'd forget everything else.

"Why?" He didn't look disappointed by her suggestion, so much as patient.

"I know my daughter," Jenna explained, "and something happened tonight. She might need to talk with me."

"Not yet." Stan pressed her into the swing and then crowded in close beside her. With one big foot, he gave the swing a push.

Under the porch roof, the moon's illumination couldn't quite penetrate, leaving them in heavy shadows. A sense of intimacy enveloped them, crowding out other, more restless thoughts.

Then Stan said, "Rachelle fancied herself in love with Terrance. Earlier, before she left, she considered sleeping with him."

Jenna jerked around to face him. "She *told* you that?"

"No." Stan's voice remained calm and even despite her disbelief. "She'd even had thoughts about marrying him some day. But tonight he moved too fast, pushing her, not being very nice."

Lost, Jenna stared at Stan, her gaze seeking in the darkness.

"The good news is that her eyes were opened to the type of guy he really is. The bad news is, she's hurt." He squeezed her shoulder. "But your daughter is smart, Jenna. She won't be seeing him anymore."

Everything inside Jenna went still. Stan acted as though he knew it all for fact, when that couldn't be. "What are you talking about, Stan? You can't possibly know what my daughter is thinking or feeling."

"I know." Stan stared down at his lap, then abruptly turned and pointed at the moon. "You see that, honey? A big, fat full moon, just hanging up there in the sky, lighting the yard like midday. And not just any full moon. This is the second full moon this month. A rarity. A blue moon."

A little spooked, Jenna turned her head and glanced up at the sky. The yard did seem unusually bright, and suddenly, the air settled, not even a leaf rustling.

A chill of alarm went up her spine.

"Don't get spooked," Stan told her. "But this is what I've been trying to tell you."

Jenna had nothing to say to that, so she remained quiet, waiting.

As if he knew her every thought, Stan smiled. "For some people, maybe for you, a full moon heightens emotions. It's not turning forty that made you think more about me. It's the moon. Obviously, for a blue moon, the effect would be exaggerated. It definitely is for me."

Jenna frowned. "Exaggerated how?"

His jaw worked. With his arm around her, her side pressed into his, Jenna felt his muscles tightening. "I was in trouble with juvy—juvenile hall—three times. All three times, I did things people couldn't understand. I jumped one kid, put myself in front of another, refused to let a girl ride her bike home . . ."

Awareness dawning, though it didn't make much sense, Jenna asked, "This all happened during a full moon?"

He gave one quick nod. "The guy I jumped was going to buy dope from some creeps, just to impress his girlfriend. After they tossed me in juvy, he did it anyway. And got in a shitload of trouble—just as I knew he would."

"Buying dope is never a good idea, Stan."

Rather than look at her, he stared straight ahead. "The guy I got in front of was going to challenge a bully who would have beat him up and humiliated him in front of everyone. That kid had enough troubles without adding more to his list."

Idly, almost as if he didn't realize it, Stan's fingertips teased over her shoulder, caressing, stroking—keeping her close.

In a faint voice, somehow tortured by memories, he whispered, "The girl had lost her mother. She was feeling suicidal. I know, because . . . I felt what she felt. I couldn't let her leave, knowing what she'd do. I caught hell for detaining her, but as a result, she got caught up in the same chaos that surrounded me. She got attention." He shrugged. "It helped." And with insistence, "At least she didn't kill herself."

The knocking of Jenna's heart made her tremble. She didn't move, not to pull away from Stan and not to move closer. "I think you need to just spell it out, Stan, whatever it is you want to tell me."

"You're right." After a deep breath, he faced her. His glittering gaze pierced the darkness, holding her captive. "From the time I was a kid, the moon heightened my ability to read other people's thoughts. When there's a blue moon, the thoughts are as clear as written text."

Jenna barely had time to assimilate what he'd said, to consider the ramifications of what he believed, when he cupped her face in his big hands.

"Jenna." He bent and kissed her forehead. "Don't be afraid of me, honey. And don't try to placate me. I know it's farfetched. Hell, my own parents thought I was mental. I can only tell you from experience that it's true."

"Stan." Jenna eased herself away—and he let her go. On her feet, she backed up one step, then two.

He watched her. "Think something, Jenna, other than the obvious." He didn't leave the swing. "I know you're worried about me, and about your kids. You want to help me even as you're wondering if I might be dangerous." He half laughed. "But then, anyone would know that just by the look on your face. Think of something else. Anything."

Dear God, Jenna mused. *For him, it's some warped game.*

"No game." He leaned forward, elbows on his knees. "Warped or otherwise. It's just the truth."

Her eyes widened. *Could he have . . . no.*

"Yes."

Her breath caught in her throat, strangling her.

Hands fisted, Jenna tried to think of something totally off the wall, but instead, she remembered the way he'd kissed her, how much she'd wanted him—

"I hope you still do," Stan whispered, pushing slowly to his feet. "Because I want you like hell."

"Oh, God," she said out loud.

"I'm sorry, baby. I don't mean to intrude on your privacy. It just happens. Sometimes I can block it out, but with you . . . the things you think just work their way in." With a cautious stride, he moved toward her. "Do you have any idea how hard today was on me? I knew every single time you thought about me."

"No."

"You pictured me naked. You thought about kissing me all over, and me doing the same to you. You thought about sex in a dozen different ways. Your visuals of my naked body are off a little. Hell, Jenna, I'm forty, not twenty-five."

Her mouth went dry.

"But I won't disappoint you." Another step brought him closer. "I'll fuck you as hard and fast as you want. I'll make love to you slow and easy. I'll kiss you from your eyebrows down to your knees—and I'll damn sure linger at all the best places in between."

"Stan, stop it."

"Like hell I will. Do you know what it's like for me, wanting you, already in love with you, and knowing you consider me incapable of commitment? To you, I'm a free-wheeling runaround. I'm a guy who'd be ideal for a fling, a stud to fuck a few times, but not good for much more."

"That's not true."

"No? You're willing to have an affair, but you don't want to love me."

Jenna gasped. Her stomach knotted and her chest hurt. Love him? She didn't want to, but—

As if sensing an advantage, he pressed forward. "Your kids like me, Jenna. They've both missed having a dad around. There's this huge empty hole left in their lives, a hole you've tried your best to fill, and God knows you've done an incredible job. But you're their mother and that's role enough."

Defiance became her only defense. "You're saying you want to play Dad?"

"No playing to it. You've got great kids, and they'd be easy to love."

"I need time to think." Never in a million years had Jenna expected so much to be dumped on her at once. Stan didn't want an affair. Did he mean he wanted forever?

"Damn right." He stood only a breath away, invading her space, heightening her awareness of him. "Tonight, tomorrow, and every day after. I want your kids. I want to make a home with you. I want family vacations and budgets and grocery shopping and trips to the school. Forget my damn past and the trumped-up reputation and the stupid borderline celebrity status. Just concentrate on how you feel with me."

Jenna shook her head. "Stan, this is . . . too much. Too over the top."

"You think I don't know that? Do you think it was easy reading my wife's mind and knowing she'd slept with other men? You think it's easy knowing how badly you want me, but also knowing you don't trust me?" He moved against her, pulling her close. His gaze searched hers, his dark eyes mysterious in the moonlight, then filled with awareness. "You're not afraid of me, Jenna. What I've told you . . . it doesn't scare you."

"No, of course not." Jenna realized it couldn't have been easy for him to share such a personal experience. He'd said his parents thought him mental. How hard must that have been on him?

"It made my life hell," he admitted. "After their re-action, I kept it to myself until I met my college room-mate. He was totally into the moon and luna effects, and after he swore secrecy, I shared with him. He helped me understand how it works."

"You've never told anyone else?"

"Not till you." His fingertips smoothed away a long tendril of her hair, tucking it behind her ear. "I had to tell you."

Jenna stared up at him, her heart full. "Why, Stan?"

He kissed her, long and hard and deep, lifting her to her tiptoes, letting his hands cup her hips and bringing her body into stark contact with his erection. "Because I want to make love to you," he rasped. "I want it so bad, it's eating me up. But I couldn't sleep with you until you understood. You have a right to know what you might be getting into."

His sense of fair play astounded her. Most men would have used their ability to take advantage of a woman—

"I want you forever. Not just for a quick lay. Believe that. Years from now, I'll still know your thoughts. At least once a month you'll have no privacy at all. When-ever there's a blue moon I'll be a part of you, in your head, absorbing your every thought like it was my own."

Again he kissed her, gentler this time, as if in apol-ogy. A bubble of renewed desire swelled inside her. Re-gardless of their uncertain future she had to reassure him. "You're a good man, Stan."

Of course, he read her every thought, and his eyes narrowed. "Right. Good at knowing things I have no right knowing."

"You said you can block the thoughts . . ."

Stan shrugged. "With most people, sure. I don't give a damn what they think anyway. After getting that suspended sentence for battery, I knew it'd be safer for me to ignore trouble, rather than try to help. The voices were still there, like birds in the trees, making background noise. But I was able to focus on other stuff so that it didn't register. With you . . . I can't block you, Jenna. Your feelings hit me like a sledgehammer."

She blushed. "It's embarrassing, knowing you were aware of my fantasies." As things became clear, she groaned. "That's why you asked me to go to lunch today, isn't it? You *knew* what I was imagining . . ."

"Yeah, I knew." He cuddled her closer, rocking side to side, his hands low on her hips. "But don't be embarrassed. Hell, woman, you turned me on until I had a damn boner all through the interview. I haven't come in my pants since I was a green kid, but you had me there, close to totally losing control." He nuzzled against her cheek, and Jenna could feel his smile. "Can you imagine how the interview would have turned out?"

She covered her face, chuckling, but also vividly aware of him as a man and how his honesty brought out more fantasies—of making him lose control, of watching him . . .

"Jenna," he groaned, "we'll be good together, I swear it." Only a whisper separated them, so Jenna could feel the faint trembling in his hard frame. "Your kids would love to have me around. Your daughter could go to Savannah, and I'd take Ryan fishing every weekend until he got sick of worms."

Jenna pressed a finger to his mouth. There were a few things she had to make perfectly clear. "I want my kids happy, Stan. But I'd never use a man to make that happen."

"I know that, damn it. That's not what I meant." His fingers tightened on her, then abruptly loosened so that he caressed her, stroking from her hips to her waist and finally up to her breasts. He palmed her and growled in satisfaction when her low moan filled the quiet night.

"*Stan.*"

"Think about us in bed together, Jenna. Every night. Sometimes during the day." His mouth kissed a damp path from her lips to her cheek and up to her ear. "Anything and everything you want, I want, too. There's nothing you can imagine that I'm not willing to do." His fingertips moved over her, finding her stiffened nipples, moving back and forth, back and forth—then tugging, rolling.

Her nails dug into his biceps where she held him. Her breath became choppy. God, she'd wanted him for so long.

"Think about just the two of us, honey. Have you wanted any other man like this?"

"No." This wanting was almost awful, so strong that she felt lost in its grip. Helpless.

His mouth ravaged hers, his tongue stroking, claiming. He continued to toy with one nipple while his other hand went to her waist, then her belly—and below.

It wasn't easy, but Jenna caught his hand, stopping him.

Breathing in harsh pants, Stan said, "Sorry. I know. Not here. You make me forget myself." He held her tight a moment more, then released her and took a step back.

She forgot herself, too. And she was almost tempted . . .

"No," he said. "We'd both regret it."

Jenna put her hands in her hair. "Stan, even if you know my thoughts, quit spitting them back at me. It's disconcerting."

His dark eyes glittered. "Sorry."

Back-stepping, Jenna removed herself from temptation. When she stood several feet away from him, she met his gaze squarely. "I need tonight to think."

"There's nothing to think about." His face was hard, his expression hurt. "You either want me or you don't."

"I do, you know I do." He had to understand that much. "But I've been thinking in the short term, and now you're talking about so much more. You can't rush me, Stan. I can't rush me, because there's not just me."

"You're a package deal." His hand slashed through the air. "I know that. And I already told you, I like your kids. They like me. No problem."

It took an effort, but Jenna held herself still and kept her voice firm. "I have to think about how this will affect them. The fact that you could read their thoughts, too, has to be considered. Can't you see that? It's not just my privacy you'd invade, but theirs as well."

"I could try to block their thoughts, but . . . I don't know if I can. Not every time. I care about them. That seems to make a difference. If Rachelle looked upset and it was in my power to understand why—" He stopped, propped his hands on his hips, and glared out at the moon.

Voice strained, he rasped, "It's only once a month at the most. And I can't pick up every little thought. Just the glaring ones."

"Unless there's a blue moon," she reminded him, "like tonight. Then you'd be in our heads every minute of every hour."

He cursed low, looking hurt and needy—that thought made him scowl.

Before he could protest, Jenna took the few large strides she needed to reach him. "Give me tonight, Stan." She went on tiptoe and kissed him, a quick goodbye peck. "I'll talk with you tomorrow, okay?"

And then she turned and hurried inside.

Stan stood there, watching the door close, hearing

the lock turn. Fuck it, he thought, but at the same time, he listened to Jenna, hearing her loud and clear even through the door. Her indecision scraped over his already raw nerves. He felt her sadness, her warring confusion, and he jerked around to leave.

He didn't have a gift. He had a curse. And in the end, it just might cost him the thing he wanted most—marriage to Jenna.

Wearing only jeans, Stan stood on his covered deck, coffee in hand, showered but not shaved. He stared out at the wet, gloomy morning and wished he wasn't alone. A lingering rain, accompanied by the occasional low rumble of thunder and distant lightning, obliterated plans for landscaping work.

After a sleepless night, he'd shoved out of his rumpled bed at five A.M. and started drowning his problems in caffeine. Because his house sat next to his garden center, and both backed up to the lake, he could see the turbulent waves rolling to the shore with a splash.

Usually he loved days like this—perfect for lingering in bed, making love all day long, slow and languorous, letting the pleasure build and peak while the wind whistled and the rain beat against the windowpanes.

Stan cursed. Today he hated the damn weather.

He needed the distraction of his work, sweating in the hot sun, digging and planting until his muscles ached. But all he could do was wait—and think about Jenna.

He considered calling her, but knew he shouldn't. She wanted time to herself, and even though he figured too much thinking would bring her to conclusions he wouldn't favor, he had to respect her wishes.

Working on his next book, *Season by Season Gardening*, was out. He doubted he could hold a thought long enough to get anything down on paper. He detested early morning television. He wasn't hungry.

And so he stood there, his skin chilled from the early morning rain-cooled air, his gaze directed blindly at the lake, his muscles twitchy and his soul in turmoil.

When his doorbell rang, Stan didn't at first move. Seconds ticked by while he held himself immobile . . . and then Jenna's thoughts sank into him, alerting him to her presence. They were too jumbled to decipher. Or maybe he was too jumbled, too filled with satisfaction and surging lust and possessiveness.

She'd come to him.

He left the sliding doors to the deck open as he strode inside. Even before he went down the hall and opened the locks, he knew what he'd find—Jenna standing there with her crooked smile and her dimple and her gentle green eyes. She wanted to make love, but did she want him forever?

He jerked the door open.

She blinked up at him, and he was afraid to hope, to open his mind to her for fear she'd come to tell him things he didn't want to hear.

Holding the coffee mug in one hand, Stan used the other to brace on the doorknob. How long they stood there staring at each other, he wasn't sure. With no expression at all, he whispered, "Hi."

Her smile wobbled. "Morning." Then her gaze dipped to his naked chest—and stayed there.

Lust. That's what he felt from her. Desire. Need. Nervousness and urgency and determination—

"Come in." Stan pushed the door wide and stood back while she crept over the threshold. And she did creep. As though she had reservations, or was afraid . . .

It hit him, a storm of sensation, exploding inside his brain like a migraine. Jenna badly wanted to talk to him, to clear the air by her own choice before he read her thoughts. Stan struggled to abide by her wishes. He tried thinking of things the total opposite of Jenna—his mother, grub worms . . . It didn't work.

Singing to himself to drown out her feelings, Stan took her arm and trotted her down the hall and into the family room that opened out to the deck. The open sliders had let in the humidity, leaving the room damp and cool and as turbulent as the storm itself.

He led her to a soft striped couch, pushed her down onto the cushions, set his coffee on the end table and crouched in front of her. His heart hammered and a sudden erection made his old faded jeans uncomfortable. "Talk to me quick, sweetheart. I'll do my best to hear only what you say, not what you think."

Jenna's lips trembled. She touched his face with one small, cool hand. "Stan." Her hair was loose, and very little make-up colored her face. She wore an old, soft sweatshirt with a pair of drawstring shorts and flip-flop sandals. Her knees pressed into his chest and she licked her lips, bringing her thoughts together. "I spoke with Rachelle."

He hadn't expected that. A dozen other possibilities had occurred to him, but not that. "Yeah? And?"

She licked her lips again. If she didn't quit doing that, he wouldn't be responsible for a delay in conversation. Already he wanted to push her flat on the couch, to open her thighs and settle between them and strip off her sweatshirt—

"I told her everything."

Stan had been studying her taut nipples beneath the soft cotton sweatshirt with interest, but at her confession, his gaze shot to her face. *"Everything?"*

Scooting forward to the edge of the sofa, earnest in the extreme, Jenna tunneled her fingers through his hair and launched into explanation. "I had to, Stan. I couldn't sleep and I was up all night pacing and trying to sort things out, and finally at five this morning, I gave up."

Stan stared at her. "I got up at five, too. Same reason. Couldn't sleep."

Her expression softened. "I'm sorry," she whispered. "I know this isn't easy for you."

Damn, she made him feel like a wimp. "I'm fine," he said, his voice gruff. "What the hell did you tell Rachelle?"

"She was concerned. She wanted to know if you'd done something mean to me, something to upset me. She told me about Terrance—you were right, by the way. He is an ass. He made my daughter cry."

"If he was a little older, I'd stomp him for her."

Jenna smiled, and she had her heart in her eyes. "I told Rachelle you weren't like that, but then she kept prodding, telling me how perfect you are. She thinks you're smart and nice and sexy—"

"Sexy?" he croaked.

Her smile widened. "Yes. But she said it in an attempt to convince me, not out of personal interest."

Burning heat came into his face. "Damn it, I know that."

"I told her I thought you were wonderful, and she wanted to know why I was up moping and pacing instead of in bed dreaming about you. So . . . I told her."

"She knows I can read her thoughts?"

"Yes. We talked through an entire pot of coffee."

Shit, shit, shit. Stan's shoulders slumped a little. "She thinks I'm a wacko."

With a quiet chuckle, Jenna leaned forward and wrapped her arms around his neck, hugging him tight. Stan could feel her breasts on his bare chest, her warm breath on his shoulder.

He closed his eyes and whispered, "You're killing me, babe," and then he pulled her closer still.

Jenna pressed a small kiss to his throat, another to his shoulder. "Rachelle said, in a rather admonishing tone, that most men never have a clue what a woman thinks or feels, and they're even more lost as to what a woman wants."

"True." But given the female psyche, how could you blame them?

"She told me that I should grab you with both hands and never let you go."

Stan's heart almost stopped. "Is that right? And what did you say?"

"I reminded her that it wouldn't only be my thoughts you could listen to. But Rachelle says she has no secrets, and when she does, she won't be around during full moons."

Some of Stan's tension started to ease. He stroked his hands over Jenna's back, down to the swell of her hips.

"I thought about that," Jenna admitted. "About how it'd be between us, how you'll know what I want, even before I realize it."

"You mean in bed."

When she nodded, her hair teased his cheek. "I've waited long enough, Stan." Her teeth closed on the muscle of his shoulder, sending a rush of sensation through his veins. "I don't want to wait anymore."

"Neither do I." Jenna hadn't said anything about love or the future, but in that particular moment, Stan needed her too much to care.

In one smooth movement, he pushed up from his knees to sit on the sofa, cradling Jenna on his lap. She curled against him, right at home, her rounded tush pressing against his boner, her arms around him, her big cushy breasts smooshed against the hard wall of his chest.

He struggled to catch his breath, but her thoughts

penetrated. It had been an effort, letting her talk without reading her feelings, her mind. Now he couldn't
stop the tide and it flattened him. Like an inferno, she
burned from the inside out. Stan knew that her breasts
were throbbing, that between her thighs she was wet
and aching, trembling all over.

He caught her face and kissed her hard, giving her
his tongue and accepting hers in return. Her urgency
became his own, and he shoved up her sweatshirt, desperate for the feel of her body, her soft breasts and
stiffened nipples.

As his rough thumb stroked over her nipple, pressing, circling, Jenna jerked her mouth free and cried
out.

Raising the sweatshirt higher, Stan lowered his head
to kiss her. Jenna struggled, trying to free herself of the
shirt while squirming under him. When his mouth
closed over her nipple, she arched her body and gave a
long, ragged groan.

Jesus, she was on the ragged edge, and he knew,
knew that she wanted his hand on her now, his fingers
inside her, stroking and working her. Without a word,
Stan levered himself up and off her, stripped her shirt
away and went to work on the drawstring of her shorts.
Jenna helped, kicking off her sandals, but once Stan
prepared to remove her shorts, she froze.

He felt her lack of confidence and paused long
enough to cup her face. "Listen to me, Jenna. You're
beautiful. Every inch of you."

"I'm forty."

"You're stacked."

Pleasure at his compliment warred with uncertainty.
"I've . . . I've had two kids."

Stan continued to look into her eyes while he slipped
his hand over her rounded belly, circled once, relishing

her softness, then pushed into her shorts. Her lips parted on a sudden breath.

He found her pubic curls and fingered them briefly before pressing lower, into damp, hot flesh, swollen and ready. His chest labored.

Her eyes grew unfocused—but she didn't break the connection of their gazes.

For a time he just petted her, lightly prodding, exploring. Then he found her clitoris, already turgid, and using his middle finger, touched her gently.

Her shattered moan filled the air. "Oh, God, Stan."

She needed release more than foreplay, Stan realized. It had been a very long time for her. Jenna wasn't a woman to indulge in one-night stands, and in a small community where everyone had known her husband, there'd be no such thing as privacy. She'd been in a position of all or nothing, and so, putting her kids first, she'd chosen nothing.

But now she had him.

Stan looked at her breasts, and his lust kicked up another notch. They were big and soft, very pale with rosy nipples drawn tight. Slowly, deliberately building the anticipation, he closed his mouth over her, suckling softly, tonguing her—and all the while, he teased her clitoris, lightly abrading, moving his finger back and forth.

Her hips lifted and her thighs opened. Stan paused long enough to tug her shorts over and off her hips, then threw them aside. Without haste he looked at her, lying naked on his couch, her belly trembling, her chest heaving, her face flushed.

All his.

Every muscle in his body strained with the savage need to take her. Her timidity wasn't strong enough to overpower her sexual yearning. She wanted him and, at least for that moment, didn't care if her body lacked perfection. Stan shook his head. To him, she was better than perfect, everything he'd ever wanted, more than he thought he'd ever get.

"Stan . . . please."

He shifted his position at the side of the couch so that he faced her feet, then levered himself over her. He slid his arms under her thighs and pulled them farther apart. With his fingertips, he explored her, opening her swollen lips, tracing along her opening, up and over her clitoris.

Her small moans and soft gasps urged him on. He kissed her belly before pressing his mouth lower.

Yeah, she wanted this, had dreamed about it, fantasized for long, endless nights about how it'd feel to have his mouth on her, tonguing her. Sucking. Making her come.

Her excitement was a live thing, invading his head, obliterating his concentration.

Harsh, trembly sounds of anticipation mingled with her fast breaths. Her heels pressed into the sofa cushions. She groaned, and her fingers curled over the waistband of his jeans at the small of his back.

Stan inhaled the hot scent of her sex, gave his own groan of excitement and closed his mouth over her. Being very gentle with her, he circled her clitoris with his tongue, finding a rhythm that made her wild. The weight of his body held her still, but she jerked hard when he pushed one finger into her.

With each new pulse, each throb and shiver that coursed through her, his own pleasure expanded. She tasted so good, he could have eaten her for hours, but only a few minutes later, with two fingers buried deep inside her, pressing hard, alternately sucking and licking her, she came.

Stan was so wrapped up in her pleasure, so into the

moment and so turned on, that he forgot about reading her thoughts. Everything he did was out of love for her, because he wanted her pleasure and enjoyed kissing and touching her—as much as he'd enjoy her touch in return.

Attuned to her every sigh and moan and movement, he knew just when to increase the pressure to give her the most explosive orgasm. He knew when to ease back, when to slide his fingers free, when to gentle her.

Because he was a man in love, not because of the twice cursed moon. It astounded him that during her climax, her thoughts hadn't been clear to him at all. He hadn't needed them to be. Jenna was an open, giving lover.

She was all his.

He had his cheek on her belly, his fingers idly tracing circles on her thigh when her soft sobs reached him. Still, without delving into her thoughts, Stan smiled with pure male satisfaction. Jenna's tears weren't from sadness, upset, or disappointment. She cried out of an excess of emotion, because she knew that what they'd just shared was special.

Enjoying her femaleness, this sign of her caring, Stan kissed her pelvic bone. "Shhh, sweetheart," he whispered, feeling very indulgent. "Don't cry."

She made an endearing little hiccupping noise, then stammered, "I'm sorry. I don't know why I am."

Carefully, Stan eased his arms out from under her thighs and began kissing his way up her body. "You," he said with his lips on her belly, "enjoyed"—he lingered on her breasts—"what I just did to you."

Her eyes were liquid with tears, sated and filled with love. "You already know I did."

"Yeah." Using one fingertip, he brushed away a tear clinging to her lashes. "Because I'm not unfamiliar with a woman's body or her response." Uncaring if she understood his statement, Stan stood, then unzipped his jeans. "You'll enjoy me inside you even more."

As he shoved his jeans down and off, she caught her breath. "God, Stan, you are so gorgeous." She quickly sat up, tucking one leg beneath her bottom, reaching out with both hands to touch his abdomen, lower, over the trail of hair that thickened at his crotch. Fully erect, his cock throbbed as her soft fingers wrapped around him.

Tipping his head back, Stan locked his knees and let her explore him at her leisure.

In an absent voice, she asked, "Do you have a condom, Stan?"

"Yeah." He dropped one onto the coffee table. "I stuck three in my jeans pocket as soon as I knew you wanted me."

Using both hands, she squeezed, slid up his length, then slowly back down again. "Three, huh?"

Stan swallowed his groan. "Yeah." Talking wasn't easy. "You never know when opportunity might knock, and I believe in being prepared."

"That's because you're such a great guy." The last whispered word no sooner left her mouth than her lips brushed the head of his penis, and Stan growled out a low curse.

"Jenna."

"You already know how often I've thought about doing this." The hot interior of her mouth closed around him and he felt her wet, velvet tongue moving, sliding . . .

He couldn't wait any longer. Not with Jenna.

He caught her shoulders to pull her away, then tipped her to her back on the sofa cushions.

Rumbling thunder nearly drowned out her laugh as Stan stretched out over her. The lights flickered and a strong wind brought the storm into the room. "Why such a hurry, Stan?" Jenna teased.

He kissed the smile right off her mouth, then kept on

kissing her until she clutched him again, until her skin heated and she moaned and writhed under him. Again, he pushed his fingers into her, and he felt her muscles clamp down, squeezing him, making him desperate to feel her on his cock.

When she again made those sweet female sounds he adored, Stan sat up long enough to roll on the condom.

"Look at me, Jenna."

Her heavy eyes opened, but grew dazed as he guided himself into her. Straightening his arms, Stan stayed above her so he could see her every reaction as he became a part of her. "Christ, you feel good, Jenna."

Her neck arched and she sank her teeth into her bottom lip, whimpering. The tension grew, until finally she gasped. "Stan, I'm sorry."

And before he'd seated himself fully inside her, she groaned long and low, rocking out another climax. Her heels pressed into the backs of his thighs and her fingers dug deep into his shoulders. Stan took great pleasure in just watching her, feeling her contractions rhythmically squeezing him, knowing that he had the power to satisfy the woman he loved.

When she quieted, her forearm over her eyes, her body damp with sweat, he began thrusting, shallow, easy, slow deep thrusts.

"Oh, God, Stan," she whispered.

With his right hand, he gripped the cushion beside her head and with his left, he braced on the arm of the sofa. He clenched his jaw, driving into her with more force, shaking the couch, feeling the power of the storm in his blood.

Restless, Jenna turned her face away from him, but she came right back, eyes barely open, lips red and swollen. "Unbelievable," she moaned, and then her hands slid up and over his shoulders, her fingers delving into his hair.

Stan bent to take her mouth, ravaging her, eating at her soft lips and sucking at her tongue, and then he exploded, great waves of pressure shuddering through him again and again. He lowered himself to hold Jenna tight until finally it all began to ease away. He felt replete.

He felt whole.

Jenna stirred as goose bumps rose on the naked flesh of her waist and hip and upper thigh. Idly, Stan stroked her with his open palm, warming her skin. "You are so soft." He kept his voice low now that the storm had moved past them, leaving only a steady rain. "I love touching you."

She sighed and curled into him. "You didn't close your sliding doors. Your floor is going to be wet."

"Storms turn me on." Stan loved her so much, it hurt. But so far, she hadn't said a word about love. She'd screamed out her pleasure, hugged him with her thighs, begged him and praised him and been as open and giving as a woman could be during hot grinding sex. But she hadn't said a single word about the future.

She was so lethargic, her body, her thoughts. Stan felt her smiles inside his heart. He felt her satisfaction and her contentment. He felt . . . a lot of things. But he didn't know if they equaled love.

"So," she whispered, twining her fingers in his chest hair. "I need to wait for another rainstorm during a full moon to get a repeat of today?"

He swatted her hip, smiled as she yelped, then went back to smoothing her skin. "I was edgy as a junkyard dog when you showed up, and I knew even before I opened the door that you were here to get laid."

Her lips curled. "I was here for you, Stan. If all I wanted was sex, I probably could have found another willing guy."

Shoving up to one elbow, Stan almost toppled Jenna to the floor. His hand gripping her ass stopped her from falling off the sofa. "Who? Where?"

This time she laughed outright. Slumberous, sated eyes mocked him. "I don't know, Stan. I've never offered before. But I figure *someone* would be willing if I started giving it away. I mean, I know Delicious can be a little backward, and there aren't that many single guys my age, but—"

In one swift movement, Stan pinned her beneath him. Catching her wrists in a fist, he stretched her arms up and over her head. "Tell me you love me."

Those green eyes widened, no longer teasing. At the same time, Stan felt the response of her body, the accelerated beating of her heart, the shifting of her thighs, the warming of her skin.

She liked being in a submissive position—and her turn-ons became his own.

Distracted, Stan trailed the fingers of his free hand along the underside of her arm, down, down, until he cupped her breast. Staring into her eyes, he caught her nipple between his fingertips, lightly pinched and tugged.

Jenna's gasp sounded of surprise and excitement and encouragement.

"Tell me, sweetheart," he insisted. "Tell me that you love me and want to marry me."

She turned her face away—but shifted back quickly when he increased the pressure on her nipple. Stan smiled at the wild beating of her heart, the excited flush of her skin. "Yeah, keep looking at me, Jenna."

"Okay."

Such a soft, needy voice. Stan leaned down to lick her bottom lip, then her throat. "Tell me, Jenna." He closed his mouth over her nipple and sucked hard.

"*Stan.*"

The way she said his name did him in. "Damn it."

He quickly grew hard again, and this time he knew he'd last at least an hour. Hell, he hadn't come twice so soon in years. "Don't move."

She watched him with the same fascination she might give a snake. "What are you going to do?"

"Grab another condom."

That earned him a groan—but she didn't move.

The second Stan had the protection rolled on, he settled over her again. "Open your legs, Jenna. Now."

Slowly, her thighs shifted apart, and he thrust in with a long, ragged groan. She was wet and swollen and so hot. "Fuck yeah. Squeeze me. Tighter."

Her muscles clamped down, and Stan ground his teeth. "God, yeah. You feel good, Jenna. So damn good."

"I love you, Stan."

He froze. His gaze locked on to hers.

Smiling, she slipped her hands out of his slack hold to twine her arms around his neck. "I thought you were reading my mind, so you'd already know that I love you."

Shaking his head, his whole body throbbing, Stan swallowed hard. "You were naked, Jenna, here, with me and ready. What you thought didn't seem as important as what you did. What we did together."

"So you couldn't read my mind?"

Stan thought about it, easily picked up her suspicion, and grinned. "I could. I guess your naked body was enough of a distraction. I was too busy feeling you, the texture of your skin and hair. And your scent makes me nuts. And the sight of you when you come . . ."

"Stan, stop."

He took her mouth in a long, tongue-twining kiss. "There's just so much of you to enjoy, it's like sensory overload. I forgot about hearing your thoughts."

Relief had her laughing. "Stan, that's . . . wonderful." Then her brow drew down in a frown. "But if you weren't reading my mind, how did you know to—"

He moved against her and caught her gasp. "Jenna, sweetheart, your body language is very easy to read."

She lifted into him. "Is that so?"

On a groan, Stan muttered, "Damn right." Holding still took gigantic effort.

Her small hands moved up his arms to his biceps. "I love you, Stan, so much that it almost consumes me. I never thought to meet a man like you."

They were intimately joined, their bodies sealed together by the humidity and sexual heat and their own sweat, as close as any two people could get.

Stan didn't want her influenced by sex. "You're sure?" He narrowed his eyes, very aware of his own vulnerability. "Be sure, Jenna."

"Stan Tucker, I love you." Her voice was firm but scratchy with emotion. "I want to marry you and be with you forever."

Staring into her eyes, Stan withdrew, but sank back in. "Say it again."

"I love you."

His guts knotted. His heart pounded. He shifted to wedge a hand beneath her hips, tilting her up, giving him deeper penetration. Through clenched teeth, he ordered, "Again."

"*Stan.*" Her head fell back and her pale throat worked.

Deliberately, Stan opened himself to her, to the physical sensation and the emotional bombardment, to her thoughts and her love and her pleasure. He greeted the churning of a building climax, savored every nuance of sensation burning through her, shivering through her thighs, her breasts, her belly . . . around his cock as her orgasm broke.

He squeezed his eyes shut and kept his rhythm steady, delighting in each high, female sound of excitement that burst from her throat.

When she sank back into the cushions, her breathing still choppy and her face damp, Stan kissed her throat, tasting the salt of her skin, rubbing his nose over her, inhaling her scent. "I love you, too," he told her. "Enough to last three lifetimes."

Jenna put one limp hand to his cheek and managed a sleepy smile. "I know."

Too tired to lift his head, Stan grunted. "So you're a mind reader now, too?"

Her gentle fingers stroked over him. "No, I'm just a woman who feels very loved. And I don't mean the sex, which is . . . well, there aren't words. But the way you look at me, how you touch me . . . I didn't think I could ever be this happy again. And I owe it all to a full moon."

Finally, Stan found the strength to raise himself up, to look at her cherished face and smile with her. "I always figured the Lunar Effect to be a pain in the ass. But every once in a blue moon, things really do work out."

Jenna gave him a coy look. "No way am I waiting for blue moons to have my way with you, Stan, so forget that. Once we're married, I expect you to love me each and every night."

Stan let the smile take him, let his heart fill with love. Then he tipped back his head and howled, and when Jenna laughed, he knew he'd never again resent the effect of the full moon.

MOON
MAGNETISM

Lucy Monroe

One

"Holy crap!" Ivy Kendall stared at the innocent-looking pink memo slip and crossed herself. Not being Catholic, she wasn't sure what good it would do. Did God have issues with that kind of thing?

Oh, man, she didn't have time for a one-sided theological discussion with herself. Not when she needed to book tickets to Alaska, or maybe Zimbabwe, or how about the North Pole? Did they have computers at the North Pole? Sure as certain they didn't have Blake Hawthorne—gorgeous, sexy, business mogul who just happened to run the hotel conglomerate she worked for.

A man who wasn't content to use a mere Palm Pilot, his Rolex watch had been custom-made with alarm and messaging functions. His cell phone had a built-in GPS device as well as Internet capability. She'd seen him use it, but one minute in Ivy's company would have every last personal technology device malfunctioning.

"Poop sticks."

She frowned. Her twelve-year-old niece uttered the phrase with a lot more relish, knowing her mom couldn't get her for swearing, but it didn't satisfy Ivy's sense of the moment at all.

Besides, *her* mother was in Florida living it up with Dad. *She* didn't have to worry about this time of month anymore. *She* could walk into a computer lab and not worry about erasing a single hard drive. Ivy wasn't so lucky, and Blake Hawthorne, king of techno-toys, was on his way this very minute.

It was a darn good thing Mom was far enough away not to hear the words bubbling up inside Ivy, ready to spew forth any second.

"Shit. Damn. Umm . . . never mind the f-word . . . Hell. Mary, Mother of Joseph . . . " Was that even a curse if you weren't Catholic? *"Crap,"* she said again for good measure, but none of her admittedly limited vocabulary of swear words did the least bit to relieve her panic.

Pretty soon, she was going to break out in hives, and wouldn't that be just what she needed?

Her boss was coming. *Today.* In less than an hour if the memo had gotten the time correct.

She banged her head against her desk and groaned. How could she have missed the memo?

It had been sitting in her in-box under a message to call Ed, that's how she could miss it. She'd rather have her teeth cleaned than go on another date with the man, but she was lousy at saying no to fragile people. Ed was more boring than a rerun of the Bob Hope Chrysler Golf Tournament, but he was also sensitive.

She'd convinced herself that if she didn't actually pick up the message, she hadn't really gotten it, and she didn't have to call him back. She'd been very careful not to read it once she got past the "from" line.

Unfortunately, she hadn't thought to check if there was anything under it . . . until five minutes ago. Way too late to get on the next outbound flight for a remote village in Botswana. Even if she *could* get the flight, she couldn't take it. She'd never be able to complete the drive between Delicious and Cleveland, the closest city with a major airport.

She'd stopped driving during this time of month after her last fender-bender. Admittedly they didn't happen every full moon, but she wasn't taking any more chances. After all, the last one had been how she'd met Ed.

"Is that a new pose for meditation?"

Her heart stopped beating. She was sure of it.

The message had been wrong, or he was early; either way, she was screwed.

Desperately sucking air in an attempt not to hyperventilate, she lifted her head. After a moment of shoring up her mental fortitude, she opened her eyes, too. One look had her mentally cursing her inability to have the hi-tech phone system her staff could have used to warn her of her boss's arrival.

She didn't get up. Her legs were shaky, her body reacting predictably to the sight of the gorgeous blond man standing so relaxed in her doorway. And why shouldn't he be? He had nothing to fear . . . or at least didn't realize he did. If he came much closer, thousands of dollars' worth of personal technical gadgets were going to stop working.

Heck, maybe they already had. It was a blue moon coming up after all.

Nevertheless, she had to try to stave off disaster. Didn't she? *"Stay back."*

His brows rose in question, and his blue eyes pierced her with curiosity. "Not finished meditating?" he asked sardonically.

"I don't meditate."

"I didn't really think you did."

Right. "Then why . . . never mind. Uh, I . . . um . . . I think I've got a bug, and I'm pretty sure it's contagious. You should leave. Now."

He smiled, even white teeth reminding her of a tiger drawing back its lips to reveal the deadly fangs of a hunter. "I never get sick." Then he stepped into the room.

"I guess germs are too intimidated by you to take up residence," she muttered, her self-preservation instincts buried under stress.

His mouth quirked, but he kept coming, across the room, around her desk, and finally, she had to swivel in her old-fashioned wooden office chair to face him.

He stood over her, his big body giving off messages she had to be misinterpreting. Sexy, sensual, in her face with his masculinity messages. "Do I intimidate you, Ivy? Is that why you do everything short of quit your job in order to avoid the management training seminars?"

She swallowed, trying to wet a suddenly dry throat. "I don't avoid the seminars."

"You weren't at the last one."

"Something unavoidable came up."

A full moon. No way was she going to New York City to stay in a hotel with thirty-eight floors of rooms (all of them with their own computer-operated climate control systems) when that big white nemesis hung so brightly in the sky.

"Something unavoidable has come up every seminar except two in the last three years."

What could she say? The coordinator's timing stank worse than a skunk's after-trail. But maybe her boss had gotten tired of her excuses.

"I only missed two seminars."

"Which means you're at fifty percent; that's a failing grade in anyone's book." Why did he have to look so incredibly yummy while telling her off?

And he smelled nice, too.

"I'm sorry."

His blue gaze pierced her. "I was, too. I couldn't help wondering if I had something to do with you avoiding the management training."

"You?" she squeaked and cleared her throat, trying for a look of insouciance she didn't feel.

He leaned against her desk and crossed his arms. "You said I intimidate you."

Standing this close he did a lot more than intimidate her. He turned her on. Big time. Why couldn't Ed have this effect on her? *He* wanted to marry her. Heck, he probably even wanted her to have his babies, and then the whole women in her family's curse-slash-gift it-depends-on-how-you-look-at-it thing would be solved. Did it matter that she would probably die of terminal boredom in the first year of her marriage?

Yeah, it probably did. She'd rather deal with a full moon and all its consequences.

"Ivy?"

"Huh?" Great. Now she sounded like an idiot times six, or something. This man was her boss. He ran a huge conglomerate of hotels and resorts. He was used to intelligent conversation from his employees, probably even expected it considering the type of testing you had to go through to get a job with HGA, Inc.

He sure wasn't getting intelligent coherence right now. She tried really hard to remember what he'd said. Oh, yeah. "Not attending the management seminars had nothing to do with you. It was entirely personal."

"Hmmm . . ." He rubbed his chin with fingers she'd really rather have on her. "I suppose I have to believe you. After all, if I really did intimidate you, you would hardly turn down every *request* I've made for you to modernize the inn."

"Not every request. I was thrilled about the new carpeting, and you must have noticed that we're redoing the woodwork as well."

"Redecorating is not modernization." His eyes flicked to the open ledger on her neatly ordered desk. "Most recently, you've resisted implementing a computer reservation and guest check-in system."

She scooted her chair back, unable to deal with his intense presence so close to her for one more second. "Old Orchard Inn is quaint. People who come to stay here like the old-fashioned atmosphere, including signing into a guestbook. It's not one of HGA, Inc.'s big properties. We don't need a fancy computer to keep track of eight guest rooms."

Blake had to agree. They didn't *need* it, but why the hell was she so against having one?

Was she a technophobe? She was smart, and quick to pick up new things; he had a hard time believing she was intimidated by technology. But what other explanation was there?

Blake bit back a sigh and an impatient retort in the same moment of frustration. He'd bought the property three years ago with the intention of building the business and selling. It was too small for a company like HGA, Inc., to take seriously, and he'd known that going in. He'd seen the Old Orchard Inn strictly in terms of short range ROI.

Then he'd met the inn's manager. Ivy had passed the corporate employment tests and been offered a job with HGA, Inc., continuing in her current position before he'd met her face to face. He'd regretted that sequence of events many times over the last three years.

Ivy Kendall made his dick hard and his head feel like exploding within sixty seconds of coming into a room. Her slight body and heart-shaped face weren't exactly centerfold material, but she'd starred in more than one dream that left him hard and aching when he woke up.

He wanted her, and *he could not have her*.

He never dated HGA, Inc., employees. It was too damn messy. Not only was there the whole potential sexual harassment thing, but there were a host of other complications that could arise as well. None of which he'd ever been willing to risk, but his rock-solid commitment to that stance was wearing away as his need for the tiny technophobe grew.

That need was driving him crazier than her unwillingness to upgrade even to the minimum of putting in computer-controlled central air and heating. He hadn't pushed too hard, knowing that once the inn was upgraded, it would have to be sold. He got the impression Ivy had no interest in working for HGA, Inc. at another property. If the inn was sold, he would probably never see her again. The thought bothered him more than it should. It had certainly made him more accommodating with her than he was with any of his other property managers.

That accommodation was coming to an end. "The inn has the lowest percentage of customer complaints of any of our properties."

She smiled tentatively, her brown eyes wary. "That's good, right?"

"Yes, except every single complaint says the same thing."

She chewed on her bottom lip, an expression of resigned understanding stealing over her sweet features. "The guests want central air-conditioning."

"Yes."

"We can give them that without giving up the old world ambience of the inn and getting rid of the radiator heaters."

"What would be the point? If we have to run duct work, it might as well be for the whole shebang." There was such a thing as taking the whole ambience thing too far.

"But do eight rooms really need separate, computer-controlled climate controls?"

"Yes, and if you had attended the last management seminar, you'd know why."

"Seventy percent of our business is repeat customers." She sounded almost desperate.

"Who are also paying only about seventy percent of the room rates they would be paying in a more modernized facility."

"I don't like the idea of modernizing just so we can gouge our customers."

"Your resume says you have a degree in business." It was only a two-year degree from a correspondence school, but even so, she should have gotten some idea of normal business practices.

Her brow pleated in a way he found too cute to be even remotely professional. "Yes."

"Raising rates to accepted industry levels is not gouging your customers."

She winced. "I guess not."

"So, are we agreed that the inn will have to be upgraded?"

Her eyes filled with a sadness he did not understand. "Even if I don't agree, you're going to go ahead with it anyway, aren't you?"

Right in that moment, he wished he could say no. She looked so damn forlorn. "Corporate's made the decision."

"I thought you were corporate."

"I am responsible to a board of directors." Which he could have bucked, but what would have been the point? He agreed with the consensus.

The inn needed to be upgraded and then sold.

"Ivy, Ed's at the front desk. He asked if you were in?" The desk clerk made what should have been a sentence sound like a question. Younger than Ivy, her eyes were alight with both interest and some sort of female telepathic understanding.

Ivy groaned and stood up. "That's all this day needs. Um . . . Trudy, I don't suppose you could tell him I'm busy with my boss?" She turned to Blake. "I am busy, aren't I?" she asked with a tone that implied his interruption into her otherwise neatly ordered existence should count for something.

"Yes, and you will be busy in consultations with me for the next several days." Where the possessiveness came from, he didn't know, or care to analyze, but he did not want Ivy going out with another man while he was in Delicious, Ohio.

Trudy's eyes widened and then narrowed on Blake in obvious appraisal, but she only said, "I'll tell him," and left.

Ivy stood up and pushed her chair into place at her desk with precise movements, then stepped back two paces and faced him. The smooth lines of her small face were tight with determination. "So, will two weeks' notice be sufficient, or do you require a month?"

The words were still reeling in his brain when Trudy came back, her expression pure female commiseration this time. "He asked, what about dinner?"

Blake turned smartly on his heel and walked out to the front desk counter. He would deal with Ed while his usually super efficient brain grappled with the implication that Ivy was willing to quit her job over the proposed improvements to the inn. The sound of a gasp and his name being called in confused appeal from behind him did not slow him down.

Ed was encroaching on his territory, and like millions of the male species before him, Blake had every intention of pushing back. If his behavior could be construed as pissing a circle around Ivy Kendall, that was too bad. She worked for him, and for the next few days she was his.

That the territory of boss and boyfriend should be mutually exclusive did not deter his purpose.

Ed did not belong here at the inn with Ivy, not when Blake wanted her undivided attention. Not when she was threatening to quit over central air-conditioning.

Blake stopped when he reached the front desk. A tall man with brown hair and an impatient glint in his narrowed gray eyes stood on the other side. He was dressed like a businessman without even a hint of country hick about him. In Delicious, Ohio? Who was this guy?

A female guest walked through the lobby toward the inn's small restaurant and gave Ed the once-over on her way. Right. Definitely no trouble attracting women. So why did he have to pester Ivy when she so clearly wasn't interested? Or had Blake misread her and Trudy's silent communication? He wouldn't be the first man misled by that kind of thing.

Maybe her consternation had not been at Ed's arrival, but the fact it coincided with her boss's. The thought pissed him off so bad he scowled at the other man.

Ed didn't even blink, but his eyes narrowed further, and his jaw took on rocklike solidity.

Blake figured they matched in that. His back teeth ground together. "Ivy will be having dinner with me. I am only in town for a few days and expect my property manager to give me her undivided attention."

His words came out clipped, surly even, and shock at his own behavior warred with anger that this man wanted *his* Ivy.

Ed blinked then, his eyes going from angry to speculative. "Isn't that a little presumptuous? She's your employee, not your slave."

The image of Ivy's sweetly feminine form trussed up to play love slave flashed in Blake's mind, and his semiaroused flesh went fireman pole status in three seconds flat. Thank whatever architect had designed the sturdy, concealing guest check-in counter that hid the lower half of his body from the other man's view.

"Expecting my manager to be available to discuss business when I am in town is hardly an indication I see her in a subservient capacity." *But maybe I wouldn't mind it,* a certain very dark part of his mind suggested . . . *just once.*

"Ed, what's the matter with you? You can't go around insulting my boss." Ivy had arrived.

"I'm not insulted. His accusation is too ludicrous for the serious consideration it would take to be offended." Blake didn't dare turn to face her with the raging hard-on pushing against the confines of his custom-tailored slacks. So, he said the words with his focus fixed squarely on the other man.

The intruder.

Ed frowned, his body shifting into a stance any other man would recognize. It was a challenge, plain and simple.

Ivy gasped. Apparently, she recognized it, too. "What's gotten into you, Ed?"

"You haven't returned my calls, Ivy. I want to talk to you."

That did have Blake turning his head at least to see her.

Her cheeks stained a guilty pink. "I didn't read your message until today."

Was that what her head banging on the desk had been about? She'd missed her boyfriend's message?

"Have dinner with me tonight. We need to talk about the direction our relationship is headed."

Cripes. He was one of those new men, the sensitive ones, who discussed his feelings *willingly*, without even being prodded. Blake snorted, and Ed glared at him, his jaw jutting pugnaciously.

"You are not helping things, Mr. Hawthorne," Ivy muttered from behind him.

"I'm sorry, I can't," she said to Ed before stepping around the counter and moving closer to him—too damn close—in an obvious bid to keep her conversation private.

Both Blake and Trudy eavesdropped shamelessly.

"Look," she said quietly, "he's my boss, and if he wants to have dinner with me, that's what I've got to do."

Would she be that submissive about other things? Would she let her big, bad boss dictate sexual preferences to her vulnerable, sweetly nervous, but definitely amorous self? It was his favorite fantasy where she was concerned.

Not one he'd ever get to play out and not just because she worked for him. Some of the sensual desires that rode him around her were definitely the antithesis of politically correct or even socially acceptable. He doubted the innocent Ivy would consent to them, much less be the enthusiastic partner she was in his dreams.

He wanted to tie her to a bed and make love to her until she screamed.

Did that make him a deviant, or just creative?

He didn't know. He'd never had these kinds of fantasies about other women.

Ed was saying something low, but then his voice rose. "You don't have to put up with this. You know I want to marry you. You don't have to work at all."

What the hell?

"She's working right now, and you're doing this little scene on my time. I don't appreciate it." The words were out of his mouth before he realized he even meant to say them. "Take a hike, Ed."

Ivy's head snapped around, her silky reddish brown hair floating in a whirl around her face and her pretty brown eyes round with surprise. "Mr. Hawthorne, I assure you, there is no need for you to get involved."

"It's Blake, Ivy, and has been since the first time we met."

She rolled her eyes at his nitpicking. "Blake, then. Stay out of this. It's not company business."

To hell with that. "You planning to marry this guy?" he asked in another uncontrollable burst of male aggressiveness.

"I . . . uh . . ." She looked back at Ed, and her body went tense, her cheeks stained with embarrassed color.

If Blake couldn't read that sign, he'd turn in his Eagle Scout badge. She didn't want the poor schmuck, but didn't have the heart to tell him.

"I'll give you ten minutes." Now that he knew the lay of the land, Blake felt a lot more charitable toward the other man.

He turned and went back into Ivy's office, passing Trudy, whose mouth hung open in pure, unadulterated astonishment.

Two

She was going to boil Blake Hawthorne in oil and serve him up as the deep-fried turkey for Thanksgiving.

"He'd better have his life insurance paid up," she muttered.

"What?"

Ed . . . darn it. Ed had to be dealt with before she could turn her arrogant jerk of a boss into fricassee.

She met his rainwater gaze straight on. "I can't marry you, Ed. I'm sorry."

"I kind of figured that out when Hawthorne came out snorting fire and belching brimstone."

"What has that got to do with anything?"

Ed shook his head. "I'm not as boring as you think I am, but when you're in love with someone else, any other man is just going to be a poor substitute."

She stared at him, her heart twisting in her chest, her breath coming in shallow, desperate pants. "I'm not in love with someone else."

She couldn't be. Loving Blake Hawthorne would be criminally stupid. She could get ten years in Sing Sing for that kind of thing.

"But you do find me boring."

"You're an actuary . . . I don't get numbers the way you do," she said lamely in an attempt not to hurt him or have to lie.

"I hope he knows what an incredible woman he's getting." Ed leaned down and kissed her temple before moving to cover her lips with his own.

He drew the kiss out, even teasing her lips with his tongue, and if she hadn't been so shocked by the move, she would have jerked back. His mouth on hers did not feel right. It didn't belong there. Though he wasn't a bad kisser, she had to admit.

When he lifted his head, there was an unholy gleam in his eye, and he nodded at something . . . or someone . . . over her shoulder. "Goodbye, sweetheart."

A strange noise from behind her said the kiss Ed had just given her had definitely been for *someone* else's benefit.

A strong hand landed on her shoulder a second after Ed walked out the door. Blake spun her to face him.

"You're quitting?" he gritted.

"Yes." She had no choice.

His mouth slammed down on hers with the power of a conquering army, and her brain short-circuited in a blaze of sparks and hissing nerve endings.

Firm, warm lips devoured hers, and she devoured them right back, tangling with his tongue and savoring the taste of a mouth that had been created for kissing. She wrapped her arms around his neck and pressed her body against hot, hard muscles not even remotely disguised by his conservative business attire.

Superman lived.

A growl emanated from his throat, a sound so primitive, it sent shivers down her spine and her thighs. Maybe not Superman. Blake Hawthorne was more like Conan the Barbarian.

His hands cupped her bottom and lifted, pressing her into the awe-inspiring proof of his desire.

Heat radiated between her thighs, making her aware of dampness there as well.

"Um . . . Mr. Hawthorne . . . " from somewhere behind them.

He squeezed her butt, and she groaned, sucking on his tongue.

"Ivy!" A high-pitched, woman's voice near her ear, but it still didn't register as something she had to respond to.

Blake broke his mouth from hers, and she buried her face against his neck, licking and sucking salty, utterly deliciously masculine tasting skin.

"What?" rumbled up from his chest.

Was he talking to her? She lifted her head to look, dazed and needy in a way she'd never been before.

"Mr. Hawthorne, there's a call for you." Trudy's voice saying something that didn't make sense to Ivy's sensually drugged brain.

"Damn it." Blake dropped her and pushed her away.

Ivy tottered on legs wobbly from her brush with a wild barbarian and looked around her.

Horror was clawing at her insides before her gaze even reached Trudy's shocked and clearly appalled countenance. Ivy, Trudy's boss and manager of this inn, had stood necking like a horny teenager right in front of the reception desk. Anyone could have seen her. Probably lots of people had.

Close to lunchtime, the restaurant was filling up, and Ivy could not help wondering in appalled fascination how many patrons had walked past the passion-locked couple in the lobby.

"I'll take the call in Ivy's office," Blake said, sounding entirely too self-controlled and unaffected for the man who had been squeezing her bottom and pressing her against his erection only moments before.

"Okay," Trudy said, her eyes still fixed on Ivy as if she'd sprouted tentacles and a third eyeball.

Ivy didn't even try for unaffected detachment. She turned tail and ran. Right up the stairs, both flights to the top floor where she slammed into her small apartment with less relief than a sense of desperation.

The small window air conditioner was on maximum cool, but her living-slash-dining room was still uncomfortably warm. Darn it. Blake was right. The inn needed central air, and of course it made sense to cater to the guests' needs by installing individually controlled systems.

She flopped down glumly on her white wicker sofa, and it creaked alarmingly. She shifted, and a twang between her thighs reminded her that though she was doing her best to block the memory of the past fifteen minutes, they had indeed happened.

How could she have lost all decorum and her sense of self-preservation in one go like that?

No way was she in the big city business mogul's league, but now he had to know she wanted to be. And why the heck had he kissed her? He'd been acting possessive and territorial since Trudy announced Ed was there. Ivy had thought at first it was all about her being a good corporate employee, but she didn't think bosses usually used kissing to keep their employees in line. Wasn't that sexual harassment or something? She certainly felt harassed, but as hot as that kiss had been, she didn't feel threatened by Blake. After all, she was the one who had told him she planned to quit.

The kiss had been no threat. To her career anyway. Her heart was another matter.

Ed had accused her of loving Blake Hawthorne.

Remembering the way she had responded to him the first time they met, and every time since—the fantasies she'd had about him, the way she felt in his company—she feared Ed might be right.

Blake was smart, and funny, too, when he wanted to be. He could also be a shark, and that gave her an atavistic thrill she didn't want to admit to, but was there all the same.

Oh, gosh . . . *was* she in love? Forget criminal stupidity, she was right on her way to total insanity.

Bam. Bam. Bam.

Her door shook with the powerful knocking, and that was saying something. The Old Orchard Inn was over a hundred years old and built with the solid construction of that century.

"Open the door, Ivy. I know you're in there."

Like it took a genius to figure out she'd be hiding after what had happened in the lobby.

The knocking resumed, and she stifled an urge to laugh, afraid if she gave in to it, she'd slip into mindless hysteria. The door wasn't even locked.

"Ivy. Damn it." Another bang on the door and then more cursing.

He had a much more expanded vocabulary of colorful words than she did.

"Ouch. Shit . . . a splinter . . . " Silence. "Do you have any tweezers?" through the door.

He was hurt? She flew off the couch and yanked the door open. He stood on the other side, sucking on his forefinger, the expression in his blue eyes scary.

She shivered even as she stepped back to let him in. "The door wasn't locked."

He glared at her.

"I'll just get the tweezers. Have a seat." She waved her hand toward one of the dinette chairs.

The light was better above the table, and she would have a better chance of seeing the sliver and getting it out.

It took Ivy only a second to get what she needed from the bathroom and then come back to Blake. He watched her walk toward him, his temper on a shorter leash than it had been in years. This woman got under his skin and stayed there.

But she had run from him.

He'd expected her to join him in her office and talk about the kiss like two mature, consenting adults . . . She had been consenting, hadn't she? With her tongue practically down his throat he was guessing yes, but no question—he'd initiated the kiss, and he hadn't given her a lot of choice in the matter.

She squatted in front of him and put her hand out. "Let me see."

He didn't even consider telling her he'd do it himself. Even though the last time he'd let a woman fuss over him, he'd been ten years old and it had been his grandmother.

Ivy winced when she saw the splinter embedded in his skin.

"This is going to hurt," she whispered.

"Don't worry about it. Just get the damn thing out."

She didn't respond to his brusque tone. She was too busy torturing him with her small fingers against his skin. Okay, she was trying to get the sliver out, but having her touch him for any reason affected his already overactive libido in dangerous ways.

He figured they needed to deal with the kiss before anything else. "It was mutually consenting." Her silence was not reassuring. "You didn't say no."

She sighed. "I know. You don't have to worry I'm going to file a sexual harassment complaint or something."

Did she really think that after a kiss like that, he was worried about federal regulations? He was a heck of a lot more worried about the possibility she didn't want to follow through on the passionate promise of her body.

She pulled out the splinter, and he sucked in air at the sting. It wasn't bad, but you couldn't tell that by the way she was blowing on his finger and moaning in sympathy.

When her lips pressed against the small drop of blood welling, he lost it.

He yanked her into his lap without a second thought and kissed her again. She gasped against his lips, and he took the sound into his mouth and gave her back his tongue.

Ambrosia.

She was so sweet, he'd get a sugar overload just tasting her lips.

She broke her mouth away, turning her head and panting. "We can't do this, Blake."

"Why not?"

"You're my boss."

"You said you were going to quit." Which reminded him. "What the hell is up with that anyway? Do you have a moral objection to central air-conditioning or something?"

She laughed shortly. "No, but I can't work here once the computerized controls have been implemented."

"Why not?"

She tried to pull away, and his arms tightened around her instinctively.

"I want to get up."

Consenting. That was key. Right. He let her go.

She stood up, and he had to fight the urge to pull her back into his lap.

"I'd rather not talk about the whys and wherefores of

my decision, Blake. I assume you brought a plan for implementation with you. It makes a lot more sense to focus on that right now."

"Not to me. I want to know why HGA, Inc. is about to lose one of its best property managers, and we are going to lose you, aren't we? You aren't interested in training to work on one of the other properties."

She shuddered. As though the thought was more than repugnant, like it was chilling. "No."

"Tell me why." His gut clenched. "It's not that Ed guy, is it? You aren't going to marry him, are you?"

"No. It's not Ed."

"Then what?"

She bit her lip and looked at him for several tense seconds. Her heart-shaped face was flushed, her lips swollen from his kisses, and her perfectly pressed general manager uniform was rumpled. She looked delectable and edible and everything in between, but her soft brown eyes were dark with wariness, and that stopped him from acting on his baser impulses.

"Why?" he practically begged.

Her full lips thinned in a line of determination. "Would you mind telling me what time it is?"

He frowned, but looked down at his watch obediently. What the hell? "It's stopped. My Rolex quit."

He sounded as stunned as he felt. He'd paid enough money for this watch to work into the next century.

She didn't look surprised, though. She looked resigned. "Maybe you could check your Palm Pilot?"

Feeling like something was going on here he didn't get, he pulled the slim case from his inner breast pocket and flipped it open. He pressed the power button and swore. None of his usual icons showed up. In fact, the only things on the screen were the basic operating system links. He tried clicking into setup, and a message came on screen offering to initialize the unit.

"My entire database and all my programs are gone. The memory had to have corrupted." That was going to be a pain in the ass. He could sync with his laptop, but anything he'd put in since the last sync was gone.

She sighed. "What about your mobile phone?"

That's right. His cell phone had a time function. He never used it because he always wore his watch. He pulled it off the clip on his belt, and this time the words that came out of his throat were vicious.

It had that little message on it that said it could only be used for emergency calls.

"What is going on?"

"I'm sorry," she said at the same time.

He pinned her with his gaze. "Why?"

"It's my fault."

"Crappy engineering is your fault?"

"It isn't bad engineering. It's me, well, me and the full moon."

"What, you're a werewolf?" he asked, laughing at the very thought of such a delicate woman getting hairy and growing fangs.

"That would be easier to live with," she grumbled.

Now, this had to be good.

"You'd rather be a werewolf?"

"Than get so magnetic I erase hard drives once a month . . . yes."

"Magnetic?" This was too bizarre to deal with on a muggy head. He stood up and walked into her small kitchenette. "You got anything up here to make coffee?"

"Sure." She started putting together an old-fashioned glass percolator pot.

"You don't have a microwave."

"There would be no point. After the first full moon, it would be broken."

He let that slide and filled the glass pot with water.

*   *   *

They took their coffee into the living room, and if the sofa creaked when she sat on it, it positively groaned when Blake lowered his over six-foot frame onto it. "So, what, a regular sofa would give you problems, too?"

She would have glared at the irritating question if he didn't sound so aggrieved. As it was, she had to bite back a smile she was sure he wouldn't appreciate. He looked so funny with his big body sprawled on her tiny sofa—if you could even call it that. Even she had to curl her legs up to lie down on it and read.

"I liked the way the wicker furniture looked in the showroom, and I figured it would be easy to get up to my apartment," she admitted.

"The unit wasn't furnished?"

"No. I took over management when the last family member that owned the inn decided she wanted to travel the world. The pieces up here were heirlooms, and her nieces and nephews laid claim to them before her first cruise ship sailed."

"I suppose wicker was cheaper than a regular living room set as well."

She was surprised a guy with his money would recognize such a consideration and said so.

His blue eyes mocked her. "I didn't get this far in business ignoring expenditure issues."

"Working for the family company didn't hurt." She said it teasingly, but he didn't smile.

"My dad owned three properties when I joined HGA, Inc. He didn't want to diversify into resort properties, but now that's the bulk of what we own."

"In other words, it wasn't nepotism that got you this job, but sound business acumen."

Burnished red accented his cheekbones. "I sounded pretty defensive, didn't I?"

"A little."

"I guess I didn't want you thinking of me as the kind of man who rode through life on his dad's coattails."

"Like it matters to you what I think."

"Obviously it does. I'm not real sure why that should surprise you after me practically inhaling you with my lips twice in less than an hour."

"Has anyone ever told you that you're—"

"Bold?"

"Blunt."

His lips twitched. "Yes. Does it bother you?"

"I just don't know how to take it. I work for you; I don't think you're supposed to kiss me senseless. It isn't businesslike."

"You told me you were going to quit."

"Is that why?"

"I'd like to think knowing you wanted to quit made the difference, but I'm not sure it would have mattered if you hadn't said anything about leaving HGA, Inc. I didn't like seeing Ed lock lips with you."

"I don't know why."

Blake shrugged. "Around you a lot of primitive feelings come out. I get possessive. I want you, Ivy."

She choked on her coffee and had to stand up to stop coughing. "Forget blunt," she wheezed, "you're certifiable."

He stood up and patted her back, the feel of his hands on her anything but soothing. "Come on, honey, it can't be that big of a surprise."

"It is." She had never known another man as uninhibited in declaring his desire for her.

Heck, she'd never known a man who wanted her with the possessive hunger Blake had exhibited since arriving earlier.

She stepped away from him. "I'm fine now."

He searched her face, as if looking for signs that she needed further ministrations, and then nodded.

They returned to their seats, but she found herself sitting next to him on the narrow sofa instead of in the chair she'd occupied earlier.

She tried to move, but his hand locked onto her knee, and she froze as sensations she wished she could ignore washed over her.

"Tell me about the moon thing."

"Are you sure you want to hear?" she couldn't help asking.

"Yes."

She marshaled her thoughts, trying to decide where to begin. She'd spent so many of her adult years trying to pretend that she was as normal as everyone else. Now that the time had come to actually admit to her gift-slash-curse it-depends-on-how-you-look-at-it thing, her heart started hammering against her ribs.

Her fingers curled into fists against clammy palms. "I've only talked about it with one person outside my family since I told my best friend, Linda Baker, in the seventh grade."

"That's a long time."

"She didn't believe me. She said a lot of stuff that hurt."

"I'm not an adolescent girl."

"In other words, you might not believe me either, but you won't call me a lunatic and tell me you'd rather be best friends with Angela Potter?"

"Linda was the idiot to choose another girl over you for friendship. I was never that stupid. Not even when I was a kid."

She smiled. Years later and totally irrelevant, his encouragement still warmed her through. "Thank you."

"My pleasure." His fingers squeezed her knee, and

jolts of sensation zinged along nerve endings that traveled a path straight to the core of her.

She had to start talking, or she was going to lose her ability to do so. "For as long as anyone in my family can remember, puberty has caused the advent of more than a menstrual cycle for the females. It's also when the moon magnetism starts."

"What is moon magnetism? I've never heard of it."

"It's not scientifically documented, but refers to the phenomenon that happens to the women in my family every full moon."

"You get magnetic?"

"Right, only it's not totally consistent. Sometimes things happen I don't expect." Like the car accidents. "And then things I least expect to be immune to me are."

He looked skeptical.

"I'm sure there is a scientific explanation for that part, but I don't know what it is. Probably something to do with the material surrounding technology I expect to be affected, or maybe a dip in my magnetism during that time."

"Give me an example."

"Of the exceptions?"

"No, of what happens when you get *magnetic*."

"Well, you've already seen what happened to your watch, your Palm Pilot, and your cell phone." What more did he want?

"All of which can be explained by technical malfunctioning."

"All three at once?" Did he really believe that? Maybe it was easier to take than the bizarre truth about her messed-up body chemistry.

"It could happen."

"I'm the malfunction, or at least I cause it."

"That's pretty conceited of you, or paranoid, depending on how you look at it," he said, his humor close to the surface.

"Do you seriously think I would make this stuff up?"

His expression turned serious. "No. I'm sure you believe what you are saying, but a few broken gadgets does not mean you're a walking magnet every full moon."

"It would be a lot more than a few if I didn't stay away from hi-tech areas during that time of month."

"Have you ever tested that theory?"

"No, but, Blake, I'm not the first woman in my family to experience it. I don't need to test the theory. I know what would happen."

"Family folklore is often based in fact, but it isn't always accurately interpretive of events."

She should have known Blake would be this way. He and Ed had one thing in common. They were both better at dealing with concrete realities than inexplicable phenomena.

"I've had four car accidents in my life, and they all happened during a full moon. Not one of them has been my fault either. It's like the other driver couldn't avoid hitting my car. They were drawn to me in some very strange way."

"If it were really a matter of you drawing the other cars, you would have had a lot more accidents than four in your lifetime."

He thought she'd come up with this as a way of excusing poor driving habits. "You have no idea how careful I've been."

He shook his head, a small smile playing around his lips. "I've been in a couple of accidents myself, and I can guarantee you the moon had nothing to do with them."

He didn't believe her. He wasn't even pretending to

give her a fair hearing. His skepticism was as palpable as his desire for her. She shouldn't be surprised, but somehow she had thought he would at least try to understand, if not believe.

"It doesn't matter what I say to you; you're going to explain it away as something else."

"Not if you don't want me to."

"But you'll be thinking it."

"I can't deny that."

"At least you're honest."

"I'm sorry."

She shrugged off his apology and his disbelief. Neither of them mattered. She wouldn't let them matter. "Okay, fine. I've explained my need to leave your employment, and whether or not you accept it won't change the outcome. I *am* quitting."

A speculative gleam entered his narrowed blue eyes. "If I can convince you that your family tradition is nothing more than an excuse for technophobia, will you stay on with HGA, Inc.?"

"I am *not* a technophobe."

"Right."

Oooh . . . he was lucky steam wasn't coming out of her ears. "Trust me when I say that you have even less chance of convincing me than I had of convincing you. And I'm not a bullheaded male too stubborn to see what's right in front of his face."

He smiled at her insult. Actually smiled. "Honey, I'm not ashamed to admit that in some ways a bull and I have a lot in common."

"I'm talking about the head between your ears, oh, master of crude innuendo."

He laughed and leaned forward until his lips hovered right above hers. "I like it when you get feisty, Ivy."

She could taste his lips on the air between them, and

that kind of thing was way too dangerous. Without giving him a chance to stop her, she slipped off the sofa and around the matching wicker coffee table.

"Stop trying to seduce me."

He leaned back, and the wicker groaned again. "Why?"

"*Why?*"

"Uh-huh."

"Because you . . . because I . . . It's a bad idea!"

He crossed his arms over his chest, his sleeve raising to reveal his dead Rolex. "Come to Cleveland with me tomorrow. There's an appliance store there that specializes in guest properties. They've got some air-conditioning and heating units I want you to look at with me."

This was way worse than Linda Baker's refusal to believe. He was not only dismissing her concerns, but he was asking her to fly in the face of them. "That would be insane."

"I take full responsibility for anything that happens while we are there connected to your supposed magnetism."

"So, if we walk into a store and all the electronic units stop working, you'll what . . . hire a repairman?"

"Something like that."

She had spent her entire life since puberty avoiding just such a situation. "No way."

"Give it a chance, Ivy. Look at it this way. Either I convince you that your fears are groundless, or you convince me they aren't. Either way, the trip isn't wasted."

"You're assuming I care whether or not you believe me."

"I know you care. The question is, do you have enough courage to do something about it?"

"I'm not a coward."

"Prove it."

"I don't have anything to prove to you."

"Then prove it to yourself."

"You don't know when to give up."

"Sure, I do. When it's hopeless. You are not a hopeless cause."

"I can only agree on one condition." Even as she uttered the words, her mind shrieked in shock at them.

Three

"Name it."

"We don't go anywhere my magnetism could cause lasting or irretrievable damage."

"I won't take you into any data entry offices."

She rolled her eyes. "For a techno-geek, you sure have a limited understanding of what can be messed up by a magnetic field."

"You think I'm a geek?" he asked, sounding really offended.

"If the pocket protector fits, wear it."

"I don't use a pocket protector," he growled, sounding more like an angry wolf than a techno-geek, but she wasn't about to tell him that.

"You use a Palm Pilot, you don't need a pocket protector, but I bet you've got an attachment to carry it on your belt."

"So what if I have? That doesn't make me a geek."

"Just because I don't own one doesn't make me a technophobe either."

His eyes narrowed. "Touché."

"We'll have to take my car."

"Why?"

"It doesn't have an onboard computer, and if you want to get farther than the entrance to the parking lot, it will have to be in a car that runs on old-fashioned mechanical ingenuity."

"What do you drive?"

"A '66 Mustang."

He smiled. "I was afraid you were going to say a Model T."

"I'm not a twenty-first century anachronism, Blake. The way I live my life isn't always my choice."

He nodded, looking pained. "I'm sorry. I didn't mean to make fun of you."

"No offense taken."

"Are you sure?" His gaze pierced her as if he was trying to read her mind. "It doesn't bother you that I think your curse is more in the realm of family folklore than reality?"

Put like that . . . She sighed. "Maybe a little, but I'm not mad at you."

"I'm glad."

He was getting that look in his eyes again, the one that said he was thinking about kissing her. She leaned back where she was kneeling on the other side of the coffee table. As if two more inches of distance would help. "Do you mind doing the driving?"

"You don't mind me driving your car?"

"I've never been in an accident when I was the passenger."

"And you're positive that has nothing to do with your driving . . . ," he teased.

She laughed, realizing he really meant no disparagement of her character. The guy had a sense of humor that needed a leash.

"I'll drive," he said with a smile.

"Okay, then. It's a date. I mean an appointment." He

just smiled at her slip, and she stood up. "Let me take you on a tour so you can see the inn's improvements."

He stood as well. "That sounds great. Are any of the rooms currently empty?"

"Actually, we're full for the next few nights. I was even on the verge of putting the executive quarters available to rent before you showed up."

"If it means saving space, I could room with you."

"Nice try, but I'm sure the inn can handle the loss of income."

"Especially at the nightly rates we're charging."

"Let's not start in on that again."

They were doing an inspection of the kitchen when Blake mentioned HGA, Inc.'s plans to sell the inn once they had improved its profitability margin.

Ivy went rigid with shock, her brown gaze narrowing in clear consternation. *"You're doing all of these updates just to turn around and sell?"*

"Yes." He didn't understand why she sounded so horrified. "The property was an investment purchase, not a long-term acquisition."

"Then, why not sell it now, before investing more money?"

"The kind of money we want to invest, combined with the inn's reputation for occupancy, should net a significant ROI."

She was silent for several minutes after that, letting Blake ask the chef questions about his special line of menu items that included apples as a key ingredient. Blake had found the practice a bit corny at first, seeing as how the Old Orchard Inn was located in Delicious, Ohio. That in itself was pretty quaint, but he'd had the baked apples the last time he visited and now thought the chef bordered on brilliant.

Ivy didn't say anything as she led him out of the kitchen and to the front lobby.

"Is something wrong?" he asked his suddenly silent companion.

"No."

Silence. Again.

"Did you want to save going over reservation procedures until later?"

She didn't look at him. "That might be best. I've got some work to catch up on."

"Me, too." He hadn't checked his e-mail since leaving Cleveland early that morning. "I don't suppose there's anywhere nearby I can get a high-speed Internet connection?"

"In Delicious? I don't think so."

He remembered the last time he had visited, he'd resorted to driving a half an hour south so he could use the wireless connection at a Starbucks. Apparently, nothing had changed since then. "What time do you want to do dinner?"

She shrugged. "Whatever works for you. You're the boss."

The words didn't give him the sensual thrill they had earlier. She said them with too much resignation.

He grabbed her shoulders and forced her to face him, recognizing somewhere deep inside that he was acting like a Neanderthal and unable to alter that reality. "What is the matter?"

She bit her lip and then frowned. "Don't you find it the least bit ironic that you're going to update the inn and force me to quit my job, just so you can sell it?"

"Honey, I—"

She shook her head, her expression pained, cutting his words off as effectively as if she'd covered his mouth. "I shouldn't have said that. This isn't about me. It's about making money for HGA, Inc."

An unfamiliar sense of guilt washed over him like a poisonous red tide. "I'm sorry."

She jerked her shoulders from his loosened grasp. "There's no need for you to be. I'll see you for dinner." She spun on her heel and left, disappearing behind the counter and into her office before he could unstick his usually eloquent tongue from the roof of his mouth.

Blake knocked on Ivy's door ten minutes before they were due in the restaurant. She'd been expecting him to be early, so she was ready.

His blue gaze traveled over her as though he was memorizing each dip and valley of her feminine form. His eyes said he liked what he saw, even if the terrain was somewhat modest. "You're not on duty anymore, Ivy. I wouldn't have minded seeing you in something besides an HGA, Inc. uniform."

She looked down at her crisply ironed blouse, no-nonsense blazer, and straight skirt she habitually wore when in her office and then back at him. "We can't have what we want all of the time, and I'm having dinner with my boss. That means I'm on duty. Ask Ed. He wanted to have dinner with me, too, but business came first."

"You didn't want to eat with him." Blake sounded so sure of himself that she almost lied just to take him down a peg.

"No, I didn't."

"You're not going to marry him." Another statement of incontrovertible fact.

She shrugged.

"You won't be seeing him anymore." This time, he sounded slightly uncertain, and she couldn't help playing out his tension.

"Maybe."

"Damn it, Ivy. Is it over between the two of you, or not?"

As quickly as the desire to tease had come, it left. He was way too intense for her to treat his question lightly. "It's over. I doubt I'll see him again."

"Good."

"Why does it matter? You're in town for what, two, maybe three days? Then you'll be gone. Who I see then is none of your concern."

"Wear something besides a uniform tomorrow for our trip into Cleveland," he said, ignoring her assertion of independence in her social life.

"Do you think that as my boss you have the right to dictate what I wear?"

"If I told you to wear your uniform, would you?" he asked instead of answering.

She thought about it. "Probably."

"So, I'm telling you not to wear it. I'm not telling you what you should wear instead."

He was being entirely too reasonable considering the aura of masculine intent emanating off of him.

"Fine, I'll wear something else." A burlap sack. Wouldn't he just love that? "Now, can we go to dinner?"

"Sure."

She stepped into the hall and closed her door, locking it before turning to head for the stairs.

"Is there a reason why we can't take the elevator?"

She stopped short. "Uh . . . no. I'm so used to taking the stairs, I never think of it."

They stepped into the elevator, and he pulled the gate closed before turning the key toward the down position. The elevator started its slow descent. "I've always loved this elevator."

She smiled. "Me, too."

"You could do very interesting things in this space."

She looked around them at the rich mahogany walls and the temporary privacy afforded by the slowly passing wall between floors. "Um, I guess so."

He stepped closer until his body hemmed hers in with his heat and solid bulk. "For instance, it moves so slowly, there's plenty of time for a stolen kiss between floors."

She got a mumbled "mm-mmm" out before his lips claimed hers. Unlike their previous kisses, this one was soft and gentle. Although, it felt just as much of a claim staking as his more aggressive behavior had earlier.

The elevator jolted to a stop as he stepped away from her. "You may look like a buttoned-down, all-business property manager, but you kiss like a woman I want to possess."

Her mouth opened, but nothing came out. She'd gotten the message he wanted her, but to have him state it so blatantly in a public place was unnerving.

It was also exciting, and the throb between her legs testified to that fact.

He opened the gate and then slipped his hand under her blazer in an intimate and proprietary move that could not be mistaken. His hand settled against her waist, and he led her from the elevator.

Trudy had left an hour ago. However, the evening desk clerk, an older gentleman who had retired from the Apple County Savings and Loan the year before, gave her and Blake the same blank-eyed stare of shock Trudy had had on her face earlier. And it was no wonder. Blake was acting like her lover, not her boss.

His hand branded her with its heat through the crisp cotton of her blouse, forcing her body to accept what her mind was still fighting. This man was going to be her lover.

They were seated at a table on the far side of the big

fireplace. It was the one place in the restaurant that afforded a modicum of privacy from the other patrons, and she couldn't help wondering if Blake had requested it.

She straightened her already perfectly placed cutlery. "Did you ask for this table earlier?"

His feet settled on either side of her left leg, and then his calves came together, pressing her leg between his and making the air hiss out of her lungs in a startled gasp. "I wanted to be able to focus on you, not the other diners."

"I thought you were here to check out the inn."

"I already know you are doing an excellent job managing it. I came to get you to agree to the upgrades I wanted."

"You could have done that over the phone."

"Then I guess I really came to see you."

"Oh," she said on another gasp of sensual delight as his leg moved against hers.

"Can you doubt it?"

Her sensible navy blue pump slipped off against his calf, and she shivered as her nylon-clad foot rubbed along the tense muscles of his lower leg. He smiled and leaned forward. Suddenly her foot was locked in strong fingers and then lifted to his lap. He pressed her arch against a truly impressive bulge in his pants.

"Blake."

"Don't you want to feel what you do to me?"

"I . . ." She couldn't say no. It excited her unbearably to know she had this effect on a man she found so amazing and delectable. "This is not the place."

"Yes, it is."

Her eyes widened and then narrowed. "You're awfully bossy."

"I'm your boss. Being bossy is part of my job description."

"Are you trying to say that my employment with

your company somehow depends on me letting you do this sort of thing?"

"And if I am?" he asked in a voice that made her insides shiver.

"I would remind you that I've already given my notice."

"So, I guess you know you've got a choice. Are you going to *choose* to let me tell you what to do?" The dark promise and obvious desire in his voice sent frissons of sensation up and down the backs of her thighs.

"You want to order me around?" she asked, never having considered the possibility a turn-on, but inexplicably excited by the prospect now.

"In the bedroom? Oh, yeah."

Oh, man. She was going to melt into a puddle of need right there on her chair.

"You want to play some kind of dominant/submissive game with me?" she asked just to clarify.

His hand held her foot against him as she tried to wriggle away. "And if I do?"

"I . . ."

"Maybe I want to take you back to my room and play sexy games with you until you can't stand because your legs are so rubbery from exertion and you can barely talk from screaming your throat raw."

Heat pooled low in her belly, and heaviness settled in her womb. "I'd say I'm glad no one is close enough to hear us talking and that it's a good thing the walls are so thick in this place." She tried to say it lightly, but her voice came out seductive and rasping instead.

Molten desire flared in his eyes, and every trace of humor left his face. "How thick?"

She could barely breathe. "The kind of walls married couples wish they had between them and their kids so they could make love without Little Johnny asking what all the ruckus was the next morning."

"Sounds perfect."

"For what?" she croaked out.

He didn't answer immediately, and all sorts of scenarios ran through her mind. Some totally implausible . . . or were they?

"Are you ready to order?" The chirpy voice from over her left shoulder made Ivy's body jerk in reaction, but Blake kept her foot firmly in his lap.

"We'll both have the chef's special tonight."

"We will?" she asked, not even remembering what it was, and she'd approved the menu for the week.

Blake had no right to look so disgustingly in control and unaffected while she could feel her face flame with embarrassment, even though there was no way Bonnie could see what was going on under the long white table cloth they used to cover the tables for dinner.

He nodded and smiled at Bonnie as if *she* were the one who had asked the question. He also ordered a bottle of wine and appetizers of Waldorf salad. Bonnie took the order, a look of bemusement crossing her perky, youthful features.

"I'm perfectly capable of ordering for myself," Ivy said as the waitress walked away.

Blue eyes challenged her with serious regard under blond brows drawn just slightly together. "Hawthorne."

"What?"

"If you want to stop playing anytime tonight, all you have to do is say my last name."

She'd read about that kind of thing. It was called a safe word, and it gave the submissive partner the power to actually control the intimacy by being able to stop it anytime. However, she couldn't quite see why she would need one with Blake, unless he had some very different ideas about lovemaking than she did.

"I'm not into pain."

His mouth twisted with instant revulsion. "I'm not either, not giving it or receiving it."

"Then why Hawthorne?"

He leaned across the table, his gaze mesmerizing with its intensity. "I want to push you past your comfort zone, Ivy. I want to make love to you like no other man has or ever will. I want everything you have to give and then some."

"You sound like an army recruiter. *Be all you can be.*"

His lips quirked at one corner. "We can play drill sergeant and new recruit another night, sweetheart."

"I didn't say I wanted to play at all."

"Then say my last name. I'll stop."

"You mean you'll stop trying to seduce me?" No doubt the man had been working on her desire to succumb since that first powerful kiss in the lobby.

"Is that what you want?"

All she had to do was say yes, and he would stop. She could see it in his eyes.

She opened her mouth, but she couldn't make the word come out. She wanted to make love to Blake Hawthorne, had wanted to since the first day they met. He wanted her, too, and that knowledge served only to fuel the fire of her own desire until it was a river of unstoppable lava flowing through her veins.

In one day, maybe two, he would leave Delicious, and she would never see him again. He was right about her not wanting to continue working for HGA, Inc. She couldn't. She would have to find another job not impacted by her monthly magnetic pull.

A job that would not include phone calls, memos,

and the infrequent on-site visit from the compelling man sitting across from her.

She closed her mouth and licked her lips nervously.

He caressed her foot under the table, doing things with his thumb against her instep that sent sensual thrills straight to her womb. "Are you going to let me love you tonight, Ivy?"

"Do you play games in the bedroom often?" she asked, trying to hedge around a direct answer.

His thumb moved to a spot between two of her toes and pressed. Oh, jeeze, that felt good. She barely stifled a gasp, but her shallow breathing had to be giving her away.

His eyes darkened to the color of the night sky. "I've never played this game before. I've never wanted to, but I feel things with you I don't feel with anyone else."

He didn't mean what her heart wanted him to mean, that he was maybe falling in love, too. However, knowing that she was unique to him on a sexual level was pretty heady stuff. Blake was the kind of man who drew women to him like hungry bees to honey. He was one of the beautiful people with a sense of personal power that never wavered.

She wasn't his type, not with her small-town lifestyle and quirky full-moon magnetism. Only he didn't seem to see things that way. In fact, he was saying she was exactly his type in a special and unique way. She wanted that to be true. Badly.

He massaged each of her individual toes with strong, steady fingers that knew exactly what to do to make her quiver between her thighs. His hard-on still pressed intimately against the bottom of her foot, and if she wasn't mistaken, it was growing. Oh, wow. *It got bigger?*

More sexy images flashed through her brain, making her hotter than she'd ever been in her life, and he wasn't even touching her intimately. Her eyes slid shut, and it was all she could do to stay on her chair.

Bonnie chose that moment to return to the table with the wine.

Ivy jerked upright and almost fell sideways when her leg didn't move with the rest of her. She made a startled sound and grabbed the table to maintain her balance.

"Are you all right, Ivy?"

"I'm fine, Bonnie." But her cheeks were blazing, and the look she gave Blake let him know it wasn't only excitement she was feeling. "Why don't you have Mr. *Hawthorne* taste the wine?"

Her foot was released immediately, and she lowered it to the floor, searching desperately for her pump. She found it and pushed her foot inside, finding it harder than it should have been because she was trembling.

Blake went through the ritual of sniffing and tasting the wine before approving it.

Did anyone ever say, *No, thank you, this Riesling is just too fruity for my palate?* she wondered whimsically and then laughed at her own joke. Both Blake and Bonnie looked at her questioningly.

She shrugged. "Uh . . . nothing. Just something I was thinking about." She was losing her mind, and it was all Blake Hawthorne's fault.

So, say his last name again and end the game, her mind taunted. But she knew she wouldn't do it. She *wanted* to lose her sanity in a haze of desire and charged emotion at least once in her life, and this would probably be her only chance. No other man had ever impacted her like her soon-to-be ex-boss.

Not even Danny, the only man she'd ever shared her body with.

Bonnie poured them both a glass of the duly approved wine, put the bottle in a standing ice bucket beside the table, and left.

Blake looked at her with an enigmatic expression and took a sip of his wine. "You used the safe word."

"I almost fell off my chair."

"Was that why?"

Had he thought she meant to end the game entirely? "Yes."

"Does that mean you want to play?"

The sense of recklessness that had been growing since she realized she would soon be out of his life forever drowned her inner caution under a tsunami wave that left room for no other answer than a positive one. She nodded.

"I need the words, Ivy. I want your verbal surrender."

"This isn't a war."

"No, but it is a campaign, and I want it clearly understood that I have your permission to invade your territory."

Considering the type of lovemaking he wanted, the level of personal sexual submission he was asking for, she could understand completely his desire for absolute clarity on what she was willing to do and participate in. It just went to show that no matter how dominant he wanted to play in the bedroom, he didn't want to take anything she wasn't prepared to give.

She liked that. She liked it a lot, and it gave her the courage to give him the verbal confirmation he needed.

"Yes, I want you to love me." She meant that quite literally, but she would settle for the physical variety. She didn't have any choice.

The prospect of never knowing anything of his love for her entire life was too depressing to even consider.

"Any way you want," she added for good measure.

Passion and approval flared in his eyes. "You don't know how much that pleases me, sweetheart."

The rich satisfaction in his voice was hard to mistake.

"I think I do."

He smiled. "Maybe you do."

He didn't try to play footsie with her again, or say anything even borderline embarrassing as their meal was served and they began to eat. They discussed his proposal for upgrading the inn, and she had to admit his ideas were sound. Neither of them mentioned the fact those ideas would put her out of a job.

He probably thought she was overreacting and didn't see that as the actual outcome. She knew better, but had no desire to diminish the rapport with a negative reminder.

They were halfway through the main course, and she had just finished telling him a humorous story about one of the guests, when he got that look in his eyes again. The sexy-pirate-I'm-going-to-ravish-you look.

Her breath caught in her throat, and she stared at him with the feeling she'd just been caught in the hunter's sights and no matter how fast or far she ran, it wouldn't be enough to get away.

"I want you to go to the ladies' rest room and remove your panties, then come back to the table."

"*What?*" she demanded in shock.

"You heard me."

"But, Blake!" She'd never done anything like that in her life.

"You know what to do if you have a problem with that." There wasn't the least amount of give in his expression, and the tone of his voice challenged her.

"I'm not wearing panties," she said, blurting out the

first thing that came to her mind, just managing to keep it to a staccato whisper so other diners did not hear.

If he'd looked dangerous before, he now looked positively feral. "Hose or thigh-highs?" he asked in a guttural voice.

"Hose."

"Go to the ladies' and remove them."

Ivy stared at him. All she had to do was say his last name, and he wouldn't ask her to do it again. She was tempted. It would be safer. It would also establish limits she wasn't willing to go beyond—limits she'd never gone past before—but he'd said he wanted to push her past those limits, and the thing was . . . she wanted to be pushed.

She took a sip of her wine, wetting a suddenly dry mouth.

"Ivy?" The look of concern mixed with sexual hunger in his eyes wrapped itself around her heart and squeezed.

This man was so incredible.

She pushed her chair back and stood. "I'll be right back."

Blake couldn't believe she'd done it. He couldn't believe he'd asked. Hell, he'd always been an aggressive lover, but he'd never felt this need to obliterate a woman's sexual boundaries. Except that was exactly what he wanted to do with Ivy Kendall.

She was so controlled. So buttoned up and proper. Giving control to him in the bedroom would be hard for her, but ultimately rewarding. He knew it. They both knew it, or she wouldn't be on her way to the rest room right now, her hips shifting in a subtle rhythm that made his arousal pulse painfully against his fly.

Ivy walked back to the table, feeling free, just a little naughty, and very, very excited. She wondered if he'd taken into consideration the fact that without her hose, the moisture between her legs might get uncomfortable. Not that she felt uncomfortable. She felt sexy, feminine, and daring. It was incredible, the way the air brushed her most sensitive flesh.

She slipped into her seat, amazed at how the silk of her skirt's lining sliding against her bottom could be such an erotic experience. Her panties never made her feel like this.

Blake looked at her with one eyebrow quirked in question.

"Yes, I did it."

Four

His smile was pure sexy male bent on dominating his mate, but tinged with surprised pleasure, as if he'd been waiting to hear she would chicken out at the last minute. Once again she considered how the submissive partner actually had a lot of power in this particular game.

She ate very little of the remainder of her dinner and nothing at all of dessert. With so many butterflies doing loops and dives in her stomach, she was too charged to eat.

When he finished his dessert, he complimented the wait staff and the chef before leading her back to the elevator. Once again he had a proprietary hand on her waist, but this time the night clerk was too busy with a customer to notice.

She peeled away from Blake as soon as they entered the small enclosure, her senses overwhelmed by his nearness. The past half an hour had been an exercise in self-control for her. Every movement she made reminded her of her less than fully dressed state, and she'd had to stifle more than one moan as pleasure jolted from one synapse to another in a never-ending domino effect.

She stood against the far wall while he closed the gate and started the elevator's ascent with the key.

"You're good with the employees," she commented, unnerved by the silence between them as the elevator slowly rose.

"Am I?" he asked, turning to face her.

The look of untamed desire in his eyes made her legs weak, and she leaned back against the wall. "Yes," she said breathlessly. "They were all thrilled by your praise."

"You've got a well-run operation here, Ivy. Your employees know their jobs and do them well."

"Thank you."

"However," he said, his voice lowering to a seductive rumble, "their boss is not so cooperative about doing her job."

The dark menace in his voice sent a perverse thrill of delight spearing through her.

"I'm very cooperative," she argued, wondering where this game was going.

He reached behind him, and the elevator stopped moving. They were between floors, which meant no one could see them and they could see nothing but the wall through the brass gate.

She was locked in total privacy with him in a space that left no room to run. She didn't want to run, but an atavistic chill made her shiver all the same.

He shook his head, looking regretful. "No, Ivy, you've been a very bad employee."

"I haven't," she gasped.

"But you have. You've fought every suggestion I've made for improvement. You've missed important training meetings. That sort of insubordination has to be dealt with."

"Um . . ." She didn't have an answer for him, but sweat trickled down her back. If this was leading where she thought it was leading, she might have to stop the game.

"Come here, Ivy."

Incredibly, legs she thought too weak to move took her the steps across the elevator until she stood directly in front of him. She hadn't consciously decided to obey him; she simply had. She was forced to tip her head back to see his face.

"I think you need a lesson in cooperation, don't you?"

"Uh . . . what kind of lesson?" She wasn't sure she *hated* the idea of being spanked in love play, but she wasn't sure she *liked* it either.

He cupped her face with one hand and leaned down until he was speaking against her lips. "Are you worried?"

"A little."

His hand reached around and caressed her backside. "You need some discipline, sweetheart, and I'm just the man to give it to you."

Her breath seized in her chest, and it was all she could do not to choke on her own nervousness. "D-discipline?"

He cupped her bottom, kneading the resilient flesh with a gentle touch belied by the ruthless expression in his eyes. "Not all discipline is punishment, Ivy."

"Oh."

"Do you know what the word *discipline* means?"

She should, but right now remembering her own name was a little difficult. "No."

"It means *to teach*. I'm going to teach you how to cooperate."

"H-how?"

"By demanding complete and unreserved cooperation from you from this point forward."

Her immediate relief that he hadn't been talking about a sexy spanking was mitigated quickly by one question: what would he ask her cooperation in doing?

"Are you ready to take your discipline like a big girl?"

The condescending question set her back up, and she glared at him. She could take whatever he wanted to dish out. "Yes."

"Good. Kiss me."

Now, that was no hardship. She'd wanted his lips back on hers since cutting off their kiss earlier. The gentle kiss in the elevator had been too short to come anywhere near assuaging that need. She pressed her mouth against the one he had so obligingly brought down to her level. At the feel of his warm lips against hers, a rush of pleasure whooshed through her body. She clasped his head with both her hands and deepened the kiss, darting her tongue between his willingly parted lips.

She tasted him, loving the warm, wet texture inside his mouth, the yummy essence that was his alone, and the feel of their lips locked in a battle as old as the first man and woman.

Her already peaked nipples tightened and ached for his touch. She pressed her breasts against him and rubbed like a cat. It felt wonderful, but it wasn't enough. There were too many layers of clothing between the two of them.

She whimpered.

He broke his mouth from hers. "What do you want?"

"I . . ." She couldn't say it.

"Tell me what you want."

The direct order reminded her that this was supposed to be an exercise in cooperation on her part, and she'd already decided she could take whatever he threw at her.

Then his blue gaze warmed, and he brushed the backs of his fingers against her temple. "Come on, honey, you can do it. Tell me what you want, and I'll give it to you. Whatever it is."

"You know what it is," she said breathlessly.

"Maybe. I want to be sure." He played with the skin exposed at the neck of her blouse, making her shiver in response. "Tell me."

How could one man be so caring and yet so relentless at the same time?

She forced her lips to form words they'd never formed before when speaking to a man. "I want your hand on my breast . . . on my nipple," she said on a rush of brutal honesty.

"I want that, too." His hand slid down her chest, under her jacket and cupped her small breast.

He upbraided the aching nipple with his thumb.

She groaned.

"You like that?"

"Yessss . . . "

"I like it, too. Your body turns me on." He pressed against her, giving concrete evidence to his claim.

"You excite me, too."

"Do I?" he asked, his voice a sensual caress to her ears.

"Yes."

"Are you wet for me?" he asked.

She buried her face against his chest, the bluntness of the conversation getting to her. "Yes."

"I want to feel."

Her head jerked up. "What?"

His eyes were set on her with serious intent, his mouth a firm line of uncompromising strength. "I want to see how cooperative your body is right now. Lift your skirt."

"But I'm not wearing any underwear."

His lips twitched. "I know."

His amusement mixed with the cool challenge in his devilish blue eyes decided her before she even considered whether or not she wanted to use the safe word.

She reached down and grabbed her skirt by the hem on either side of her hips. She inched it up until it barely covered the apex of her thighs.

"All the way, sweetheart."

If he'd been watching while she did it, she probably wouldn't have been able to, but he was looking into her eyes, his gaze compelling her to acquiesce. She didn't even know how he knew she hadn't uncovered herself completely. Nevertheless, she brought the skirt up the last couple of inches. Air tickled her damp curls and caressed her bare bottom.

He moved back slightly, reaching down between them. His fingertips played gently over the top of her mound and upper vulva. It felt so good, she closed her eyes and savored each small movement.

"Spread your legs."

Without opening her eyes, she shifted until her thighs were far enough apart for his hand to slip between them, but he didn't trespass her outer lips. His fingertips barely touched the sensitive hairs covering her sex, making her yearn for more and whimper with that need.

"Do you want me to touch you?"

"Please . . ."

One finger slipped between her slick folds and probed her entrance. "Yes, you are wet for me, aren't you? That's a very good sign of your cooperation. In fact, that kind of cooperation deserves a reward, don't you think?"

She couldn't think, couldn't make sense of his words in order to make a response. She could only react to her body's needs, rocking her hips, seeking deeper penetration with his finger. But then the heel of his hand was pressing against her clitoris.

And it felt so good. "Oh, Blake . . . oh, oh, oh . . ."

"Keep your skirt up, Ivy, do you hear me?"

What? Oh . . . "Yes."

She tightened her grip on the skirt's hem until her fingers ached from the pressure.

His mouth claimed hers again, the kiss hot and hungry.

He slipped another finger between her thighs and then used them to tease up and down the sides of her labia, the heel of his hand continuing its teasing stimulation of her swollen sweet spot. Tension like she'd never experienced spiraled inside her until she was shaking with preorgasmic muscular rigidity.

She moaned against his lips, the sound shocking in its carnality. She needed more, but couldn't make herself break the kiss and tell him. She moved her body against him, riding those fingers in a wanton abandon she would never have considered herself capable of.

He added a third finger, using his middle one to caress her clitoris directly while his others continued the massage of her vulva, and then he pinched the nipple he had been teasing with his thumb. She detonated, pleasure exploding inside her with the power of an atomic split.

Blake swallowed Ivy's scream, his own body perilously close to going off.

She was so damn responsive.

A rush of hot moisture covered his fingers as she jerked against him in spasmodic convulsions in the longest climax he had ever witnessed in a lover. He kissed her through it, gentling her with his fingers and his mouth until her quaking had been reduced to a mere quiver.

Finally, she sagged against him as if she'd lost the ability to stand on her own. Hell, she probably had. This was not your average cop a feel in the elevator.

He slid his mouth from hers, placing calming kisses against the corner of her lips and against her temple. "You are amazing, sweetheart."

Her head fell against his chest, and a sigh shuddered out of her. "You're the amazing one. That was incredible."

He removed his hand, and then he tilted her head back so she could watch him as he cleaned his fingers with the only thing handy, his mouth.

Her eyes widened. "Oh . . ." But she kept watching him, an expression of fascination coming over her features.

He popped the last finger out of his mouth. "You taste good."

"Do I?" she asked in a voice barely above a whisper.

"Want to taste?" he asked, pressing his fingertip against her lip.

Several emotions swirled in her soft brown eyes. Confusion. Alarm. Curiosity. *Desire*. "I don't think—"

He pushed his finger between her open lips. "Taste."

She closed her lips around him and sucked tentatively.

His dick pressed against his pants like a tidal wave trying to break over a dam. It hurt in a very good way. "Use your tongue, baby, taste it."

She obediently swirled her tongue around him, and his body jerked and shuddered against her as his sex pulsed in a short beat that left the tip wet and the shaft ready to finish.

His control was hanging by a thread, and her hot mouth clinging to his finger was going to be the scissors that snipped it.

But he didn't want to take her for the first time in the elevator. He wanted her in his bed and under him. He wanted to do more than join their bodies; he wanted to stake a claim.

He reached behind him with a hand that trembled and turned the key. The elevator started its ponderous ascent upward.

The movement jolted her, and she catapulted from his arms, landing against the back wall with an audible thump. She still had a grip on her skirt, and the sight of her glistening red curls almost did him in.

"I can't . . . I can't . . ." She closed her eyes and swallowed. "I can't believe we're doing this."

"What's the matter? You liked it, Ivy. Don't try to pretend now you didn't."

"Of course I liked it. I'm not insane, but someone *could see us.*"

And if they saw her now, they'd get an eyeful. "Honey, your skirt is still up around your belly button."

She looked down, her expression horrified. "Oh, my gosh!" She yanked it down. "I can't believe I forgot."

"You were preoccupied."

She covered her face with both hands. "I'm going to die of embarrassment right now."

The old-fashioned elevator got very little use, and being at the back of the inn, it wasn't a glaringly public place either despite the open grillwork of the gate that left its occupants exposed through the matching grillwork gate in the doorway of each floor. "Don't worry about it."

"That's easy for you to say. You're not the one who looks mussed," she mumbled through her hands, spreading her fingers so she could peek at him.

He grinned. Her hair was a little messier than its usual silky smooth flip, but the biggest giveaway to what they had been doing was in her eyes. She looked devastated.

Good, because touching her devastated him.

"No one is going to know what you've been doing by the state of your dress."

"Anyone who has been waiting for the elevator is going to speculate." Her voice came out trembly.

He liked knowing that despite her embarrassment, she was still reeling from his effect on her.

They were passing the second floor. The area in front of the gate was empty. "No one is around on this floor, and the only rooms on the third floor are your apartment and corporate quarters."

Her stance did not relax appreciably, but she lowered her hands so she could look at him fully. "Blake?"

"Hmm?"

"Why did you stop?"

The question surprised him. "You wanted to make love in the elevator?" he asked, his voice raspy from desire that had had no outlet.

"A minute ago, I wouldn't have cared if we were in the lobby."

The admission did things to him that weren't related entirely to how tight his pants had become in the crotch area. "I like your honesty."

"I'm not sophisticated enough for sexual games."

"Aren't you?"

Incredibly, she blushed. "I meant head games, pretending I don't want you when I do, that sort of thing."

He grinned. "I'm glad. I hate *that sort of thing*, and for the record, I want you, too."

"I got that impression, only why . . ."

"I want you fully naked and under me the first time I come inside of you."

Her eyes widened until she resembled a shock victim. "You're so blunt."

"So you've said." He stalked her to the other side of the elevator, stopping when she was pressed tightly against the back wall and his body barely touched hers. "That makes us a good couple. Blunt is just another way of being honest."

The air vibrated between them, and her breath came in shallow pants. She licked her lips and gasped when he followed suit, tasting her while placing his hands on either side of her head against the wall.

He pushed his tongue inside her mouth, unable to resist deepening the kiss, even though one part of his brain was telling him what a stupid choice that was. If he was going to make it out of the elevator without dropping his pants and impaling her against the wall, he had to keep his raging libido under control.

Tasting the sweet warmth of her mouth was not going to help him do that.

The elevator stopped with a gentle jolt, and he managed to pull his mouth from hers and step back. "We're here."

The only sound that came out of her mouth was a low whimper. Her eyes were shut again, and her lips were parted as if inviting further kisses. He would take that invitation, just as soon as they made it into his room.

He swept her up into his arms and pivoted on his heel. "You'll have to pull the gates open."

She did, her fingers fumbling with the locking mechanism, but finally managing to get both gates pulled open and then shut after they stepped from the elevator.

It was only a few feet down the hall to his door, but it felt like a mile, each step excruciating. Not because she was heavy, but because holding her excited him. To his already overstimulated nervous system, the feel of her body against his was enticement it took every ounce of his self-control to ignore.

Once inside his room, he let her stand, but kept an arm around her. She was wobbly.

"I want you naked, Ivy."

She stared at him, her expression uncomprehending.

He stepped back. "I. Want. You. To. Take. Your. Clothes. Off."

The glazed desire in her eyes faded a little. "Just me?"

"Yes."

She crossed her arms over her chest in a defensive gesture that intensified his desire to push her farther than any lover had ever pushed her before. "Can't we undress together?"

"Are you refusing to cooperate?" he asked silkily, knowing that would prick her pride, push her toward proving her mettle.

She saw his attempt at dominance as a personal challenge. It also excited her. He liked knowing that. It told him they were on the same wavelength in every way.

Her eyes narrowed. "I'm not refusing; I just want it to be more mutual."

"It is mutual." He cupped her face and kissed her, branding her lips with his barely restrained passion. "It will give me a lot of pleasure to see you undress." He kissed her again. "And you will enjoy undressing for me."

"That's not what I meant." But she didn't deny she would enjoy him watching her.

She'd loved revealing herself to him in the elevator. Her arousal had been strong and blatant. Remembering the way she'd climaxed in his arms sent arrows of awareness straight to his dick. He stepped back.

"Are you having a problem with our game?"

"Um . . ." She licked her lips.

He reached out and ran his fingertip down her cheek, letting it settle against the rapid pulse at the base of her neck. "If you don't want to do it, all you have to say is my last name."

She glared. "I'm not giving in."

"This isn't a contest."

"Isn't it?"

Maybe it was, but it was more about exploring feelings and needs that had never surfaced with another woman.

She covered his hand against her neck with her own. "I want to undress, but I want you to undress, too. You've already seen me half naked, but you haven't even taken off your tie, for goodness sake. Please, Blake."

Please was not the safe word. Please was part of the game. "Does the thought of you standing there naked while I'm dressed make you feel vulnerable?" he asked, knowing the answer and ready for her to admit it.

"Yes."

"I *want* you vulnerable. I don't want any barriers between you and me."

"My clothes aren't a barrier, not in the way you mean."

"Yes, they are. You've used your uniform and professional image as a defense mechanism with me. Tonight that ends."

She flinched as if his words had struck deeply. "That's not fair. I dress this way as part of my employment with *your* company. How can you hold that against me?"

"You dressed for work to go to dinner with me. You were trying to keep me at arm's length tonight, and I intend to be as close to you as your skin."

He waited, to see if she would deny it, or if her innate honesty would carry over even when it made her uncomfortable.

"I was . . ." She sighed, her face averting. "I was trying to keep a barrier between us, but I'm not anymore." She looked at him again, her eyes filled with compelling brown warmth. "That's got to be obvious."

"I want the barrier gone."

"It is gone."

"Get naked and it will be gone."

"Why are you being so stubborn about this? Why

does it matter?" she implored, the very tension in her voice telling him she knew damn well why it mattered.

"You tell me."

"I don't want to be that vulnerable."

"If you trust me not to hurt you, not to take advantage of your femininity no matter what the circumstances are, it won't be a problem for you."

"But—"

"There are no buts. Either you trust me, or you don't." Suddenly this need, this compulsion to push her, to dominate her as his sexual mate, made sense. Ivy Kendall kept herself separate from other people; she'd been doing it since the first time they met. She had emotional barriers that protected her from getting involved, and he wanted her involved with him.

He wanted everything, and everything included her unwavering trust. Each time he pushed her and she complied, it knocked another chink out of the wall around her and put another piece in the bridge between them. He wanted that bridge rock solid.

"Do it." His hand fell away from her, and he took another step back, challenging her with his eyes. *"Do it, or say the safe word."*

Her eyes snapped dark fire at him. "Fine." She yanked her jacket off, the thin cotton of her blouse not enough to hide nipples still hard from their time in the elevator.

She started unbuttoning it. "If you need the juvenile thrill of having me naked while you are dressed, I'll take my darn clothes off."

"You're pretty mouthy for a woman who is supposed to be learning how to cooperate more fully with her boss."

"I am cooperating," she practically growled. "Can't you tell?" She ripped the shirt off and tossed it on the floor.

He didn't watch to see where it landed; his focus

was too fixed on the beauty of her creamy breasts revealed in the stretchy lace cups of her bra. "That's a scandalous piece of underwear."

She shrugged. "No one can see it under the blouse and jacket."

"I'm seeing it now."

She reached behind her to unfasten it. "For a second longer anyway."

"Stop."

She froze with her hands behind her back, a question in her eyes. Her delicate curves pressed forward in an intensely erotic display, the blush of arousal unmistakable on her fair skin.

"Peel it away slowly."

Her breath hitched, and she did as he said, revealing the flawlessness of her form one delicious centimeter at a time, until she finally let the bra fall to the floor.

He sucked in air, but he felt like all the oxygen had gone missing from his immediate vicinity. "You're perfect."

"I don't feel as vulnerable as I thought I would."

"Why should you? I'm the one ready to have a heart attack."

She laughed, the sound soft and ultrafeminine. Was she amused by him?

He couldn't drag his gaze from her gorgeous breasts to tell. They were small, but deliciously round and firm with tip-tilted nipples that were turgid points, colored a deep red from the blood rushing through them.

He wanted to taste those tantalizing berries, but that would have to wait. "Now the skirt."

Without so much as blinking, she reached behind her and undid the button and zipper. The sound of it sliding down set off a burst of libidinous hormones in his body, making his muscles clench in primal preparation for taking his mate.

She shimmied it down her hips, and it, too, fell to the carpet, revealing curls more red than the hair on her head. They were fluffy from his earlier ministrations, and he knew if he touched them, she would quiver just as she had in the elevator.

He walked toward her, the draw of her body an irresistible pull. She wasn't the vulnerable one right now. He was because he needed to touch her more than he needed to breathe, more than he needed to eat to survive, more than he needed warmth, or shelter, or satisfaction in his job. He could live without those things, but he couldn't live without touching her.

When he reached her, he reached out and shocked himself by not touching the erogenous zones on her body, the parts of her now revealed to his gaze for the first time.

He cupped the side of her face with one hand and pressed his other one against her heart. "You are the most beautiful woman I have ever seen."

Five

Her eyes filled with tears, an inexplicable agony surfacing in their brown depths. "You said we would be honest."

Had he? Or had he said that his bluntness was a good counterpart for her honesty? It didn't matter. Either way, right now he was telling the absolute truth. "I mean it."

"You can't."

"Why not?"

"There are so many glamorous women in your world."

"And none of them come close to matching you for sheer feminine magnificence. How can you doubt my words? The inn could burn down around us and I couldn't let you go."

One tear spilled over and rolled down her cheek, but her sweet lips tilted in a smile that touched places inside him he didn't even know existed. "Oh, Blake . . ."

He kissed her and lost himself in her lips. He was kicking off his trousers before he realized he'd even started undressing, but he had to feel skin to skin, warmth to warmth.

The minute he was naked, she pressed herself against him, cradling his aching erection against the smooth softness of her belly and pressing her hardened nipples into his chest.

She moaned at the contact.

He groaned.

They fell on the bed, and he started touching.

Blake's hands were everywhere. Ivy loved it. He'd been so controlled in the elevator, but he'd lost that control now, and she reveled in his overwhelming passion.

One big hand cupped her backside while the other fondled her breast. His mouth was voracious on hers, and she responded with a renewal of excitement that made her ache for his possession. She hooked one leg over his thigh in blatant invitation and felt the head of his sex nudge her swollen folds.

She pressed forward, but he reared back, a loud groan issuing from his throat. "Wait a second, baby. We're going too fast."

Cooperation was all well and good, but she was done with games tonight. "Blake, I want you inside my body right now."

He laughed, the sound strained. "I wasn't going to make you wait, honey, trust me."

He was stretching toward the nightstand beside the bed. He pulled the drawer open and fumbled around inside, all the while keeping her from going anywhere with the hand still clamped to her butt. Like she wanted to. It would take a crow bar and a very powerful winch to get her from his side.

"Got one," he practically shouted as he drew back toward her, a foil packet in his hand.

"You brought condoms? To Delicious, Ohio?"

"I wanted you the first day I saw you. My self-control has been deteriorating ever since. I wasn't going to be caught flat-footed if it disappeared all together."

"Oh."

He ripped the packet open with his teeth and pulled out the condom with a shake that sent the packet flipping over his shoulder. "Can we talk about this later?"

"Yes, of cour—"

He surged into her with a thrust that stretched her, filled her, and took the last bit of breath from her body.

He pulled back, she sucked in air, he surged forward again, this time seating himself to the hilt. She cried out and instinctively tried to move back from the marauding intruder so intent on dominating her inner flesh.

He stilled, his body vibrating with barely suppressed savagery. "Are you okay?"

She couldn't talk; her lungs were still frozen, that one breath all she'd managed in the last few seconds.

He squeezed her, and she took a choking breath.

"You're big."

"Does it hurt?" His eyes searched her face with desperate appeal. "I didn't mean to hurt you. I'm sorry, sweetheart."

"It *doesn't* hurt. It's just . . . so much."

"Too much?" he asked, primal need lacing his voice, but concern for her was there, too. Sweat broke out on his brow.

"Not too much. I love it." *I love you,* she wanted to say, but held the words in check. Just barely.

"Good." He gripped her hip with strong fingers, adjusting her leg over him so she was blatantly open to his possession and then started to move.

His pelvis collided with her mound with every pounding thrust, and she knew another orgasm was not far off.

The pleasure built and built and built. He grunted with each thrust, the veneer of sophisticated businessman completely gone in the face of this primordial male so intent on dominating her body with his own.

He didn't have to be on top for her to feel like he was in complete control. Only she didn't mind. She wanted this no-holds-barred intimacy. She'd craved it forever, even if she hadn't known it.

"I'm going to come!" he shouted.

And then he started grinding his pelvis against her in a deliberate attempt to take her with him. It worked.

She screamed.

He shouted.

They shuddered together in sweaty, orgasmic bliss, but he wasn't done. He ground against her, groaning with another body-arching pulse from his sex. He did it again, and each one prolonged her own pleasure, the starbursts going off in her head in one pyrotechnic display after another until it felt as if her mind exploded. She gasped, her heart raced, her body locked in an orgasm that could have been measured on the Richter scale, and everything went black.

Blake could not believe it. Ivy was utterly limp against him. Her heart-shaped face had gone from tight with orgasmic tension to smooth and serene in the space of a heartbeat. He released her hip, and she fell onto her back in unconscious abandon.

He had never given a woman a fainting orgasm before. In fact, he'd sort of always thought that particular sexual myth was just that . . . a fairy tale. Sudden fear made him rear up and over her as he looked for signs of any kind of physical distress. What if it was more than her climax? What if she'd had a heart attack? Or an aneurysm? Or . . .

Her beautiful brown eyes slid open, and her swollen mouth creased in a gentle smile. "Hi."

"Hi, yourself." His voice was weak from the unexpected worry and scratchy from shouting his pleasure out loud enough to strain his vocal cords.

"That was pretty amazing."

"Yes. I lost control there at the end."

She arched toward him just the tiniest bit at the reminder, and his still semi-erect flesh slipped inside her slick opening. He couldn't help it; he pressed forward for total possession, or as much as he could achieve in his current state. She didn't seem to mind, but sighed out in what sounded like bliss to him. Then she tightened around him, and he grunted.

This woman was incredible.

"I didn't hurt you, did I?"

He'd pounded into her like a sledgehammer, and the fact he hadn't been on top of her hadn't stopped him from hitting deep with each thrust. In fact, the way her thigh had been hooked over his had laid her completely open to him.

"You might have bruised my hip a little, but I don't mind."

He looked down at her right hip. The soft white curve was such a perfect feminine shape, but it was marred by small blue splotches. He swore. "I held you too tight."

She touched his face, the feel of her fingers against his skin warm. "You held me just right. I loved it. Couldn't you tell?"

"I've never had a woman faint on me before."

"That makes us even. I've never fainted. Not in any circumstance."

Why that should make him feel so proud and primitively possessive, he had no idea, but the connection between the two of them seemed to be weaving tighter every second.

Pretty soon he was going to start pounding his chest and saying stupid stuff like, "My Ivy."

The fact those two words sounded anything but dumb inside his head was scarier than her faint.

He went to pull away, but her arms locked around him.

"I've got to take care of the condom."

"I know, but I don't want you to move."

But he had to, and they both knew it.

She sighed and let her arms fall back to the bed. "All right."

Holding on to the condom, he carefully slid from her tight heat and then rolled to his feet. He grabbed a tissue from the box on the bedside table and dealt with the condom. The wastebasket was in the bathroom; however, he didn't head there immediately. The view in front of him was too incredible to easily walk away from.

Her hair was a cloud of reddish brown silk against the white comforter. A sheen of perspiration covered her luscious body, her still erect nipples and scent telling him that she might be satisfied, but she wouldn't object to him touching her again.

"You're extremely sensual, Ivy."

"I never have been." She stretched languidly, her body twenty-two karat enticement. "Not with anyone but you."

He found himself swaying toward the bed in shock and renewed desire. He stayed upright purely by strength of will. She wasn't the only one their intimacy had laid waste to.

"You didn't enjoy sex before?" he asked, unable to contain his astonishment.

She was the most amazing lover he'd ever known and more responsive than he'd ever even fantasized about.

She didn't seem offended by his surprised reaction, not with that warm, sated smile still directed his way. "I've only ever made love with one other man."

"Who?"

"Doesn't matter; it was a long time ago."

"It couldn't have been that long. You're pretty damn young now."

"Been peeking at my employee records?"

"I'm the boss. It's my prerogative. Now stop trying to change the subject and tell me who it was. Did he hurt you? Traumatize you in some way?" She didn't make love like a woman who had had a bad sexual experience in her past.

She laughed, the sound soft and appealing. "No, nothing like that, and it happened my senior year of high school."

It happened? Had she only made love the one time? One man he could believe. One encounter? Impossible. "And you haven't had sex with anyone since?"

"No."

"Was it that bad with him?"

She came up on her elbows, striking a provocative pose. Her expression wasn't sensual, though; it wasn't amused any longer either. If anything, she looked thoughtful and just a little sad. "Making love with Danny wasn't like it is with you, but it wasn't terrible either."

"Then why?"

She sat up and slid her legs over the opposite side of the bed so her back was to him. "Because it hurt too much when he walked away."

"But everyone breaks up with their high school flame." And they didn't all stop having sex because of it.

She stood up and started hunting for her clothes. "Not everyone."

"Well, okay, a few end up getting married, but just because you didn't shouldn't have turned you off dating."

She spun to face him, the look on her face one of surprise. "I didn't say it put me off dating. I've dated plenty of men since high school."

"But you haven't made love with any of them." He tried not to make it sound like a question, but he was still having a hard time wrapping his mind around the idea of her years-long celibacy.

She cocked her head to one side and looked at him as if *she* was the one who needed to see inside *his* head. "Not everyone thinks sex is a natural component of dating."

Okay. Touché. "But if you were holding out for marriage, you wouldn't have made love with him, and you sure as hell wouldn't be here with me right now." He certainly hadn't offered her anything permanent.

She winced, and he realized how that had sounded, as if he was ruling out a future between them before the sheets had even cooled from the most explosive sex he'd ever had.

"I didn't mean—"

"Don't worry about it. I'm not looking for marriage or even a long-term relationship. I know that's impossible for us."

"Not impossible . . ."

She just smiled and shook her head. "I made love with Danny because I loved him. I *wanted* to marry him, but I knew he couldn't have his dreams with me around. He did, too."

"Are you talking about this moon thing?"

"Yes."

"Ivy—"

"I know you don't think it's real, but Danny knew it was. He wasn't ready to get married and start a family. Who is at eighteen? So, he had to move on, and so did I."

Blake didn't know what getting married had to do with her moon thing, but he understood the implication of what else she'd said. "So, he made love to you and then walked away?"

She shrugged. "Neither of us had a choice."

The little prick could have chosen to keep his dick in

his pants. It had to have been harder for Ivy to let Danny go after making love than it would have been before. She'd just said it had hurt, enough to make her very cautious about having another sexual relationship.

But she'd also said she didn't see making love as a given component to a dating relationship.

He was trying to get this, but it felt like one of those male-female things that he found incomprehensible most of the time. "So, tell me again why no sex since then."

She took a deep breath, as though preparing to say something that she rather wouldn't. She crossed her arms over her stomach and let the air out. "I've never loved another man enough to want to share something so intimate and sacred with him."

He felt like he'd just been gut punched. *"Are you saying you love me?"*

She winced again, her face pinkening with embarrassment, and she tightened her arms in a blatantly defensive move. "Yes."

He didn't know what to say. He wanted her like he'd never wanted another woman. Hell, his hard-on had grown to aching full mast again, and all they were doing was talking. About stuff that usually gave him a worse case of the jitters than a triple-shot espresso.

He hadn't considered the l-word, though. "Ivy, I—"

"Don't worry about it. I'm not expecting you to love me back." Her gaze flicked down. "Uh . . . are you going to take care of that?"

"I can't until I get rid of the condom and put a new one on."

Her mouth dropped open in an "O," and then she laughed. "I *meant* the condom."

He was still holding the tissue bundle. "We're talking."

"There's not much else to say, is there?"

He couldn't help feeling she was hoping there was, and he just didn't know if he could give her the words and mean them. If he didn't, he couldn't say them. She deserved the same level of honesty she had given him.

She could have lied and said she didn't love him when he asked, or that she didn't know, but she hadn't spared her pride at the cost of her integrity.

"I guess not. Not right now, anyway."

She nodded, the flicker of disappointment in her pretty brown eyes quickly masked. But he'd seen it and felt like a jerk for putting it there.

He turned and went into the bathroom without another word.

When he came back out, Ivy was dressing. She had her blouse on and the first several buttons done up.

"What are you doing?"

"Putting on my clothes."

"I can see that. Why?"

"Walking to my room stark naked doesn't appeal." She smiled, inviting him to share the joke. "I've never had even a slight hankering to streak naked down hotel corridors."

"Why are you going back to your room?" Was it because he hadn't said he loved her? Did she regret letting him into her body now because of it?

"You know the answer to that," she said lightly.

"If I did, I wouldn't be asking," he growled.

Her eyes widened at his tone. "Management Training 101: you're on duty even when you aren't." She finished buttoning her blouse and smoothed it down with a grimace obviously meant for the wrinkled condition. "If the staff needs me, they aren't going to come looking in your room. At least, I hope they aren't. That would be more than a little embarrassing."

"Oh."

She bent down and grabbed her skirt off the floor. It

was all he could do not to go over there and take her sexy butt in his two hands and squeeze. She was so perfect, shaped like a dream and as hot as reality could get.

She shimmied into the navy blue uniform skirt. "You could come with me, if you like." She said it casually, but her tense posture and the way she didn't meet his eyes when she asked gave away her nervousness.

"I like."

She looked at him then and smiled—a beautiful, happy, white teeth, lips bowed lusciously grin. "Good."

"You had to know I'd say yes."

"I thought me telling you I love you might have scared you off."

"Technically you didn't say the words," he said, apropos of nothing. He didn't want to hear them, did he?

She laughed, actually laughed. "No, I didn't, did I?" She didn't look heartbroken or miserable that he hadn't said he felt the same way, far from it, and how was he supposed to feel about that?

Her smile never faltered. "I love you, Blake."

Oh, man . . . that sounded good, too good.

It also turned him on. He started toward her, smiling with intent when her eyes widened in alarm. "We can go back to your room after."

"After?" she parroted, backing up a step.

"Yes, after."

"But . . ."

"I'm the boss, sweetheart, and right now your most pressing duty is to let me pleasure you stupid."

"Some duty." Her breath hitched, and her gaze grew hot. Just that fast.

"I think so," he said, forcing her back one more step, knowing it was the last one he needed to get her right where he wanted her to be.

Ivy backed into the bed and tumbled backward when Blake kept pushing forward.

Feeling the brush of his erection against her as she fell, she expected him to pounce immediately, but he didn't. Instead, he used his mouth and hands to sensitize her feet in a way that impacted every erogenous zone of her body as if each of her toes was some kind of remote control device.

The slow seduction of her senses had her begging for his possession before he'd even gotten her skirt off, but he showed with one tormenting caress after another that he was in no hurry to put himself inside her.

He slipped her skirt down her legs in an excruciatingly slow glide.

"Blake . . . "

"Shhh . . . honey, let me pamper you."

"Pamper me?" She gasped as he leaned over her naked bottom half. "You're driving me crazy."

He laughed, the warm air from his mouth stirring the sensitive hair on her mound. What was he doing?

Her legs were pressed apart by strong hands, and then his mouth was against her most private flesh. His tongue swirled and dipped, making her arch toward his mouth in hungry, shivery excitement. He surrounded her clitoris with his lips, flicked it with the tip of his tongue, and started humming . . . not singing, but making a sound with his mouth that made her flesh vibrate. Then he slipped his finger inside her more than willing flesh. She clasped him as tightly as she could, moaning with the pleasure that inner clenching gave her. He pressed with his long finger against a spot that made her shudder and cry out.

He added a second finger, but kept up his attention to that secret spot she hadn't even been sure she had.

Without so much as a preliminary muscle rigor, she came. "Oh, Blake, oh, yes . . . it feels so good, so perfect. I love you, Blake." Having the freedom to say the words again intensified her pleasure, and her body continued convulsing around his fingers and arching toward his mouth.

The feelings grew unbearably intense, and she couldn't take any more. She tried to pull away while shoving at his head with her hands, but his grip on her was unshakable, and the pleasure that was close to pain continued to spear through her.

"Blake, please, you've got to stop . . . I can't stand it."

But he didn't stop, and she had another orgasm, this one even more intense than the first. Her whole body tightened to frozen immobility while her womb contracted and her inner core radiated the most amazing sensations outward she'd ever known. Then, again without warning, her body went limp, and every muscle that had been rigid was now totally incapable of moving or sustaining her in any way. Even her head lolled to the side in boneless abandon.

He kissed her, paying thorough homage to every centimeter of quivering nerves between her legs. Then he lifted his head, and she managed to turn hers enough to see him. Her essence glistened wetly on his mouth, and his blue eyes were dark with sexual pride. And hungry need. He'd given her pleasure; now he wanted to take his.

"You said it again."

"What?" she slurred.

"That you love me."

"Yes." And she'd liked saying it. Loved the freedom to express feelings she would get to revel in for a few short days at the most. There would be plenty of time to grieve his loss later, just as she had grieved Danny's, but right now she could do nothing but celebrate being with this man.

Instinctively, she knew Blake wasn't comfortable with emotion. It wasn't controlled enough for him, and this was one man who really liked to be in control. He'd given her a tremendous gift when he hadn't allowed her honesty about her emotions to drive him away.

He didn't say anything else, just started making love to her again, removing her blouse, caressing her, making her want him. Passion burned in his gaze like an inferno fed with gasoline, but his touch was gentle, and incredibly, he incited her own desire until it matched his once again before taking her with an excruciatingly slow, but inexorable thrust.

He filled her completely, and she wrapped her legs around his waist to keep him that way.

"It's not too much, is it?"

"No, darling. Not too much."

His eyes closed, and his head went back, a look of utter bliss on his features. "You can take all of me."

Their pelvic bones ground together. "Yes. I love taking all of you."

Then he started to thrust, each movement slow and measured.

"Blake . . . I want . . . I need more!"

"I was too fast the first time, but this time I'm going to be slow and careful. You're a lot smaller than me, Ivy."

"Just because you're some kind of freak of nature doesn't mean I'm a fragile midget. Go faster, darn it." She pounded his back.

But all she got for her trouble was another slow, deep glide.

She reached up with her mouth, latched on to a patch of skin just above his left nipple, and started to suck.

A strangled sound that could have been her name came from his throat.

She kept sucking and pinched his right nipple, then

played with it, delighting in the way the small, hard nub felt against her fingers.

Suddenly he was rearing back, breaking the hold her legs had on him and tossing her over onto her stomach.

"Hey," she yelled and then gasped as he slammed into her from the back.

He went so deep, he was touching her heart; at least that's how it felt. "You are a vixen."

"Vixen? Who says vixen?"

"I do. It fits the beautiful tease I've got in my bed."

"We aren't technically in your bed; we're on it," she panted.

"And I'm on you."

"Yeah, couldn't stand the heat, huh?"

"If you've only ever made love with one other man, where'd you learn that stuff?"

"I read."

A deep laugh rumbled against her spine. "I'll have to borrow some of your books."

"Any time."

"But right now, I want to love you without any of your little tricks, got it?"

If he'd said screw her, she would have said something equally sexy and tried to get the leverage to flip over, but he'd said love, and even though he didn't mean *love*-love, it still just melted her.

It wasn't a good idea to go gooey on him, though. That probably *would* scare him away. "Are we playing your game again?" she asked in an effort to keep it light.

"What would make you say that?"

"The fact you have me on my stomach and I can't do anything but what you want."

"Don't you like it?" He thrust deep and pulled out slowly only to thrust deeply again.

When she got enough breath to talk again, she answered. "I like it just fine, but I don't like you thinking you can always be in control."

"Would I think that?" he asked, reaching around and under her with one hand, his voice all rumbling innocence and his fingers a temptation to sin. The questing hand slid along her belly and down to her pubic hair; then fingers pressed between her labia and touched her clitoris.

"You might think it, but you'd be wrong." And she tried something else she'd read about.

He cursed, a word she never, ever said, but described spectacularly what they were doing.

She squeezed and released her inner muscles in a rhythm that matched his thrusts. Pretty soon the rhythm increased until all she could do was squeeze and hold the contraction for as long as possible, then release and start squeezing again.

Six

He panted in her ear, his fingers playing her sweet spot as though they knew her every secret. He did. More than any other person on the earth. Minutes later, she and Blake came together with lots of noise and passionately rocking bodies. Afterward, he collapsed on top of her, his weight warm and solid against her back.

He kissed her temple, her cheek, and her lips when she twisted her head at an uncomfortable angle so he could do so. Then he rolled off of her, but she couldn't move. She didn't even have enough energy to turn over. She felt him get off the bed, but she couldn't work up enough energy to wonder if he'd gone to take care of the condom again as her eyes slid shut.

She didn't go to sleep, but lay there in a state of semidoze until he came back. Without a word, he lifted her to cradle against his chest like something precious and carried her into the bathroom.

He stepped into the claw-foot tub with her still cradled in his arms and sank down until they were both submerged in the hot water. "There are times I positively love the quaintness of this inn."

She smiled and drowsily nuzzled his neck with the back of her head. "Me, too."

"Your words are slurry."

"Mmmm."

"You're so tired, you're barely awake."

"Mmmm."

"Go to sleep if you want. I'll take care of you."

But she didn't. No matter how tired she was, she wouldn't have missed the following half hour to save her life.

He washed her whole body. Using the glycerin soap the inn provided for its guests, he gently massaged muscles she hadn't known she had, or hadn't remembered. He also gently touched her between her legs, carefully cleansing her swollen vulva and opening. His touch was light, as if he was being careful not to arouse her again. It was pure tender care, and she adored every soothing caress.

When he was done, he lifted her out and dried them both off before carrying her back into the bedroom.

She looked at her rumpled clothes on the floor and shuddered. "I have to get dressed and get back to my apartment."

He put her down on the bed and then opened a drawer and pulled out a black T-shirt. "Put this on. It will cover everything, and it's clean."

"But—"

"It's late. Your apartment and this room are the only things on this floor. It's highly unlikely we'll run into anyone in the hall."

We? She hoped he meant that literally. She wasn't sure he remembered her invitation to join her for the rest of the night in her bed. She also hoped he was right about no one being in the hall, because the black T-shirt looked way more comfortable than her rumpled clothing.

He helped her pull the T-shirt over her head and tuck her arms through the big sleeves. She should feel like a child being dressed by a parent, but instead she felt cherished.

When the T-shirt hung on her like an oversized mini-dress, he went back to the dresser and got out a pair of shorts and another T-shirt. He pulled them on and then led her out of the room, one arm around her waist as if he knew that walking on her own would be way too much for her rubbery legs.

If someone saw them, the fact she was wearing his T-shirt wouldn't be the first thing that gave away their status as lovers. She couldn't make herself care. She wouldn't be working here much longer anyway, but even if she would . . . the prospect of having her employees know she'd slept with the big boss wouldn't have deterred her from taking him to her bed.

She loved him.

And he gave her more pleasure than she had ever believed she would feel.

When they entered her apartment, they went straight back to the bedroom, and he didn't even complain when he had to curl around her body to fit on the double bed.

Blake woke the next morning to Ivy's small hands exploring his body. He rumbled a good morning, she kissed him in response, and they made love, this time without any games or attempts at one-upmanship.

Then they showered together, and she experimented on him with soap, emulating something else she'd read in a book.

This time, he was the shaky one drying off. "I need to check my e-mail and get some work done before we drive into Cleveland."

She bit her lip as if worried about something, but nodded. "All right. We can have muesli and yogurt for breakfast, then. It will only take a minute to put together."

She made coffee to go with it, and he took his mug with him to his room.

He powered on the computer and left it to boot up while he shaved. He looked at the blond stubble on his face in the mirror and frowned, remembering the red spots on Ivy's delicate breasts and cheeks this morning. She hadn't seemed to mind the rough texture of his morning beard against her sensitive skin.

In fact, she'd gone a little crazy when he rubbed it over her nipples, but he still should have at least *thought* of shaving.

"Selfish bastard," he said to the man in the mirror.

And then remembering Ivy's screams of pleasure, he smiled. Maybe not totally selfish.

He came back into his room and went to check his e-mail and froze. The screen had a blinking white cursor and nothing else. He tried rebooting, but the same thing happened. It never made it past the bios commands. Damn it. It was a brand-new, state of the art laptop, and the hard drive had crashed. The manufacturer was going to hear from him.

Ivy came out of the bedroom after blow-drying her hair to find Blake at her kitchen table drinking more coffee. He was scowling.

"I thought you were going to check your e-mail."

She knew how slow the land line connections were. He could only be done if he'd gotten very few messages—unlikely—or hadn't been able to access them, which was all too likely considering how much time she'd spent in his room last night.

She bit the lip she'd been worrying all morning

since Blake had mentioned his computer earlier. Last night had been the full moon, a *blue* moon, and from the looks of things, her gift-slash-curse it-depends-on-how-you-look-at-it thing had run true to form. She'd wiped his hard drive clean.

"Stop biting your lip, sweetheart. It's swollen."

"Why didn't you check your e-mail?" she asked, feeling so cold even his endearment and indulgent smile didn't warm her.

"My hard drive crashed." His teeth snapped together in annoyance, all indulgence gone. "It's a brand-new computer."

"Blake . . ." She didn't want to say what had to be said. This was why Danny had left, and as long as Blake had believed she was superstitious rather than dangerous to hard drives and Swiss watches, he had wanted to be with her.

"Yeah, honey?"

She loved the way he called her sweetheart and honey. He'd even called her baby once, and she'd liked it, too. It meant she was unique to him, special. He didn't go around using endearments with anyone else.

"I was in your room last night."

His blue eyes warmed, the irritation melted away by male appreciation. "I know."

"It was a full moon."

"So?"

"Blake!" He wasn't stupid; he had to get the picture.

"Are you trying to tell me you erased my hard drive?"

"Not *on purpose*, but yes."

He shook his head. "Hard drives crash."

"And watches break, even Rolexes. I know, but please think about this. What are the chances your computer, your watch, your cell phone, and your Palm Pilot would all break within the same twenty-four-hour period?"

"It could happen."

"You are a whiz with numbers . . . tell me the chances."

He looked disgruntled. "Not very damn good."

"And yet it happened."

"Yes."

"Because of me."

"N—"

"Yes," she hissed, tired of trying to convince the stubborn man of something she hated having him come to believe.

His eyes narrowed. "I know you believe—"

"Do you think I like living like this? No computer, no microwave, no cordless phone even?"

"I didn't say—"

"Stop being so stubborn." She gritted her teeth and counted backward from ten. "Granny Smith's Apothecary and Soda Fountain is right next door. They carry cheap watches that aren't anti-magnetic. Go buy one. Make sure it works and bring it back."

"Ivy, this is ridiculous."

"Just do it."

He could have argued they didn't have time, or that he had better things to do, but he didn't. He sighed and got to his feet, his expression disgruntled. "If it's that important to you, I'll do it."

She spent the next fifteen minutes trying not to dwell on what was going to happen once she convinced him of the moon magnetism.

When he returned, he walked into her apartment without knocking. He was carrying a small paper bag. "It's in here."

"Did you check to make sure it works?"

"Yes."

"Good. Take it out."

She was always more magnetic the days leading up to the full moon and during it than after. She didn't understand it, but she knew her body's cycle. To a point anyway. The level of her magnetism varied in intensity before and after the full moon, but she was guessing that since it had been a blue moon last night, she'd still be magnetic enough to prove her point.

He fished the watch from the bag.

"Look at it."

"What am I supposed to see?" He didn't sound irritated, or dismissive, just curious.

"The second hand moving. Is it?"

"Yes."

She put her hand out.

He gave her the watch.

She closed her fingers over it.

"I don't know what you're trying to prove."

"Oh, you know, you just don't want to deal with it."

He let out a frustrated breath, running his hand through his perfectly groomed blond hair and leaving it mussed.

The cold metal of the watch back warmed in her hand. She held on to it longer than she thought she needed to because when she let go, when she let him see, it would be over. Finally, she forced herself to open her fingers and let him see.

He looked down and scowled. "It stopped."

"Are you going to try to explain this away, too?"

He looked at her, and the expression in his eyes made her stomach knot. "It's true, isn't it?"

"I tried to tell you it was."

He nodded, but said nothing.

What was he thinking? That she was a freak? A weirdo? Definitely not a woman he could have in his world.

"What did your high school sweetheart want to be that he couldn't take you with him?"

"He works for NASA."

"You still talk?"

"Yes, he's the only person besides family who knows."

"I know now."

"True."

"You really can't manage a hotel with computerized check-in procedures and maintenance systems."

"No."

"Why not?" She opened her mouth to answer, exasperated by his willful ignorance, but he raised his hand to shush her. "I mean, why can't you just stay away during a full moon?"

"For one thing, I'm not always sure when the problems will start. Sometimes it's not until the day of the full moon; sometimes it happens several days before."

"But you know when the full moon comes every month."

"And you would be okay with your manager taking off for several days every month to cover my bases?" She shook her head, knowing the answer. "Even if that would work, where would I go? I can't exactly stay in a hotel."

"Where will you go when you leave here?"

The question sliced into her heart, slashing her deeply buried hopes. "I don't know."

The phone rang, and Ivy sprang to answer it. She'd convinced Blake about her moon magnetism, but now that meant he would leave, and she welcomed any interruption that would stave off the final break.

"Ivy?"

"Yes, Trudy?"

"The maintenance guy who is redoing the woodwork is here. He wants to talk to you."

"I'll be right down."

She hung up the phone and turned back to Blake. She couldn't read anything in his expression. "There's someone at the front desk I need to see."

"Ed?" he asked in a harsh voice, masculine hostility radiating from every pore.

"No. I told you, I'm not going to marry Ed, even if it would get rid of my gift-slash-curse it-depends-on-how-you-look-at-it thing."

"You stop being magnetic after you get married?"

She shook her head. "That's what the women in my family believed for generations, but I did some research. Pregnancy is what actually changes the chemical balance and ends the moon changes in our bodies."

"So, if you had a baby, you wouldn't have to worry about this anymore?"

"Right, but I'm not going to run out and get artificially inseminated just to change my body's chemistry. Children deserve a better start than that in life." She turned to go, trying really hard not to cry and afraid the wetness on her cheeks meant she wasn't succeeding very well.

"I could make you pregnant."

She stopped with her hand on the door. "What?"

He could not have said what she thought she'd heard him say.

She spun back around to face him, swiping at her cheeks. "What?" she asked again.

He came to her and laid his hand against her neck, his thumb brushing her pulse point. "I said I could give you a baby."

She couldn't help it; her eyes flicked down to the front of his pants, and he laughed.

"Not right this second, honey, but it wouldn't take much."

Despite the intimacy of the night before and that morning, she felt a hot blush stain her cheeks. "That's not funny, Blake."

"I'm not laughing."

"But you can't mean it."

"Why can't I?"

"You can't just give me a baby to change my body chemistry. You'd be a father. That's a lifetime commitment." And she had absolutely no doubt he would see it that way too. She'd known this man for three years. He took family seriously.

"So?" he asked, just as if the prospect of a lifetime tied to her through a child didn't upset him in the least.

The phone rang again. Ivy didn't have to pick it up to know it was Trudy reminding her to come downstairs. "I've got to go."

"Ivy—"

"I . . . we . . . let's talk about this later, okay?"

"Okay." He removed his hand from her, and she felt as if all the heat in her body had taken a vacation.

Cold loneliness rushed across her heart, and she shivered.

Get a grip on yourself, girl. He wasn't here two days ago, and he won't be two days from now. You survived then. You will survive later.

"Think about it," he said as she stepped out the door.

She rushed down the hall toward the stairs. If she appeared to be running, she could be forgiven. She was running, but leaving Blake physically behind didn't get him out of her brain.

He'd offered to give her a baby. He had to be losing his mind. Why else would he make such a preposterous suggestion? Did he pity her? Would a man make such a far-reaching suggestion based on pity? What else could it be? Blake wanted her, there was no getting around it, but she'd told him she loved him, and he had not said the words back to her.

He wanted to make love to her, not get saddled with her as the mother of his child for the rest of his life.

* * *

Blake stood in Ivy's tiny apartment, the shock of her revelations starting to wear off, but the seductiveness of his suggestion to give her a baby was not.

He got hard thinking about her swollen with his child. He'd have to marry her. She was right; a child deserved a better start in life than to be the solution to its mother's physical problems. He would love his child. Ivy would love the baby, too. She was good at loving.

The alternative—leaving and never seeing her again— was not one he could face. Not now. Not after he'd shared a level of trust in intimacy he'd never known with anyone else. Never wanted to know with anyone else.

He loved her.

Why had it taken him so long to realize it?

He'd fallen for her the first time he'd seen her. He'd avoided dating other women for the last couple of years and used work as an excuse. The truth was, he didn't want anyone but Ivy.

He had to tell her. She didn't know he loved her; how could she when he'd just realized it himself? She was going to say no to having his baby and marrying him if he didn't explain how he felt.

And he knew just the way to do it.

Ivy was sitting in her office chair, working on her ledgers, when Blake walked in. He'd left word with Trudy he was going to be gone for a few hours, and apparently Ivy had opted to put that time to good use getting some work done.

Her dedication to her job and to her employees was just one of the many things he loved about her.

He shut the door behind him.

Ivy's head came up at the click of the lock sliding into place.

His expression was as serious as a heartbeat; he knew because that's how he felt. "I think we need to have another lesson in cooperation."

She blinked, her mouth opening and closing, but no words came out. "C-cooperation? *Here?*" she finally stuttered.

He smiled, loving the catch in her voice, the feminine wariness combined with grudging interest in her beautiful brown eyes. "Here, sweetheart."

He crossed the room, just as he had the day before, but when he reached her side of the desk, instead of looming over her, he dropped to kneel in front of her.

"Blake?" Her voice was so tiny, almost scared, and he wanted to take her in his arms and tell her everything was going to be okay, but there were other things that had to be said first.

He took her hands in his. They were trembling, but then so were his. "I love you, Ivy Kendall. Will you marry me?"

Tears started sliding down her cheeks, and she shook her head. "You can't. You don't. It's just pity. Please, Blake, don't . . ."

He kissed her until her mouth went cooperative against his; then he pulled away. "I can. I do. It's not and I will, for the rest of our lives."

"But you didn't say anything when I told you I loved you."

He took a deep breath. "I'm stubborn. You may have noticed."

She laughed, a small, breathy sound. "Yes, I had."

"I didn't want to admit what I felt was love, not the times I was so disappointed I wanted to hit things when you didn't show up for the management training seminars, not when I realized my desire for you was out of control and spurring me on to fantasize about you in a way I hadn't ever done with another woman, not when you said you loved me and turned me on so bad, I lost what was left of my mind, not when seeing you getting dressed to go back to your room scared me worse than going sky diving for the first time, not even when you told me you couldn't be with me because of your moon magnetism. But, honey, when you ran away from me and my proposal, even I wasn't stubborn enough to keep denying my love."

"You didn't propose. You offered to give me a baby."

"Same thing. I'm not a sperm donor; I'm a man. If I'm going to give you a baby, you are going to be wearing my ring on your finger."

"Oh, Blake."

"Is that a yes?"

"I—"

Wait a second. He let go of her hands to dig in his pocket. He came up with a small black velvet box and flipped it open. The square-cut moonstone with diamonds on either side of it winked up at them.

He pulled the ring out and put it partway on her finger. "Yes?"

She grinned, her eyes glistening with tears. "Yes."

"Thank you, God."

She laughed, and he pushed the ring all the way on and then kissed her until she was plastered against his front, kneeling on the floor with him.

Then he gave her another lesson in cooperation and had to stifle her shouts of pleasure with his mouth.

Much later they were snuggled into his queen-size bed after Ivy announced their upcoming marriage to the staff.

Everyone congratulated them, but none of her employees were surprised. Trudy said it had been obvious to all of them for months that Ivy was in love with the big boss. They were just glad he had shown enough smarts to return her feelings.

"I'm not going to like being separated from you during full moons until I get pregnant," she said, rubbing her hand over his tight abdomen.

They had made love again, this time *her* giving *him* a lesson in cooperation. He'd even let her tie his hands to the old-fashioned bedposts to do it. He was free again, and his arms were locked around her as if he'd never let go.

He lunged up and over her, his face fixed in a scowl. "Who said anything about being separated?"

"You can't—"

"You've got to stop making erroneous assumptions, woman. They're going to get you into trouble one of these days."

"Thanks for the advice, but—"

"I've got a fishing cabin in Vermont, and we can retreat there for a few days every month."

"You can't leave your business like that."

"Actually, I can. I *am* the boss, but my plan is to work remotely. I've been thinking about it, and we can insulate the second bedroom against magnetic fields and make it my office. I'll do the same for my study at home as a safety precaution. You won't be able to go in those two rooms. I'm sorry about that, but it's better than being separated once a month."

"You would do that for me?" she asked, making no effort to hide the awe she felt at the prospect.

His scowl deepened. "Of course. I love you, or did you think saying that meant I just wanted to get you in the sack?"

"No, but . . ."

"Look, I want to be with you. Always. And I'd like to wait to have kids for a year or so. That means we need a solution to your monthly magnetic moments."

"You want to wait to have children?"

"Is that okay with you?"

"Yes. I'd like to be married for a while first, but I do want your babies, Blake."

"And the idea of you having them is the biggest turn-on I've ever known except for when you tell me you love me."

But waiting for a year or so sounded good. It meant he really was marrying her because he wanted to be with her, not because he was trying to help her fix her problem. The man had to love her a lot to have already worked out the solution he had.

She wiggled her hips against him. "You said me telling you I love you turns you on?"

"Yes," he growled.

"I love you, Blake. I love you. I love you. I love you . . ."

His laughter ended on a groan of desire, and they made love again, this time both of them totally secure in the knowledge this marriage was going to happen for all the right reasons and their love was real and strong enough to last a lifetime.

FULL MOON
PIE

Sarah Title

To Mary Ellen – Because nobody loves you like your sister.

One

"Is she out there yet?"

Dan Fields dropped the blinds to the office window at the sound of his assistant's voice. Mrs. Harris came up behind him, filling his nostrils with the sweet, powdery smell of her . . . well, he wasn't sure where the sweet, powdery smell came from. But it was a smell he always associated with sweet, gray-haired ladies of a certain age, which Mrs. Harris certainly was.

Maybe not so sweet.

Especially now, as she pinched the blinds open and gave a knowing "ah."

Yes, of course she was out there. A few days a month, every month, she was out there from late morning until well after most of the businesses downtown had closed. And she always had a steady stream of customers for the entire day. A few days a month, and then she disappeared.

And every day, he looked for her.

Mona and her stupid pink truck.

Apple of My Pie.

Who would have thought that a small town in Ohio would embrace something as trendy as a food truck?

But the people of Delicious had always been pretty open-minded, especially when it came to food, and especially when that food highlighted the golden delicious apples that made the town famous. Well, famous in Ohio.

Everybody said Mona was a genius with her baking; she managed to create treats that combined cutting-edge flavors with the comfort that only homemade baked goods could provide. She always managed to get the apples to taste just right, even this early in the season.

Not that Dan would know.

"I'm going to go down and see what she has this morning. You sure you don't want anything?"

He knew Mrs. Harris was a professional, distinguished, accomplished woman, so there was no possible way that she had just winked at him. He just grunted at her and returned to his desk.

No, he didn't want anything from Mona Miller. He had spent the past few years very specifically not buying anything from Mona. Not that he wasn't tempted. The first time she came to a meeting of the Delicious Small Business Association, her idea for a mobile bakery was just that, an idea. Dan loved it, at first. He thought it was creative and had great growth potential. And judging by the way his colleagues fell on the samples she brought in, she would be successful. He had watched as they grabbed every last crumb, leaving nothing for him, but he didn't mind. He was distracted.

He had tried to be professional about it, but there was no denying that Mona looked, well, delicious. She was short but curvy, and she had a mass of crazy, brown curls that framed her eyes, eyes that were such a pale green they were almost gold. They were amazing eyes. And that smile. When he offered her suggestions on how to file the right paperwork for her permits, she had smiled at him, and her whole face lit up.

That was them, in a nutshell. She had wild, inventive ideas; he had paperwork. Not that there was a "them." Just a smile that made his heart stop, and a business plan that he could, if he was being generous, call erratic.

Normally he made a point of buying local—after all, his accounting firm would never survive without the support of the Delicious business community. "Accounting firm" might be a slight exaggeration – it was just him and Mrs. Harris. But they did all right. They had regular customers and a solid reputation, and he was even thinking of taking on a business school intern when the semester started.

So how could he, as a responsible small business owner, one who paid his taxes and his bills and had a lease on an actual building, support a woman who clearly did not take the rigorous work of owning a small business seriously? One who worked frivolous hours and ignored the tremendous growth potential in this town so she could maintain those frivolous hours?

A food truck! She couldn't get a real bakery? And pink! Ridiculous. Branding was important, he got that, but pink? A pink truck and pink shirts—and apples weren't even pink!

And the name—Apple of My Pie. When he had first heard it, he liked it. It had a whimsical quality that suited what he thought were her start-up plans. Apparently, though, whimsical was a way of life for Mona. Every time he heard that business name now, it made his teeth hurt.

He hated the cutesy name and the cutesy truck and the cutesy little pink tank top she wore as she handed out muffins and tarts and pie and . . . whatever else she sold. So far Mrs. Harris had just brought back turnovers and the occasional pie to take home when her grandchildren were in town. Each one smelled amazing, and if the satisfied sighs Mrs. Harris emitted as she licked her fingers clean were any indication, each one tasted amazing, too.

But that was not for Dan. He turned back to his e-mail. He had work to do.

Mona grabbed a bite of an apple turnover before turning back to Joe Gunderson. She probably shouldn't help customers with her mouth full, but Joe didn't care. He liked a girl who ate, he told her. And if he wasn't eighty years old and half blind, she would have been flattered.

Frankly, she was still a little flattered. It was nice to be appreciated.

The turnover was good. The golden delicious apples that made the town of Delicious famous were a little early, but they had baked up amazingly well. She shouldn't be surprised; it was a full moon. She couldn't mess it up if she tried. She thought Joe would probably like them, so she threw one into the white box she was loading up with assorted fruit tarts for him. It would be a nice surprise for him when he got home.

She handed Joe his change and tied his box with red-and-white string. That was probably her favorite part of the bakery. She loved that string. It reminded her of small towns and neighbors who liked each other, and it suited Delicious to a T. She slapped on a pink Apple of My Pie sticker and handed the box across the little counter that folded down from the window cut into the side of the truck. As soon as she was sure he had a good grip on it (he promised he would never drop any of the stuff he bought from her—but he was eighty, after all), she stood up to stretch her back.

She loved her little pink truck, but leaning over to help all of these customers was rough work. It was better than when she first started out, when she was selling baked goods out of the trunk of her hatchback. That had been one really good thing to come out of her limited interactions with the Delicious Small Business Association. Its members were all really supportive in helping her get funding to upgrade to her dream vehicle, even if some of them balked when she proved that she was serious about painting it pink. Dan the Accountant, known as Khaki Dan among her girlfriends, had been especially . . . not into it. But she knew he saw a food truck as just a stepping stone to a "real" bakery, as he called it. Mona humored him, even though she also knew a full-time business was impossible for her.

Her truck had shelves and refrigeration, and she did her best to make it look homey and welcoming. After a lot of false leads, she'd finally found it cheap on eBay. The guy selling it said it was a retired cupcake truck from Chicago, but it smelled suspiciously like falafel when it was delivered. Fortunately, she had had plenty of time in between baking spurts to fix it up. Joe's nephew, Dylan, owned a kitchen supply store and he'd agreed to work on it in exchange for her catering his daughter's college graduation party (fortunately, the party fell on a full moon) and a selection of goodies for his wife's monthly book group. So Dylan had ripped out the old gas grill that didn't work anymore and put in a warming oven, and tuned up all of the refrigerators and the solar generator on top of the truck.

Then Mona had given it a thorough cleaning, scrubbing every surface within an inch of its life, scouring out any unsavory old-food smells. When she could move her arms again, she contemplated the peeling paint job, and her future. This venture had to work, and going halfway was not an option. So, despite Khaki Dan's protests, she had painted it pink.

And so Apple of My Pie, Mobile Bakery, was born. She still did most of the baking at home, where she had spent all of the money she inherited from her grandmother on a massive kitchen overhaul. The demand for her food was so great that she still relied on insulated shopping bags for the extra inventory. Business was good. Business was really good. So good that she was finally ready to stop worrying about the fact that this venture would only be part-time, because she could finally afford to live on the money she made with her limited schedule.

She checked her watch. The lunchtime rush was about to begin, so she pulled the German apple cake out of the warming oven, then switched it off. Even with the fans going, Apple of My Pie could turn into, well, an oven, especially as the summer sun beat down in the afternoon. She pulled a pink bandana out of her jeans pocket and wiped her forehead, then tied her hair back with it. She had pulled her hair up into a ponytail that morning, but her curly mop was no match for Ohio summer humidity, and she knew she looked like a frizzy mess.

She started slicing the cake into squares and putting them out on the little paper trays she used for plates, then stacked them under the dome of the old-fashioned cake plate she had superglued to the counter. Apple cake was a specialty of hers, and a lot of her regulars came by just for a slice of it. She laid out a tray mixed with cookies and berry tarts next to it—her regulars could usually be counted on for an impulse buy.

She wasn't sure exactly why she looked up when

she did, but, then, it always took her by surprise. There he was, going into the mom-and-pop diner down the street.

Khaki Dan.

She thought he had been avoiding her ever since Apple of My Pie hit the road. He hadn't accepted the invitation she'd extended to the whole SBA when she had her opening day street party. He never stopped by like the other small business owners did. He never even seemed to look at her food truck.

She thought she had done something to offend him, but whenever she saw him anywhere else—in the park, at the library, at the one bar in town—he was nice enough. He smiled and exchanged small talk, and she thought she even saw some interest in those piercing blue eyes of his—interest she was definitely willing to reciprocate. But then she would pull up in Apple of My Pie, and it was like she had put a sack over her head. A sack filled with month-old garbage that said, "I Hate Accountants." He didn't just ignore her when she worked; he seemed insulted by her.

Not that he didn't have opportunities to be cordial. Every day, like clockwork, he and his well-fitting khakis went into the diner at noon. Every day, according to Marylou, he ordered a turkey sub with lettuce, tomato, light on the mayo, extra pickle. He drank black coffee, never pop, and always skipped dessert.

Which was probably how he stayed so fit.

Truth be told, that was what Mona had noticed about him first. After all, it's not every day that you see a nicely dressed, not-wearing-a-wedding-ring, good-looking guy in a small town like Delicious. She sort of resented that such a catch could be such a jerk. It seemed like a cruel trick on womankind.

But apparently Mona, or Food-Truck-Mona, was his only pet peeve. Marylou said he was actually a very

nice guy and a good tipper, and Mrs. Harris, one of her
best customers, worked for him and had nothing but
good things to say. But he sure didn't like Mona. And
she wanted to find out why.

By the time the lunch rush was over, she had almost
forgotten about Khaki Dan, but then she heard the distant tinkling of the bell to the diner, and out he came,
briefcase in one hand, to-go coffee in the other. Black
coffee. Who could drink coffee without anything in it?
This was a man who needed some sweetness in his life.

"Hey!" she called out, and waved. He looked up,
startled, then looked behind him. "Yes, you!" she
shouted, then gestured for him to come over. Even from
down the street she could see his eyebrows scrunch up
in consternation, but he started toward her anyway, his
loafers leading his reluctant legs. And what legs they
were. Damn, that man could fill out a pair of khakis.

"Hi, Dan," she said as he approached, and leaned
out the window.

"Hi," he said back. She noticed that his gaze flicked
down to her tank top but went straight back to her eyes.
She appreciated the effort. And she appreciated the attention from Dan a little differently than she did from
Joe. A down-low-in-her-belly appreciation.

"I've seen you just about every day and you never
come over to say hi," she said.

"OK. Uh, hi."

"Been a while." She brushed an errant curl behind
her ear. His eyes followed her fingers.

"Been busy. You?"

"So far, so good. Is your office around here?"

He pointed to an office across the street. She knew
that, of course. It said Fields Accounting LLC across
the door. Mrs. Harris came out of there every morning,
and every morning she talked about her boss, Dan, and
how he would never take a break for a cookie or a slice

of cake but that he was just as nice as could be. Worked too hard, so he sure could use a break. She thought Mrs. Harris was trying to either help Mona make a sale or marry them off. Probably both.

"Ah, Mrs. Harris's building," she said, letting this charade that they didn't really know each other continue.

"She works with me."

Mona knew that Mrs. Harris was his secretary, and that she preferred to use that old-fashioned job title instead of the more twenty-first-century administrative assistant. But Mona appreciated that Dan said Mrs. Harris worked "with" him, and not "for" him, even if that was technically true. She took it as a touching show of respect.

"Mrs. Harris is one of my best customers," Mona said, as if Mrs. Harris had not been planting the seed for this conversation for the past several years.

"I know." He sighed.

"You want to try something?" she asked. "On the house." His gaze flicked down her body again, then quickly back up to her eyes. Ha, she thought. Do that again, her belly said.

"No, thanks, I'm not much of a sweets person," he said as his eyes lingered over the fruit tarts.

She shrugged. "A little sugar could do you some good."

"Why are you only out here once a month?"

It was a question she got a lot from customers, and she was pretty good at deflecting it. But most people just asked out of polite curiosity or because they wanted her to feed their sugar cravings more often. Ever since she'd started Apple of My Pie—even when it was just an idea and a hatchback—Dan had been up her butt about making it more permanent. He just wouldn't let it go, and here he was again. He didn't even know if her goodies were good enough for a full-time business!

It made her hackles rise. It made her defensive.

Because she had a feeling he wouldn't take polite deflection for an answer, that he wouldn't stop until he got the truth.

He couldn't handle the truth.

The truth was, she was cursed.

It had to do with the moon. Every full moon, she baked. No, that was an understatement. Her baking skills erupted into an almost maniacal inspiration around the full moon such that she could not ignore them, compelling her to bake and bake and bake. She couldn't do anything but bake—she couldn't read, she couldn't check her e-mail, she could barely sleep. She definitely couldn't hold down a regular nine-to-five job—not unless she would be allowed to take a few days off a month. To bake. When the moon told her to.

She was grateful, usually. Her curse gave her a talent that enabled her to do something she loved to make an OK living. But in moments of self-pity—usually about halfway between full moons—she began to feel that maybe her full-moon-inspired baking bursts were holding her back. She would never be able to open a real shop, or make more than her modest living. She didn't want riches—although she wouldn't turn down some sparkly jewelry—but it would be nice to know that she could pay both her mortgage and the electric on time without scraping under the couch cushions for lost change.

Sometimes, she just wanted to be normal. Khaki normal.

It didn't matter. Her grandmother had the curse, and her mother before that, and they passed it on to Mona's father, who, with typical Dad efficiency, tried freezing his pies and tarts to be able to enjoy them throughout the month. But full-moon baked goods don't freeze well. They don't keep at all. She learned that you just have to get them while you can, and enjoy them while you got 'em.

It took her father a long time to accept that, but it was a lesson he made sure Mona learned. And she had. So, yes, there were times when she wanted to be normal. But her curse had forced her to create a life for herself that was unique and satisfying, one that left her exhausted during the full moon but with plenty of free time to foster friendships, volunteer around the community, and use her nonbaking talents to make people happy. It wasn't perfect, but no life was.

And this guy, she thought as she stared down Dan the Accountant, King of the Khakis, this guy comes up here and accuses me of laziness. That's what he was doing. He wasn't the first one. Her curse wasn't commonly known—outside of her family, only her best friend Trish knew, and she was sworn to secrecy. A lot of people found it strange that her work schedule was so . . . flexible. (When in reality, it was more rigid than they knew—she was at the mercy of the moon, after all.) But something about this guy, with his obsessive routine and his smart-looking briefcase, really pissed her off. Mrs. Harris told her he hadn't ever eaten anything from Apple of My Pie, at least not that she'd seen. So what did he even care!

And the fact that his blue eyes nearly crackled with fire when he confronted her, that pissed her off, too. Those were some really nice eyes. The nerve of those eyes.

"Wouldn't you make more money if you didn't have such a capricious business model?"

Mona stood up straight. She was short enough that

she never towered over anyone, but she towered over him now, her inside the food truck, him on the sidewalk down below.

"What's it to you how much money I make?"

He flushed. Good, she thought.

"Maybe I don't need to make money," she said, leaning back down. "Maybe I'm a baking empire heiress, just slumming in Ohio." Uh-oh, she thought. Her imagination tended to go wild when she was mad. And her mouth tended not to be able to stop it. "Maybe my business is backed by a handsome desert sheikh who tasted a slice of my apple pie and decided he had to have me, all to himself, but once a month he sets me free into the world as long as I promise to return to him in his desert lair."

His eyebrows went up. "Desert lair?"

"Yeah, a desert lair."

"In Ohio?"

Stupid logic. She wanted to disarm him, badly. "You think I couldn't get a desert sheikh?"

Down his eyes went, again. She wanted to tease him, ask him if he had a muscle spasm or something. But she sort of liked it. Dan the Accountant did not seem like the kind of guy who was out of control very often. The power to unnerve him was intoxicating.

Not that it meant anything. Despite Mrs. Harris's assertions to the contrary, Khaki Dan was an egotistical control freak. He wasn't even a customer, and here he was, trying to tell her how to run her business. And now there was a line forming behind him.

"Listen, do you want something or not?"

This time his eyes didn't wander. They just honed right in on hers, and she felt a jolt. She wasn't sure of what—recognition? Lust, at least. Definitely lust.

Oh, he wanted something.

She would be happy to give it to him.

Two

Dan sat at his desk, willing the figures on his monitor to stop swimming. He had taken some data entry from a pile on Mrs. Harris's desk, thinking he could lose himself in the almost-mindless task. It didn't work. He needed only half his brain to make sure he was using the right column of the spreadsheet, and the other half of his brain . . . well, the other half wasn't focused on his work at all. He was aching and uncomfortable, and three times already Mrs. Harris had asked him if he felt all right.

No, he did not feel all right. His office was filled with the smells of Apple of My Frigging Pie. Mrs. Harris had picked up a pie for dessert—caramel apple pecan pie with Kentucky bourbon—and the scent of it was so strong, he could practically taste it. And he had a raging hard-on. Not from the pie, he was pretty sure.

No, definitely from the woman who'd made it.

So what if she was hot? So what if she was funny and smart and quick?

He was sure he had impressed her by acting like an uptight asshole.

He cringed when he remembered the look on her

face when he'd asked her why she didn't work more. He might as well have said, Why are you so lazy? He didn't mean it like that, though. He meant it like, Your food is so popular and you seem so happy feeding people, why wouldn't you try to do that all the time?

There had to be a reason. Maybe she wasn't really the baker. Maybe she had a hired gun, like a hidden Grandma or something. Maybe she kept wood sprites locked in her basement, and they only came out during the full moon to bake up a frenzy. Maybe she bought her baked goods from a grocery store, but a really nice one that was really far away and she could only get there once a month.

She was probably a fraud.

She didn't seem like a fraud.

She seemed genuine, and sweet. And soft. And she smelled really, really good.

Had his desk chair always been so uncomfortable?

"You sure you feel OK, Dan?"

Mrs. Harris paused on the threshold of his office— her version of a knock—and came toward his desk. "You look, I don't know, nauseous. Did you eat something weird for lunch?"

"No, I—"

"Of course not. You always eat the same thing. Maybe the mayo at the diner is bad. Should I call over and have Marylou smell it?"

"No, don't ask her to smell the mayo!"

Man, he really was boring if half the town knew what he ate for lunch every day.

He liked turkey sandwiches, dammit.

But Mrs. Harris was already at her desk and on the phone. He started to get up and follow her, but, well, hard-on. He didn't need to have a conversation with her about that. Because she would definitely make him talk about it.

That actually helped the situation a little.

"Marylou said you hardly touched your sandwich." Mrs. Harris charged into his office with a white paper bag in her hand. "That's not like you, Dan."

"Maybe I'm getting tired of turkey."

"Well, don't tell Marylou that. She'll be heartbroken. Although her meatloaf is delicious. You might switch to that?"

This conversation was really depressing Dan. His middle-aged secretary was trying to set him up with a new regular lunch menu. When had his life become so sad? Was this really how he liked to live?

Since when had he had so many existential crises in one day?

He was sure it was Mona's fault. He never had existential crises before he talked to her.

"You must be hungry, that's it. Eat something, and then you'll be able to concentrate." Mrs. Harris dropped the bag on his desk. "I know, I know, you're not much of a sweets person, but you can run an extra mile tomorrow morning. Besides, a little sugar might do you some good."

Dan eyed the white paper bag warily. There was no grease dripping out of the bottom making a stain on his desk. He couldn't even smell what was inside, not with the top turned down and scrunched closed. He could leave it there. He could let it sit there, on the corner of his desk, and get on with the rest of his day. He could ignore it.

He couldn't ignore Mrs. Harris, though. "Thanks." There. Now he could get back to work.

She rolled her eyes. "For a grown man, you can be such a child," she said, then turned on her sensible heel and went back to her desk.

What was that supposed to mean? He almost got up to ask, but getting up would mean he would have to walk past the white bag haunting him from the corner of his desk, and there was no way he was going to give Mrs. Harris or Mona the satisfaction of knowing that his indifference was all a lie.

So, OK, maybe that was a little childish.

Whatever.

He had work to do.

Data entry.

Here we go, he thought. Enter the data.

He got about three cells in before the bag called out to him.

This was stupid. He wasn't even hungry! He had eaten most of a sensible lunch! Well, he didn't eat much of the sandwich, Mrs. Harris was right. It did taste weird to him. No, it tasted fine, but it didn't feel right. It wasn't what he *wanted*. He had never *wanted* anything for lunch in his life—it was just lunchtime, and he ate. He didn't know what he had wanted for lunch, but a turkey sandwich on wheat, light on the mayo, was not it.

Maybe what was in the bag would be.

What's the worst that can happen, he thought. He could really like it, and prove everyone in town right and become a regular customer of hers. Or he could hate it. He could hate it, and then he would be the only weirdo in town who didn't go to Apple of My Pie. Which he already was, but if he hated it, he would have a good reason. Or it could be poisoned. Mona could have known that he had bad feelings about her professionalism and she could have made a special poisoned batch of whatever-it-was and sold the piece to Mrs. Harris knowing Dan would not eat his whole lunch and Mrs. Harris would be her usual generous self and offer it to him, and then Dan would eat it and his insides would melt and he would die, and Mona would sit outside in her pink truck and laugh and laugh because her revenge was finally complete.

Where the hell was that coming from? He was starting to sound like her. The possibility that she had that amount of nefarious foresight was just as likely as the nefarious desert sheikh with a sweet tooth.

He didn't like the idea of a desert sheikh. Not a nefarious one, anyway. And not one who would hurt Mona.

Or do other things to her.

"Stop it!" He thought he said it to himself, but he heard Mrs. Harris get up, and a second later her head was poking in his office. He looked up, imagining how ridiculous he must look to her, standing over his desk, pointing at the most innocuous white paper bag in the world like it was a naughty puppy.

She rolled her eyes again. "Just eat the damn thing, would you? I've got work to do."

"Fine," he said. He picked up the bag, unrolled the top. Oh, man, it smelled good. Apples and cinnamon, and something else he couldn't identify. He inhaled deeply.

Mrs. Harris chuckled. "I'll leave you two alone," and he barely registered that she shut his office door.

Slowly, carefully, he lifted the contents out of the bag. It was surprisingly heavy, but he could feel that it was moist through the thin wax paper it was wrapped in. Oh, sweet Jesus, apple cake. He loved apple cake. His grandmother used to make apple cake.

But he knew right away this wasn't like Grandma's apple cake. This was a step beyond. The thin layers of apple on top were laid out in neat, radiating rows, and he imagined how perfect they would have looked before Mona cut into the cake. He peeled the paper down and admired the thick chunks of apple mixed throughout.

It was the best-looking apple cake he'd ever seen in his life. He wanted to take a picture and frame it. Or Instagram it. Or . . . no. He just wanted to eat it.

He took a bite and groaned. This was . . . heaven. The cake was spongy and sweet, but not too sweet, and it didn't overwhelm the slight crunch of the apples. These were definitely Delicious's famous apples; even this early in the season, he could tell. And the cinnamon was balanced with something a little tangy—ginger? What was it? It was subtle, and it was blowing his damn mind.

He meant to savor every bite. This kind of thing was too good to rush. But before his brain could finish telling him to slow down and enjoy, he was already licking his fingers clean.

That was some damn good cake.

He sat down on his office chair, hard. He was exhausted. He wanted more. He swiveled around to face the window and parted the blinds. She was still out there.

He heard Mrs. Harris chuckle at his retreating back, but he didn't care. He would have to thank her later. For now, he needed another taste.

"Ow, dammit!"

Mona dropped the hot pan on the counter, sending cookies flying. Normally she didn't have a problem remembering that when metal comes out of the oven, one needs an oven mitt to touch it. But today she was all out of sorts. Not all day, but this afternoon. She would have just driven home and said forget about it, but the customers were still trickling in and she still had plenty to sell, even with the lost sheet of cookies.

They were definitely lost. She took great pains to

keep her mobile bakery clean, but even she wouldn't eat cookies off this floor. And she would eat anything.

It was all stupid Khaki Dan's fault. Ever since he gave her that tongue lashing, she was off her game. She blew a piece of hair out of her face. Tongue lashing probably wasn't fair. More of a mild scold that she totally overreacted to. Did she really tell him her weird desert sheikh fantasy?

Just thinking about him got her blood boiling. She thought she had been doing a great job flirting with him—and not just to get him to buy a cookie. She really thought he was cute. No, she thought he was freaking hot, and she *thought* he might feel the same way about her, and she *thought* she was pouring on the charm to let him know she was open to whatever kind of flirting he might want to throw at her. And instead, boom. He called her a lazy bum.

She figured it was probably more her pride that was hurt than her feelings, although her feelings stung a little bit, too. She didn't often put herself out there, preferring to keep it strictly professional with her customers. She didn't want to get into a situation where she had to avoid certain areas of town or certain times of the day if things didn't work out. Because of her curse, she had to be very flexible with where and when she could sell, and she couldn't afford a bad romance souring her business.

So maybe fate was looking out for her. And while she wasn't thrilled with fate at the moment—Dan was really freaking hot—she knew it was all for the best. So what if she spent more time than was strictly necessary watching Dan walk off? The man knew how to fill out a pair of khakis. And so what if she wanted to call him back and give him a free sample, just so they would have more to talk about? It was better this way.

Now he would never bother her again and she could go about her business dealing with customers who were actually nice human beings and who didn't make her want to bash their heads in and maybe also rip their shirts off a little.

Much better if she never saw him again.

She winced and yanked her palm off the cookie sheet a second time. She had forgotten it was there. Stupid Khaki Dan ruining her day. She took two pies—apple crumble and straight-up apple—out of the cooler at her feet and placed them on the cookie sheet. She kicked a few cookies out of the way and pulled open the keep-warm oven that was still nice and toasty, and shoved the pies in. They were already fully baked, but letting them cool and then heat up right before she sold them didn't seem to affect the taste any, and she liked to have a few ready to go for the after-school rush. She'd do the same in a few hours for the after-work crowd, then she'd focus on cookies (she had a few containers left) and slices of cakes and tarts that could be eaten in hand for the after-happy hour crowd. And then she would go home and put her feet up and drink a glass of wine and not think about how she had to get up at the crack of dawn tomorrow to see if her magic would work for one more day. It should; this was the second full moon of the month, and that usually meant extra baking days as it waned. But even though her gift (because when it worked, it was a gift; when it didn't, it was a curse) was as predictable as, say, the orbit of the moon, she had a constant niggling worry that, someday, it would up and disappear. She had to take advantage of it while she could. She had to hold on to this life she loved for as long as the moon would let her have it.

So that meant no more throwing her inventory around, and no more thinking about hot accountants. Only hot buns from now on.

Oh, buns.

No. Only baking. Baking baking baking.

"What did you put in this?"

She jerked around at what sounded like an angry customer, only to be confronted by the very thing she wasn't supposed to be thinking about. Dan. Khaki Dan, whose eyes were wild and whose hair was disheveled, and who was waving a crumpled paper bag at her. It looked like one of her paper bags. And it looked empty.

"Hello, Dan, nice to see you again," she said through gritted customer-service teeth. "Can I help you with something?"

He gave her a wild look and shook the bag. "The apple cake! Mrs. Harris gave me the apple cake—"

She loved Mrs. Harris. Had something gone wrong? "What happened to her?"

"Nothing happened to her!" Now his arms were really flailing. He was going to hurt himself if he didn't calm down.

But he still looked hot.

"It didn't happen to her! It happened to me! I ate it! I ate the apple cake!"

"Are you hurt?"

His eyes, unbelievably, got wider. "No! No, I'm not hurt, but I think I just had a sexual experience eating a piece of cake!"

Well. That was a new one.

"Um, thanks?"

"What did you put in there? I tasted cinnamon, and apple, obviously. But there's something else, some kind of kick—"

"You can't really expect me to give away all of my secrets, can you? How would I be able to fart along with my capricious business model if I did?"

That seemed to calm him down. His arms dropped

to his sides and he looked down at the ground. He mumbled something.

"What was that? I can't hear you when you're apologizing to the sidewalk."

He looked up then, and she almost gasped at the look in his eyes. It was, somehow, everything. Laughter and regret and lust. Definitely lust. Again.

Mona gulped. That was a lot of look.

"I'm sorry for the way I spoke to you before. I don't know why I was so rude. I mean, it does kind of frustrate me that you work so sporadically, especially now that I've tasted your—"

"Yes, you mentioned the apple cake."

"Mona, it's amazing! I've never tasted anything like it before in my life, and I grew up eating this stuff. How did you do it? And how can you not do it all the time?"

She sighed. She couldn't tell him. The truth was ridiculous, and he was not a ridiculous person. If she told him that she was cursed with baking talents that followed the lunar cycle, he would never speak to her again. That might not be so bad. But he would also never give her that look again.

She was kind of into that look.

She needed time to think this through, but she didn't have time since he was standing right in front of her and he looked so apologetic and still a little lustful. She started to pace; pacing would help her think. But her pacing space was limited by the square footage of her food truck, and by the mess she had made earlier. A mess she forgot all about in the face of that lustful look. She turned, took a step to think, and the cookie she stepped on slid right out from underneath her.

She landed on the floor.

Hard.

"Mona!"

She heard Dan's panicked cry from the side window, and then she heard the back door being wrenched open. Then she didn't hear much because suddenly Dan was in her face, leaning over her and clutching her arms.

"Mona, are you all right?"

She looked up into those deep blue eyes and said, "My butt hurts."

Nice, Mona.

He kneeled back. "You didn't hit your head? It sounded pretty loud."

She took the hand he offered and let him pull her to a seated position. "No, that was my butt."

"Do you want me to, ah, look at it for you?"

She laughed and put a hand to her forehead. "I can't believe I just wiped out on a cookie."

"It's sort of a mess back here." She watched him take in the crumbled cookie mess all over the floor.

"It's not usually. In fact, it's your fault that it's such a mess."

"Me? What did I do?"

She sighed. "You yelled at me and it messed up my groove. I've been dropping stuff and messing up all afternoon. I gave Bobby Warner change for a twenty, and he only gave me a dollar."

"Oh."

"His mom made him give it back. Which was nice of her. I gave her a pie."

"Wow."

"See? So you cost me a pie. How am I ever expected to turn a profit if you keep messing me up like this?"

"I'm sorry." He was still kneeling in front of her. She looked up at him with an expression she was sure was full of reprimand and disgust. So she was completely taken aback when he reached out and tucked a lock of hair behind her ear.

It was a sweet gesture. She thought he didn't like sweets.

And whatever look she thought she was giving out, she could read his clear as day in those blue, blue eyes. The lust was back. He was smoldering.

She almost looked away—that was a lot of smolder, and she was starting to get whiplash from the way her own feelings were bouncing around—but that smolder was magnetic. When he started to lean forward, she just followed the pull and leaned toward him, too. His hand cupped her cheek, gently pulling her closer.

"I'm sorry," he whispered a second before his lips touched hers.

And, hot damn, this man had *smolder*. His lips were gentle, and surprisingly soft, and she responded to everything sweet in them, tasting, exploring. His other arm came down to rest on the floor next to her hip. She heard him flick a cookie out of the way, and then he leaned in farther, caging her between the lower cabinets and his body. She put a hand up to his arm, just to anchor herself, and she almost broke the kiss in surprise because, damn, this man had *muscles*. But she didn't—she held on, running her hand up his shoulder, trying to concentrate on the way his mouth was slowly taking control of hers but also sort of wondering how an accountant—an accountant!—got shoulders like that.

But then he shifted forward a little more, and she felt herself sliding underneath him, just a little, and she clutched those strong accountant shoulders and held on as he deepened the kiss, coaxing her mouth open and swallowing her gasp and her sigh.

Three

She tasted even better than the apple cake.

And she felt amazing. Her curly hair was smooth and her skin was soft, and he wanted to wrap her in his arms and feel her whole body pressed against his. But even though she was driving him crazy with those tentative lips of hers, he was still aware that they were on the floor of her place of business.

He almost forgot that, though, when he felt her hand run up his shoulder, felt her arch up slightly and gasp into his mouth. He took the opportunity—a few cookie crumbs never hurt anyone—and opened his mouth to her, his tongue meeting hers. He moved his hand down the back of her neck, holding her closer, wanting to feel those tank top straps slide down, wanting to see if the rest of her skin was as soft as her neck. He needed her closer. He let go of her neck, but she had a strong hold on him. He moved his hands to her waist, both of his arms making a band around her, and he leaned back. She came with him so they were both sitting upright, her chest snug against his. Her legs were an awkward tangle around his knees, but she didn't seem to mind; she just held on tighter and angled her head, and he went deeper.

He felt like he could sit there all day, kissing Mona and pressing her against him. But he was still a human, and he still had to breathe. He broke the kiss, but kept his eyes closed. He rested his forehead against Mona's as he caught his breath. He could still taste her. She loosened her grip on his shoulders and slid down to the floor. Somehow he hadn't noticed that he had pulled her so close that she was sitting in his lap.

Her absence made his arms feel heavy, and he let them fall to his sides. He finally opened his eyes to find her staring at him, hard, her green eyes sparkling.

"What?" he asked, stupidly. Come on, man. The best kiss of your life, and you're asking her "What?"

"I had no idea," she said, then ran a finger over her lips. "Who would have thought?"

He thought maybe he was being insulted, or complimented, or possibly both, but the sight of those pretty fingers running over her plumped, moist lips had him too distracted to care.

"All that, inside those khakis," she said. He followed her eyes down to his lap. Yup, his high school hard-on was back. Although he felt a little more justified with this one.

"This whole time . . ." Mona was still talking, but she seemed to be mostly talking to herself. Her eyes ran up and down his body, and he pretended not to preen under her appreciative gaze.

When he had seen her before, she was always so confident and sure of what she was saying. He had never seen anyone make conversation so easily, or seem to feel so comfortable talking to such a wide variety of people. It was not a skill that came naturally to him, and, frankly, it was a little intimidating.

So it gave him no small pleasure to see her sitting

before him, stunned and blabbering, because of his kissing. It made a man feel good, frankly. She made him feel really good.

Her eyes finally reached his. This time, her stunned expression turned a little softer, and the corner of her mouth turned up, revealing a small dimple that he wanted to lean in and kiss. God, he wanted to kiss her again. He wanted to kiss all of her.

But his timing was off, as usual, and he almost jumped out of his khakis when a loud beeping sound interrupted his post-kiss reverie. She wasn't expecting it, either, if her jump was any indication.

"Crap," she muttered, then offered him a rueful smile and picked herself up off the floor. "After-school rush," she shrugged, and switched the beeping timer off and started pulling things out of secret compartments all around the truck.

So that was it, he thought as he watched her change from post-kissing puddle of mush (still good for his ego) to quick-moving, confident, efficient bakery operator. She barely looked at what she was doing, but before his eyes the empty counter was transformed into a smorgasbord of cookies and cakes and pies and tarts and . . . he didn't even know what half that stuff was. But he definitely wanted to taste it.

This couldn't be it. She couldn't just turn it off like that, could she? She couldn't have *not* felt what he felt?

"Can I see you again?" he asked. "Tonight?"

She turned, then looked down, almost as if she was surprised to see him still there. Frankly, he was surprised to still be sitting on the floor. He was so distracted by her movements that he didn't realize he was still at her feet.

"Tonight I have to bake. I'm open tomorrow, then not for a while. So tonight isn't going to work for me."

That was a reasonable enough explanation. Sensible. It was a work night for him, too. He had no business trying to get busy when he had to be up early tomorrow morning.

But he couldn't accept it. He had to see her tonight. He didn't know why, but he just knew—it had to be tonight. Maybe it was the weird double full moon, but he had a feeling about her now and it was way too strong for him to ignore.

"You have to eat, right?" He stood up so he was facing her. She reached around him for containers and toppings. He plastered himself as tightly against the wall as he could. As much as he wanted to get in her space, she had work to do.

She barely looked up at him. "Sure, I'll eat. I usually grab something on the way home."

"What if I bring you something?"

She looked up at him sharply. "You mean you'll bring me dinner?"

"Yeah. I mean, takeout or something. I can't cook. I wish I could cook, but I can't." With every sentence fragment, he saw his chances dwindling. "Whatever you want. Anything."

"Anything?" She actually paused in what she was doing, and he took advantage of it. He pulled her close so she was flush against him again. With her face so close to his, she couldn't hide the desire in her eyes. That was what he had been looking for, that it wasn't just him being crazy, that she felt it, too.

"Anything."

He kissed her on the nose, and then he was gone.

Mona stood in the center of her mobile bakery with her spatula in the air. She felt a pull toward the side door where Dan and his khakis had just departed, but she stayed rooted to the spot. She wasn't going to follow him. So what if it was the best kiss of her life? She had work to do. She couldn't follow him.

Well, she could follow him with her eyes. She watched him look both ways, then cross the street. He had his hand on the innocuous door to his accounting firm office, and she thought that was it, now she could get back to work. But he turned and caught her watching. And he waved. Embarrassed, she waved back. With her spatula.

He grinned. Damn, he was cute.

He turned to go into his office. Damn.

Anything she wanted.

She wanted him.

"I want that one."

She jumped a little at the disembodied voice that seemed to be her fiercest competition for Dan. But when she looked down, it was Serena Bradshaw, aged four. Well, it was Serena's fingers, stretching in the general direction of the cookie tray. Serena was still too short to see over the counter, but her fingers seemed to be able to sense cookies with impressive precision.

Mona smiled and leaned over the counter. "Which one, now?" She held the tray of cookies a little lower so Serena could see, but not so close that she could reach.

"She doesn't need to see them to know which one she wants," said Serena's mother, Trish. "She wants them all."

"Smart girl," said Mona, winking at Serena.

"Takes after her grandmother." Serena was Mrs. Harris's granddaughter. It was a testament to Mrs. Harris's strength of character that even her daughter-in-law, Trish, liked her. In Mona's experience, that wasn't always the case when a mother was so fiercely attached to both her son and her granddaughter.

It didn't hurt that Trish was particularly awesome and managed to balance super-mom skills with razor-sharp wit. Mona knew a little tart could make the sweetness go down a little smoother.

Trish was close to her mother-in-law.

So maybe she was close to her mother-in-law's boss.

"Did I just see Dan over here?" Trish asked, digging in her purse and coming out with her wallet and a wet wipe.

"I'm not sure." Mona practiced her most innocent face. Sweet, delicate, innocent. She looked to Serena for approval. Serena watched the cookies.

"He was walking kind of funny."

"Dan is funny!" shouted Serena, momentarily distracted from the cookies.

"Yes, Dan is very funny," said Trish. She gave Mona a conspiratorial wink. "Serena is a little in love with him."

"You must spend a lot of time with him," said Mona. Innocently.

"A little. We like to visit Grandma Jan after school sometimes."

"Grandma Jan?"

"Mrs. Harris." Trish laughed. "Serena is one of the only people who doesn't have to call her Mrs. Harris. And since I popped Serena out, neither do I."

That was all very nice, but Mona needed more intel.

Trish stepped out of the way as people started to gather around Apple of My Pie. Mostly moms, and more than a few dads, with kids in tow. Mona was used to the rush, though, so she just started laying stuff out on the little counter. People grabbed what they wanted and handed her cash. She could dig change out of her apron in her sleep. She had just invested in one of those cute little square things that enabled her to charge credit cards with her cell phone, but most people in town still used cash.

"So Dan finally became a customer, huh?"

Mona recognized the look on Trish's face. It was the same fake-innocent look she had had on just a minute ago.

"I guess Mrs. Harris cajoled him into it."

"About time."

"What's that supposed to mean?"

Trish laughed. "I think he was the last person in town to come over here, and he works across the street."

"Maybe he doesn't have a sweet tooth."

"Dan loves cookies!" Serena shouted, proudly holding up her own cookie.

Trish shrugged. "He loves cookies."

"Dan? He finally came over?" Adam Connelly, with little Brian in tow, joined the conversation. "That guy swore he'd never eat here! When I see him at our pickup game this weekend, I'm going to give him such sh—" He stopped himself before he could curse and looked guiltily at his son.

"Daddy said *shit!*" Brian shouted triumphantly.

"No, I didn't. Have a cookie."

"Dan always did have a stubborn streak," said Ms. Abrams, who ran the art supply store down the street. "I always said it would take a strong woman to break him down."

"Hear that?" Trish asked Mona. "A strong woman."

Mona blushed so hard she thought steam was probably pouring out of the top of her head. "Are you guys gonna buy something or what?"

"Darling, the only thing sweeter than your cake is gossip." Ms. Abrams winked at her. "What's going on with you and Dan?"

"Nothing! He just had some apple cake, and—"

"Ooo . . . apple cake. Good choice. That will get to his stomach and his heart."

"I didn't sell it to him. Mrs. Harris gave him a piece."

"Grandma Jan shared her apple cake?" Trish looked shocked. "He must have been really suffering for her to share her apple cake with him."

"You got any apple cake left?" asked Adam.

"No!" said all the women simultaneously.

"Listen, it's no big deal," said Mona, handing out paper bags and change. She hoped she was giving people the right change, but she didn't really care. She just wanted her friends to go away and stop grilling her about Dan. Dan, who was apparently stubborn and nice to kids and played pickup sports. "He just had a piece of cake, and then he came over to tell me how much he enjoyed it." And then kissed me within an inch of my life and then promised me dinner, she thought. So what if she wanted to marry him now?

"Uh-huh," said Trish. "Is that why you're blushing?"

"I'm not blushing! It's hot and I'm busy and you people are bothering me when I'm trying to work!"

"That's funny," said Ms. Abrams. "You were never too busy to gossip before."

"That's because we were never gossiping about her before," said Adam.

"Ha ha, you guys are hilarious."

"Listen, I think it's great," said Trish. "Dan's a really terrific guy, and you guys balance each other well."

"What's that supposed to mean?" Mona said, for the second time in this conversation.

"Dan is . . . steady. That's a good word for it, right?" Trish looked to her friends for corroboration.

"He's uptight," said Ms. Abrams.

"He's a little stiff," suggested Adam.

"Dan's soooo funny!" mooned Serena.

"And you"—Trish waved her arm at the pink Apple of My Pie truck—"you're . . . not."

"You mean I'm flaky?"

"As your pie crust," said Ms. Abrams. "In a good way," she added quickly.

"Why does everybody think I'm some kind of irresponsible nut job?" Mona asked. And these people were her friends.

"It's not like that! Not at all!" said Trish.

"But come on, Mona. You work, like, once a month," said Adam.

"So? Maybe I don't have to work more than that." There was no need to tell everyone that she couldn't. Especially not if they thought she was a flake! Telling them that her baking skills were a curse of the lunar cycle—that wouldn't improve their opinion at all.

"Listen," said Trish, reaching up and patting her arm. "We love you. We want the best for you. And we all love Dan."

The others nodded, even some of the other people in line. I guess everyone's in on this conversation, Mona thought.

"Just give it a try, that's all," Trish added.

Mona didn't remember resisting Dan, or thinking that she wasn't going to give anything a try. After that kiss—her knees got a little weak remembering it—she was probably willing to try anything he wanted her to. Even if it meant normal stuff, like . . . filing.

When her internal monologue went to filing, she knew it was time to move on. "OK, enough dissecting my love life."

"What love life?" interrupted Ms. Abrams.

"Scram, all of you. I have customers with money to deal with."

"See you tomorrow?" Trish asked, picking up a sticky Serena.

"Yeah, I should be here." Thanks to that extra full moon. That was what was making everyone crazy. Her friends getting up in one another's business wasn't exactly out of the ordinary, but she was not usually on the receiving end of their nosiness.

It was that damn full moon.

Was that what was making her crazy?

Was that what was making her give only half of her brain to her business while the other half fantasized about an uptight, stubborn man in khakis who was an amazing kisser?

That damn full moon!

Four

Dan had never talked so quickly in his life. All he wanted was for this consultation with the Shimuras to go smoothly, and to generate minimal questions, so he could figure out his grand plan for dinner with Mona. He was thinking Italian. She was surrounded by sweet stuff all day; she would probably want something salty and savory. Did DiMartini's do takeout?

"Is there even a market for a sushi restaurant in Delicious?"

Oh, sushi. That could be good. Deceptively simple, not as heavy as Italian food. Where could he get sushi in Delicious?

"Mr. Fields?"

"Huh? Yes, sushi is a great idea!"

Mr. and Mrs. Shimura looked at each other. "We know it's a great idea," Mr. Shimura said. "We're just trying to figure out if it's a viable one, remember?"

"Oh, yes. Right. Viable. Well—" Dan pulled out the market analysis he had been working on for the past week, the one he had stayed up nights thinking about. It wasn't the first time he had ever been asked for business advice, but usually it was more along the lines of, should we add a new patio to the Orchard Inn (yes) or what about a karaoke night at the Perk Up Coffee Shop (unfortunately, yes). He'd never been asked for advice on building a business from the ground up.

So he was proud of this report. He was less proud of the fact that with every table he inserted and with every piece of market data he analyzed, he compared what this report would look like to the one he could make for Apple of My Pie.

In reality, the one he was working on for Apple of My Pie was much more colorful. He thought Mona would appreciate a lot of graphs. That was what he had decided this afternoon after the mind-blowing kiss, that it would take a lot of colorful graphs to convince her to become a more permanent fixture in Delicious.

Was that it? Was he afraid of her leaving? That if she didn't have deep roots in town, she would just up and leave? Was the fact that she could just go any time what was really terrifying him about getting involved with her?

Or was it the fact that he'd thought he couldn't stand her but after kissing her he realized how wrong he was. And if he was wrong about that, what else in his life had he been missing out on? Was black coffee the best way to get caffeine? Should he be spending so much time in khakis?

He was not wrong about sushi. His report didn't think so, anyway. "I think you could really be success-ful. The market in Delicious isn't huge, but we have a good reputation for supporting local businesses like this. And people like you, so you'll get people from all over town to try out any restaurant you open. You guys have been a fixture around here for . . ."

"Twenty-five years," said Mrs. Shimura, patting her husband's hand. "Mr. Shimura brought me here right after we graduated from college. I thought, How can we raise our children here? But everyone in town was welcoming from the start. It really is our home."

"And now that we're retired . . ." said Mr. Shimura.

"And the grandchildren have moved away . . ." added Mrs. Shimura.

"It has always been a dream of Mrs. Shimura's to have her own kitchen where she can share the foods she loves with the people she loves."

That was sweet, thought Dan. He'd have to get them to include that in their business plan.

"But we need to make money," said Mrs. Shimura. "We're not running a sushi charity."

Dan went over his findings with them. With the influx of young families from larger metropolitan areas, the tastes of Delicious were changing, or at least becoming more open-minded. He really thought they could be successful.

"Oh, Dan, that's wonderful! I will cook for you tonight, OK? Something wonderful because you have been so good to us."

"Actually, tonight I have plans," said Dan. Plans he didn't want Mrs. Shimura involved in, no matter how much he liked her. He took a sip of his very cold leftover lunch coffee.

"Oh, with that cute baker?"

And he nearly choked on it. "Uh . . ."

"That's OK. Mr. Shimura says I pry too much. She's a nice girl, Dan. You be good to her."

"She found out Mrs. Shimura has diabetes, so she made her sugar-free muffins. Sugar free, I thought. Disgusting!"

"But, oh, Dan, they were delicious! Mona bakes with her heart, you can feel it. Don't you screw this up, young man."

Dan smiled weakly and decided this meeting was over. He handed the Shimuras a copy of his report and walked them to the door. Mrs. Harris was just turning off her computer, and she bid the Shiumras good night.

"So? How'd it go?" she asked him.

"I think they're going to do it."

"Good. They're good people. And Mrs. Shimura's cooking is . . . well, I've never had anything like it! Who would have thought, at my age, eating sushi!"

"You're not that—"

"You did good, Dan, I'm proud of you."

"Thanks, Mrs. Harris." He still felt a swell of pride every time she said that to him. He was happy she liked what he did. He didn't need her approval—and he knew when he didn't have it—but he liked it all the same.

"Well, it's getting late, and if I don't get dinner started, Herb will order a pizza," she said, picking up her coat. "It's a beautiful night. What have you got planned for this evening?"

She asked it in a tone that suggested to Dan that she already knew what he had planned for this evening—well, he hoped that she had only a G-rated idea of what he had planned. Everyone in town seemed to know what he wanted to do. That made him feel like there was a lot more riding on this dinner than exploring an unexpected connection with a really hot, really smart woman. In spite of its being nobody else's business at all, it still felt so public. The fishbowl feeling was just adding to the pressure.

Why was he going through with this dinner again?

"Mrs. Harris, do you think the full moon makes people crazy?"

"Crazy?"

"You know, do things they wouldn't normally do. Get crazy ideas and act on them."

She patted him on the cheek. "Dan, I think people

do what they want to do, and the full moon gives them an excuse."

That sounded right. Right enough, anyway. He said good night to Mrs. Harris and promised not to stay too much longer, then headed back to his desk. He would just put a few finishing touches on his report for Mona. Just a few more graphs, maybe. Then it would be perfect.

Mona waved good-bye to her last customer of the day. It looked like Molly and Deacon were going to share her last piece of apple cheese tart. Mona gave them a discount—the slice really wasn't big enough for two people—but the way Deacon was looking at Molly, well, he was probably going to let her have the whole thing, anyway.

That's love, she thought.

She checked her watch. It was nearly seven o'clock. She had a lot of prep work to do before the sun set, a lot of stuff to get in the oven before the moon rose. Ugh, and the piles of dishes. Well, it had to be done. The full moon would be waning tonight. That meant tomorrow was her last productive day until next month.

Her stomach growled. She was starving, but it didn't look like Dan was going to show. Well, she had no business canoodling tonight, hot khakis or no. She had way too much to do. She tipped open her cash box. It looked pretty flush. She knew it was. She had already counted it and figured that she could get by taking tomorrow off if she woke up in a sexual daze and couldn't stand up straight because Mr. Khaki turned out to be a great kisser *and* love god.

That's what she got for planning. Ha, said the moon. She was just starting to secure all of her empty pans and plates for the drive home when she heard a *bang* from across the street. She jerked up. It was Dan, running across the street—without even looking both ways first!—clutching a mess of papers and his briefcase stuffed under his arm.

"Mona! Don't leave! Don't leave," he gasped as he came up to her truck. "I'm sorry. I got carried away, and I lost track of time, and then . . ." He shuffled his papers while he spoke, his sentence barely audible through his heavy breathing. "There's no excuse, I should have been paying attention, but I was working on this, and then, and then, I'm sorry." He finally looked up at her, his eyes unsure.

And she melted like butter in a hot pan.

"I made this for you." He handed her the pile of papers.

"You killed a few trees for me?"

"No. Well, yes. Sort of. No. It's a report. Of how profitable you could be if you opened a storefront bakery. And think of how happy people would be if they could eat your baking all the time!"

This again.

"I can't," she said.

"But why not? Are you concerned you won't be profitable? The data really support this proposal. You have nothing to be afraid of!"

"I'm not afraid. I'm just . . ." She sighed, turned to lock the cabinets. "I just can't. Just forget it, OK?"

"Mona."

His tone of voice had completely changed. Before he was pleading and out of breath and a little whiny—in a cute way, but still whiny. Now, when he said her name, all of the desperation was gone. There was a seriousness, a sincerity in how he said her name, that made her turn. She was just curious, that was it. She didn't need to hear anything else he had to say, but she was still curious.

"Mona, I don't know what's happening to me." He reached up into the window for her hands. She didn't think about, she just handed them right over. "I don't know what it is between us, but ever since we kissed, I can't get you out of my head. Do you know why I made this?" He tilted his head toward the report.

"Because you're pushy and anal retentive?"

"No. Well, a little, ha ha." He raised his eyebrow, but he continued. "Because it was the only thing I could focus on. I tried working on other projects for other clients—"

"I'm not a client."

"I know! I know. I don't want you to be a client. I mean, if you want to be, that's OK, but that's not why I did this. I just had to do something to justify sitting in my office all day thinking about you. I think there's something between us, and I'm an idiot and a dork, and the only way I could think of to get you to listen was by . . ."

"Making graphs?"

"There are a lot of graphs. I thought you would like them."

Mona pulled her hands out of his and picked up the report. "I'm sorry you put all this work into this report, but I'm not going to change my mind." She sighed. She didn't want to keep having this conversation, or the one that should come after it—the one where she told him she was cursed and then she watched the dust settle on the path he beat out of her life forever.

But he was right. There was something between them. She felt it when they kissed, too. She had been feeling it since the first time she saw him, his face torn between scowling and smiling as she presented her plan for a pink mobile bakery at the Delicious Small Business Association. Because of that connection, no matter how tenuous, she felt she owed him an explanation. Or maybe she owed it to herself to come clean with him.

Besides, he had put in a lot of graphs. They were kind of pretty. "But since you put so much work into it," and since I want to get into your khakis, she added in what she hoped was just her inner voice, "I'll explain it to you. But not here," she added quickly.

"Anywhere."

"Hey, I thought you were going to bring me dinner."

He reddened a little, looked down at the ground. "I got distracted."

"By graphs?"

He looked up. "By you."

"Dammit, that was sweet. OK. Pizza."

"Pizza?"

"Who has the best pizza in town?"

"DiMartini's."

"Good, you pass the test. Get a pizza, bring it here"—she scribbled her address on the back of a napkin—"and all of your questions will be answered."

"All of them?"

She leaned forward so she was close. "I might try to distract you with kisses. But, eventually, yes. All of them."

Before she could lean back, he surged forward and kissed her. It was a quick one, quick and hard and made awkward by their strange positions, but it left her breathless all the same.

"See you there."

Five

Dan stood on the doorstep of a modest bungalow on the outer edges of Delicious, and waited. He checked the address again—this was definitely Mona's place. It stood apart from the other houses on the block, a pale yellow home with apple green shutters, surrounded by groves of trees. Apple trees. Of course.

He wasn't sure how long he had been waiting, but it felt like just about forever. He wasn't sure if that was because a lot of time had really passed since he rang Mona's doorbell or because he was going crazy with anticipation and time just seemed to be passing at a turtle's pace. But, then, the food was getting heavy, which he thought was better evidence that he had been standing on her doorstep for a while.

It had taken a lot less time than he thought it would. There was a line out the door at DiMartini's—there always was, and their food was always worth it—but someone had just called to cancel an order. Coincidentally, it was the same order Dan had just placed—one large pie, half veggie special, half pepperoni. So Dan grabbed it and still had time to get a bottle of wine before heading over to Mona's. He thought beer went bet-

ter with pizza, but this was a date, dammit. He was
going to give her wine.

He rang the doorbell again. Maybe she had changed
her mind. She'd seemed so sure, though. She'd seemed
as enthusiastic as he was. This was right. He had never
felt so strongly about something as he did about his
need to be with her. His instincts had never overruled
his head before. This had to be right.

But where was she?

Maybe she had tripped and fallen again. She did
seem to have baked goods all over the floor of her food
truck earlier that day; maybe she had a housekeeping
problem. Maybe she'd spilled some pie filling and now
she was lying helpless on the kitchen floor and it was
up to him to save her!

Or maybe she was standing him up. Maybe she was
hiding under the counter, peeking out the lace curtains
to see if he would go away. Either way, he had to get in to
make sure. He would either get answers or save her life.

He tried the doorknob; it opened easily. He shouted
out, "Hello?" but he didn't get a response. He did hear
some noise coming from the back of the house, so he maneuvered inside with the pizza box and the wine (he had
left his briefcase in the car—no need to rehash the graph
argument again) and walked toward the noise.

As he got closer, he realized the noises were coming
from the kitchen, a really nice, modern kitchen that
looked a lot more updated than the arts-and-crafts style
of the rest of the house. There were four ovens built
into the wall, stacked two on top of each other. Between the ovens was a massive six-burner gas stove
with a big, industrial-looking vent over the top of it.
There was a small island in the center of the room,
piled high with dirty pans and dishes.

The noise, it turned out, was water. There was a dish-
washer running on the far side of the kitchen, next to the

big, industrial sink. There, in front of a large window that looked out over a dark yard, was Mona. She was pulling down a spray head, rinsing off cookie sheets and standing them up in a large drainer next to the sink.

And she was dancing.

She had changed. Well, mostly. He was glad to see she still wore the cute pink tank top, even if it did say Apple of My Pie across the front. But instead of the slim cropped jeans she'd had on earlier, now she wore tiny black cotton shorts. They were . . . short. They showed off her legs, which were tan and strong and surprisingly long for such a short woman. And the shorts also hugged her bottom, showing off her curves as she wiggled and shook to the music playing through the headphones plugged into her ears.

He didn't want to stop her. God, she looked amazingly cute. But the pizza was getting cold and the wine was getting heavy and, damn, those shorts were making his hands itch.

She must have seen his reflection in the kitchen window because suddenly she screamed and spun around, her eyes wild, and aimed the spray of water at him.

"Heglb!" he sputtered

"Oh! Crap! Dan!" she shouted.

She dropped the sprayer and the flow of water stopped. She rushed toward him, and he hoped she had a towel because his head was soaked.

"Did you ruin the pizza?" she asked, grabbing it from his hands.

He was sure he had about half a gallon of water in his ears, and she was asking about the pizza?

She threw the box on the counter and tossed the lid open. "Perfect," she said as she inhaled. "The box is just a little wet on the top. We're fine." She finally turned around and looked at him. "Oh, my God, you're soaked!"

"I know," said Dan, using his mostly wet sleeve to

push his wet hair out of his eyes. "Do you have a towel or something?"

She ripped open a drawer and tossed him a dish towel, and he got to work rubbing the deluge out of his hair. "Sorry for soaking you."

"I didn't mean to startle you," he said at the same time.

They looked at each other, and he laughed. She put her hand over her heart, but eventually she laughed, too. "How did you even get in here?"

"The door was open."

"Oh, yeah. I forgot I left it open for you. That was fast, though. I thought you would be at DiMartini's for a while. I thought I'd have more time to do some of these dishes." She swept her hand over the island. "And now you're soaked."

Dan wanted to shake it off, to act like it was no big deal. But he was really, really wet. His shirt was sticking to him, and water was running down his back. He ran the towel over his waist, trying to at least keep his pants dry. He was pretty sure he wanted to end the night with his pants off, but this seemed a little soon.

"It's OK," he lied. "Do you have another towel?"

She left the kitchen and came back with a fluffy yellow towel and something folded into a tight bundle.

"Sorry, it's the only shirt I have that will fit you."

He unrolled it. It was a T-shirt, and it looked big enough. It said Apple of My Pie across the chest. And it was pink.

Mona tried not to sneak a peek as Dan peeled off his wet shirt. She turned demurely to the sink to give him some space. So what if she could still see him in the reflection of the dark kitchen windows? That wasn't her fault. That was science.

She hadn't been wrong about his shoulders when they had kissed that afternoon. They were broad and they looked strong, and as he pulled his wet shirt off, his abs flexed. Dang, he had a six-pack. And a smattering of hair on his chest, a chest that looked broad and strong like his shoulders. And those arms.

No way were those accountant arms.

She averted her eyes before he caught her gawking, and when he said she could turn around, she had to laugh. There was nothing else she could do. The shirt was silly and pink, but it fit him snugly and showed off his gorgeous man-shape and he looked so sexy. Sexy and pink.

"Hey, it's your shirt," he said.

"No, it's not that, it's—" But she stopped when she saw that he was laughing, too. "It actually looks really good on you."

"Thanks. I think?"

Mona tried to regain her composure. He was sexy, but she was hungry, and that pizza smelled really good. "Um, I guess I'll just—"

"Let me help," he said, reaching into the drawer to pull out a clean dish towel.

"No, that's—"

"The sooner we're done, the sooner we can eat that wet pizza."

Mona's stomach growled.

Dan raised an eyebrow. "We can eat now, if you want."

God, yes, she wanted to eat. She wanted to eat him up in all of that pink sexiness.

But good sense—and actual food hunger—won out. "Better do this first. I have a bunch of prep to do for tomorrow. It will be easier if I can work in stages."

They turned to the sink, and soon they settled into a

comfortable rhythm. She scrubbed, then rinsed, then passed to Dan. He shook into the sink, then dried, then piled everything on the counter in neat piles according to size and style of pan. Mona had to smile at that; she was never that organized with her clean dishes.

"You really do have a lot of work to do, don't you?"

"We're almost done," she said, pulling the last small pile of dirty pans into the soapy water.

"No, I don't mean washing all these dishes. Although it is a lot, especially for one person. I was just thinking that, at some point, you had to fill all of these pans with food."

"From scratch," she added.

She heard him give a little laugh. "I guess that's why you don't want to do this all the time."

Not this again, not already.

"Sure," she said.

"Hey, I didn't mean to . . . I'm not trying to start an argument." He put down the last clean pan and draped the towel over the side of the sink. "I'm not, I swear." He reached out, and Mona found herself pulled toward him, her hips resting against his, his arms in a light hold around her waist.

"Then what are you trying to do?" she asked, shuffling her feet closer to his.

He pushed a lock of hair off her forehead. "I'm just trying to understand you, that's all."

"Trying to understand me so you can tell me how to run my business better?"

He leaned his forehead against hers, and even up so close, she could see that he had closed his eyes. "No. I'm not. It is hard for me to understand why you won't even listen to my advice . . ."

She snorted.

He lifted his head and looked at her. "I'll respect

your decision if you don't pick a fight every time we talk about business."

Was this him flirting with her? His moves could use some work.

"I mean, we both run businesses, it's a big part of each of our lives," he said. "It's bound to come up."

"Did anyone ever tell you you're a patronizing ass?" She tried to pull away, but he held her firm with those unnaturally strong accountant arms.

"Not to my face." He shrugged.

She had to laugh at that. But she only laughed a little, because he was still a patronizing ass. Even if he was a funny patronizing ass.

"I just want to get to know you better. I mean, how long have we known each other?" he asked. "Years, right? And all we've ever talked about is business. That's all I know how to talk to you about."

"This doesn't bode well for us, then, does it?" she asked his damn clear, blue eyes.

"What I mean is, I'm going to be rusty about talking to you about other things. But I want to. I want to know everything about you, and I want you to know everything about me. I don't know why it took so long to see you, and how great you are, and how much I'm attracted to you."

She raised her eyebrows, remembering his barely controlled gaze at lunchtime.

"Fine. So I knew I was attracted to you from the first time I met you," he said, "but I didn't want to admit it. I'm not used to things I can't control."

"But now you want to pursue this," she said, waving her hand between the two of them. "Even though I am not something you can control."

"I don't want to control you—"

"Just my business."

"No! Dammit, Mona!" He stepped back and she immediately regretted pushing him. But there was something inside her, some instinct, that told her to push. She had good instincts. So she pushed.

He took a deep breath and looked back up at her, but he didn't step back into her space. She was pretty mad at her instincts for that, because the thought of him leaving did not-very-fun things to her insides. Even if he was being an ass.

"No. I just . . . I was blind to my attraction to you, and now, I don't know, the shades have been lifted."

Oh, metaphors. That was kind of like poetry. Probably the most poetry she would get from an accountant.

He looked into her eyes again, and damn those deep blue pools of feeling, where she could read every struggle, every desire. She didn't need poetry if he was going to give her looks like that.

"It was just the apple cake." She had to brush his seriousness off. Her instincts told her to laugh, that if she took this too seriously, there would be trouble.

"The apple cake was amazing, but I'm pretty sure it wasn't the apple cake. I thought it might be the full moon, but I don't think that's it, either."

"No?" Everyone blamed everything on the full moon. Mona wanted to blame this on the full moon. Otherwise how could she explain the step she took toward him, ignoring those treacherous instincts? How else could she explain the hand she put on his chest, or the one that snaked around his neck? Or the fact that when she pressed into him, his hands went around her waist and she took that as encouragement to press a little harder?

It had to be the full moon.

"It's not the full moon. It's you," Dan said, just a second before his lips descended to hers and she kicked at her instincts, told them to leave her the hell alone because this, this felt so good that how could it be anything other than what she really wanted?

Six

This was what he wanted. That was Dan's last thought as he closed the distance between his mouth and Mona's, felt her go soft under him. He forgot all about how, a few seconds ago, he was thinking he should probably just go, or at least tell his erection that it wasn't going to happen because Mona just wanted to pick a fight. But then she started talking about the full moon and apple cake and the fight seemed to go out of her. He should step back, let her work through her feelings. But then she took an infinitesimal step toward him, he felt it, and he decided he could help her work through her feelings.

With his mouth.

And his tongue. She seemed to like it. She breathed a heavy sigh and opened to him, her body melting into his, and he just held on and let her melt.

But he wasn't letting her get away.

Well, if she really wanted to, he would.

But she was pressing up against him in a way that suggested she probably didn't want to, and her pressing made it harder for him to imagine being able to let her go, so he held on. And then he realized how much he was thinking. Dammit, this was not a time for thinking!

This was a time for kissing. So he cupped her face in his hands and angled his head and took her mouth even deeper. God, she was sweet, and she was squeezing the life out of his shirt. He felt her lift the edge and he gasped a little at the feeling of her warm hands on his back. She moaned, and he ran his hands down her body, feeling the muscles in her back flex.

Those little sounds and the moving into him, all of that made him think she was thinking what he was thinking, which was that this was meant to be and it was meant to be tonight. He was sure, for himself, anyway. But even though he felt good about his powers of persuasion, he had to be sure she was sure. If for no other reason than to get his brain to stop with these ridiculous twisty thoughts so he could get to the lovin'.

He pulled back and she squeezed him harder, her mouth following his, not letting go. But he persevered because he had to be sure.

He lifted his head back to where that delicious mouth couldn't reach his. He cupped the sides of her neck and rubbed his thumbs over her cheeks until she opened her eyes.

"Are you sure?" he asked.

Hell yes, she was sure. She hadn't been sure before, but now she was. But maybe she was just physically sure? Because, physically, Dan felt pretty amazing. Beyond that, he felt a little scary, too. Looking into those blue, blue eyes forced her to admit that all of the arguing and suggestions of nefarious ulterior motives were just a way for her to keep a little safe distance.

She probably wouldn't tell him that.

She had to protect her heart. Dan was so all in, like he wasn't even thinking about what would happen if they woke up in the morning and the magic wore off and he couldn't stand to look at her again.

She reached up and stroked the side of his face, let her hand curl gently into the neck of the pink T-shirt. She wanted him, badly. But she wasn't sure.

"Here," he said, disentangling himself from her and heading over to the counter with the pizza. "Do you have plates?"

How could he just turn it off like that, she thought, practically panting against the counter. Then he turned around and she saw the tremendous tent his khakis were making under the pink shirt, and she had to laugh. Once she started, she couldn't stop. Then tears were streaming down her face and she was hiccupping, and the more she tried to stop the hysteria from pouring out of her, the faster it came. She was exhausted, she was confused, and here was this guy who seemed way too good to be true. It was like her curse. Sometimes it was a gift, and sometimes it was like a smack with a wet fish.

Wet fish? Oh God, even her inner monologue was losing it.

Then suddenly tented-Khaki Dan was in front of her, his hands strong in hers, coaxing her head upward with soothing sounds. How did he have it in him to make those soothing sounds? This man was perfect! He must not be real. That set her off again.

She leaned into him.

He was hard and solid and, well, hard, and she held on. Holding on to him felt good. It gave her strength.

He handed her a paper towel.

"Sorry about that," she said, turning away to blow her nose.

"You must be exhausted."

"You have no idea." She *was* tired. Tired of baking,

tired of this crazy rush during the full moon that left her drained. Tired of keeping her distance from people, especially man-people, because she didn't think they'd accept the truth about her curse.

But there was a part of her that wasn't tired. The part of her that was drawn to Dan was bouncing off the walls of her chest. And everything that he said—whether it was completely the wrong thing or perfectly right, and he did a fair amount of both—made her bounce even harder. He stood in front of her, hair disheveled, lips wet, cheeks flushed, and she was sure she had never felt so attracted to a man in her life.

"Let's just eat, and then . . ." Dan reached around her for the plates.

"I don't want pizza, Dan." She put her hand on his arm to stop him.

"Oh! OK, do you want something else? I can go out and get anything—"

"I don't want anything."

"Anything?"

"To eat."

He blinked at her. Then he stepped forward.

Smart man.

Seven

Dan didn't believe in luck or fate or any of that karmic mumbo jumbo that people used to explain how unusual things happened to them.

At least, he had never believed in that stuff before.

And then Mona took his hand and led him to the back of the house, to what was clearly her bedroom, and he thanked all of the stars and pennies and clovers in the universe for whatever had gone through this woman's head to make her decide that this was a good idea.

Looking at her in those little black shorts, he felt certain this was a good idea.

But when she turned to face him, her pale green eyes turned dark with desire, her skin seeming to glow from it, he knew this was a great idea.

She took a step back and he followed, deeper into the room. She ripped the Apple of My Pie tank top off, and as she did, her hair came loose and fell in soft waves around her face and over her shoulders. She was amazing. She had a little bit of a tan, that healthy glow of someone who spent a lot of time outdoors. He had noticed her skin before, and appreciated it. But tonight she seemed lighter, luminescent.

And very, very touchable.

"You're glowing," he said as he approached her, because he thought she should know.

"It's the moon," she said, indicating her open curtains. The moon was huge, and light seemed to come off of it in waves, cutting through the clear, cloudless night. Mona walked over to the window and started to close the curtains.

"Don't," Dan said, taking just a quick moment to rip his own pink shirt over his head. "You look beautiful. And the neighbors are far away, right?"

"Right," she said quietly, then turned back to the moon.

Dan came up behind her and ran his hands down her shoulders, over her arms to capture her hands and move them from the curtains. She turned, then released his hands and reached around herself to unclasp her bra. It fell on the floor between them, but Dan barely noticed. He just put his hands back on her shoulders and pulled her close, feeling skin on skin, and took her mouth in a deep kiss.

Her hands felt amazing on his back. They were warm and strong, and he shuddered as she ran them up and down his spine. He wondered if his skin felt as good to her as hers did to him. She was soft, but underneath that softness he could feel her strength. The girl had muscles everywhere—her shoulders, her arms—and she shuddered, too, as he ran his hands down her back. Her back was probably tired from all that standing and leaning, so he pressed harder, massaging, and she melted into him, her mouth opening wider. He didn't think it would be possible to do it, but he deepened the kiss, their tongues clashing, and he felt her arms tighten around his waist. God, she was sweet. She felt hot and amazing.

She sighed and let out a little moan. Part of him wanted to rub her back all night if this was how good it made her feel. But the horny part of him won out, and he ran his hands lower, over those little black shorts and over the curves of her bottom. Then he ran up her back again—she liked it, and he was a giver—and then back down, this time reaching into the waistband of her shorts, feeling her flesh under his hands. She squirmed against him, and her hands mirrored his movements. He didn't think it would have been possible for him to get any harder, but those strong hands running over his backside squeezed and he pressed closer to her heat and he thought probably he should get these pants off, soon.

She pulled away and looked up at him. She was flushed, her lips swollen, her curls in a tangle around her face. He brushed her hair away and tried to catch his breath. She was beautiful, the most beautiful woman he had ever seen.

She looked into his eyes for a moment, and something was happening in that brain of hers, because she smiled, just a little quirk on the side of her mouth, and her hands reached for his belt.

"Let's see what you've got going on under those khakis."

Holy crap. Mona thought by now she should be over it every time Dan surprised her. She'd thought he was uptight, but he turned out to be sweet and thoughtful. She'd thought he was a flimsy pencil pusher, but he was strong; he was damn muscular. His shoulders were wide and defined, and the layer of dark blond hair on his chest did nothing to hide the musculature there. And his butt. That was pretty good, too.

So many surprises.

When they'd started talking earlier, she'd thought he had a one-track mind, that he would be all business. But, surprise, surprise, his one-track mind seemed to be focused in a much more pleasurable direction.

What other surprises did this Khaki Love God have in store for her?

She undid the buckle on his sensible brown belt, the leather making a zipping sound as she pulled it through the loops. Her hands fumbled a little with the button on his khakis, but she managed. She pushed them down over his hips and he stepped out of them. He was wearing boxer briefs, and normally she would say that those were a silly kind of underwear for men who couldn't decide what they wanted, but this was no time for joking. Not when she saw what he was packing inside those briefs.

Mona took a hold of him then, and he was hot and heavy in her hand, even through his underwear. Dan swore under his breath but she heard it anyway, and it was another surprise for her that he even knew words like that. He pulled her hand away, a strangled "not yet" coming from his throat, and then his hands were all over her. She started to work his underwear down over that amazing accountant butt, but as soon as his lips hit her neck, she lost track of all of the parts of him she wanted to touch. Because at the same time as his lips hit her neck, his hands came up to cup her breasts, and he was doing amazing, reverential things to them, weighing them gently in his palms, running his fingers over her nipples. Then he started being amazing and reverential with his mouth and she almost lost it right there, right against the window with the curtains wide open and the moon shining in on them, making his hair glow.

His clever mouth stayed where it was, and she gasped and pressed his head closer to her, as if he could get any closer. But his clever hands started moving and she felt the *shush* against her skin as her panties hit the floor, and then his hands were *all* over her. He kneeled in front of her, his mouth still on her breasts and his hands firm on her hips. He elbowed her legs a little farther apart and she wanted to say, "Wait, hold on, that's not fair, we should—" but she couldn't get it out before his mouth was on her and his tongue was inside her and she was pulling on his hair and making loud, strange noises and throwing her head back, and the moon blinded her as she shouted out in ecstasy.

Mona struggled to catch her breath and concentrated really hard on locking her knees so she didn't topple all over this poor, sweet man who was still kneeling on the floor, caressing her hips gently and looking up at her with a Cheshire cat smile. She added a curse of her own, then weakly reached under his arms to pull him up toward her. She didn't think she could actually make him move at that point—she was kind of surprised she was able to move herself—but he got the hint and he kissed his way up her belly, through the valley between her breasts, her neck, her chin, then he was back at her mouth and she was on fire again. She wrapped herself around him, arms tight around his neck, legs around his waist, and he stumbled backward onto the bed, which was what she had in mind anyway, so that was fine. She straddled him, pressed her whole body against him as they kissed, then reached over into her nightstand for a condom. He grabbed it from her hand, and that was another surprise—he was the world's fastest condom putter-onner. She started to lean over to the side, to let him get on top, but he held on to her arm and pulled her hips on top of his and, oh, my God, she thought. She reared up, sitting up on top of him, her hands on that amazing chest, and she wasn't sure if she was riding or holding on, but together they found their rhythm and he was deep inside of her and then she was cresting that wave again, calling out his name as she shook. The last thing she remembered as she fell into a heap on his chest was him shuddering beneath her, banding his arms around her back and whispering her name desperately into her ear.

Eight

Dan's body was exhausted, but he felt, strangely, not exhausted at all. He barely had the strength to pull Mona into his arms. He managed, though, and she nestled in. He closed his eyes to try to sleep, just for a second, but he found he couldn't stop his fingers from running up and down her arm. Then she sighed and snuggled closer to him, and he shifted a little so he could follow the same path along her back.

He just couldn't stop touching her.

"Wow," she whispered into his shoulder.

He smiled, even with his eyes closed. He felt the same. The same, but more, and if he had had more energy, he would be jumping up and down on the bed and shouting his Wow. But he was tired. Too tired to do anything but hold Mona and sweep his hands over her soft skin.

"I should get up." She sighed.

That woke him up.

But he played it cool. At least, he hoped he did. He just banded his arms around her and wouldn't let her go.

She laughed. "I have work to do."

"Just one more minute," he pleaded.

She sighed. "Fine. One minute. I'm counting."

But then she sighed again and tossed her leg over his, and he felt her back relax and she melted even closer. Ha. She wasn't going to be counting.

"What would happen if you didn't count, and you just stayed here with me?"

"Well," she said, turning a little and looking up at the ceiling, "I wouldn't make any money and I'd miss a mortgage payment and I'd have to live in my pink truck, which is against health code regulations, so then my business would be shut down, so I would be destitute and miserable and pathetic."

"I'm impressed with your post-coital banter."

She laughed. "Sorry, I get a little defensive."

He shifted over so he was on his side and propped a hand under his head to look at her. He wanted to ask her serious questions and talk about this thing that was growing inside him, that had started when they talked and now was expanding to fill half of his chest, and that he was pretty sure had to do with her, and that he was almost positive was a good thing. But the moon was still high and still shining through the curtains, and her tan skin was luminescent and she was lying there on her back, looking up at the ceiling and not at him, and he wanted to ask her what was going on in that head of hers and he would, he promised himself, he would, but his hand wasn't listening, and he gently rubbed her stomach, up between her breasts, down her side, just feeling as much of her as he could, as if he could absorb that moonglow into him and keep her here forever.

Mona did not want to get up. She wanted more than anything in the world to lie in bed all night with Dan stroking her skin. Everywhere he touched, he left a little trail of sensation, so she continued to feel him even when his fingers had moved on. She could feel herself start to get interested in more than simple touching. She thought maybe he had a few more tricks up his khakis, and she had a few of her own she wanted to share.

But she couldn't.

She had to bake.

It wasn't as dire as she'd told Dan; missing one day probably wouldn't be the end of the world, but she had told people she would be there. People were expecting her. Adam was expecting a fruit tart, because his in-laws were coming to town and he wanted to impress them.

Plus, this was how she made her living. When the moon was full, Apple of My Pie became her life. She couldn't throw it all away just because some guy was amazing in bed.

She looked over at Dan. Man, she wanted to throw it all away.

She had to make him understand. She felt pretty sure that if she just said she had to get ready for tomorrow, he would accept her explanation and that would be it. But it wouldn't be enough. She wanted more from him. Not just more sex, although that would be . . . nice. He was nice. She felt drawn to him and it scared her, but she couldn't help what she wanted any more than she could help that the moon was pouring in the window and it was making her fingers itch to get her hands on some flour and dough.

If he couldn't accept her for who she was, curses and all, that would be it. No more Khaki Dan, back to real life.

She felt his hands run lightly over her breasts, just a breath.

She could so easily just let him sleep (surely the poor man must be tired), go to the kitchen, and then wake him up for round two. It was what she had always done.

And look how well it had worked out for her before.

She was alone. Not really alone—she had amazing friends, and she loved her life, truly. But she didn't have a partner. And she would never get one if she shied away from sharing with Dan the biggest part of her life. That she was cursed.

She could do it. She had to do it.

She just wouldn't look at him while she did.

"I have to get ready for tomorrow."

"Already?" He nuzzled into her neck.

Damn him.

"There's kind of a lot to do," she said to the ceiling, ignoring the thrill that coursed through her as his fingers roamed.

"Can it wait a few minutes?"

"How many minutes?"

He looked down at her. "If I say three, will you be offended?"

She laughed, and looked away. She couldn't face those eyes, because she saw desire and tenderness there. And soon, that would be gone.

"No."

He rolled over so he was on his back too, his arm touching hers. They looked up at the ceiling together.

"Can I help?" he asked. "I should warn you, I've never baked anything in my life."

"Wow, that's . . . a generous offer."

"I can, I don't know, grease the pan. Or cut stuff. I know how to cut stuff."

She nudged his shoulder with hers. "You're sweet, but I have to do it on my own."

"Oh, OK."

"Are you offended?"

"No! I mean, my pride is a little." He clutched his heart. "Ouch. But that's fine. Do you need me to go?"

Yes. No. Yes.

"I have something to tell you," she told the ceiling.

"OK."

"About my business."

Dan sat up. She continued to look at the ceiling.

"There's a reason I bake only certain times of the month."

"Ha! I knew it! Mafia connections? Do you have to wait for the ingredients to fall off the back of a truck?"

"That's the first thing your brain goes to? I have a weird schedule so you think I'm in the Mafia?"

"No, I guess not."

"It's just—"

"Oh! Do you have a kid? And the kid lives with her dad most of the time and so when you don't have her you bake?"

"What? Dan! That—what?"

"No kids?"

"Don't you think if I had a child you would have seen some evidence of her by now?"

"Oh, so you agree your imaginary child is a girl."

"Dan! I'm trying to tell you something here."

"OK, I'm listening." He lay back down and joined her in ceiling gazing.

"I'm cursed."

He sat up. "Cursed?"

"Well, gifted, maybe."

"The Mafia is ridiculous, but a curse is something I'm supposed to believe?" He flopped back down next to her. "Good one."

"Just . . . just listen, please." She didn't look at him, but she held on to his arm so he would stay put. "I don't know where it came from, but my grandmother had it and my father had it."

"The curse."

Without looking at him, she threw a hand over his mouth.

"Yes, the curse." She turned, finally, and looked at him. He looked like he wanted to say something, so she kept her hand on his mouth. She took a deep breath. She told him the truth. "The curse has everything to do with my business. You know how my baking is amazing?"

He nodded, but she kept her hand in place.

"That doesn't always happen. In fact, most of the time, my baking is disgusting. Like, Brussels-sprouts-and-mud disgusting."

He raised an eyebrow. She kept going.

"But during the full moon, that changes. I don't do anything different, same ingredients, same family recipes, but suddenly everything tastes amazingly good. It happens only during the full moon and a day or two surrounding it. It gets stronger as the moon gets stronger, then it dies back down. So those are the only days I bake, and those are the only days I run my truck. Because if I did it every day, the bad days would outnumber the delicious ones and people would be so grossed out that I would have no business."

She stopped talking; that was kind of all she had to say. But she didn't move her hand; she wasn't ready for what he had to say, not yet.

He took her wrist and pulled her away from his mouth, and then he smiled.

OK, she thought. That wasn't so bad.

Then he laughed, the corners of his eyes crinkling, his head thrown back and tears streaming down his cheeks.

"A curse? Mona, come on. . . . Wait, are you being serious?"

Forget it, she thought. Not worth it. She stood up and took one last look at him, lying naked on her bed. Maybe worth it, but not right now. She grabbed her robe and headed for the kitchen.

She had work to do.

Nine

Dan was not known as a spontaneous, jokey kind of person, but these past few hours with Mona he had laughed more than he had in a long, long time. Mona brought that out in him—the long-buried silliness and fun that he had somehow misplaced while building his business. She made him fun again.

So he was a little confused to find himself lying in bed, alone, after another hilarious quip about why her business was so sporadic. He watched her retreat to the bathroom, then head back out and down the hall. He heard noises coming from the kitchen—cabinet doors, pans on the counter, the fridge opening and closing.

She really was working.

What had he said that had upset her?

And how could he go back in time and un-say it?

Maybe her curse would help her turn back time and they could go back to the part where they were making love. He would be willing to relive that again, no problem.

But then he started thinking. If she was banging around the kitchen like that, she was probably pissed off. And the only thing they had talked about was . . .

the fact that she was cursed. Which was, of course, ridiculous.

Then he remembered that winter. It had been just after the holidays, and he'd been working late. Downtown was quiet, and he was trying to get some paperwork finished up for tax season. But he'd kept getting distracted, as usual, by just the idea that Mona was out there in her pink food truck. He had seen her when she'd pulled up in the morning, and when he'd gone out for lunch, and then when he'd happened to need to stretch his legs late in the afternoon, and so what if his distraction had taken him to the window that had a full view of the street where she was parked. She'd had that side window with the fold-out counter closed, but there had been a big APPLE OF MY PIE IS OPEN sign in the middle of it. Mona periodically appeared at the little side window, opened it to wave at people, handed out a hot chocolate or a warm muffin. She'd worn a bright pink knit hat and a pink-and–white-striped scarf that practically covered her entire face. Every time she'd leaned out to a customer, he saw the white cloud of her breath, and even though she'd been smiling, he thought, *Why is she doing that to herself?* It was freezing, and she was clearly not comfortable. Later, as he'd conveniently stretched his legs in front of his street-view window, he'd noticed Mona closing up for the night. Business can't have been worth it, he remembered thinking. Then he saw a few flurries start to fall and he was glad she was going. That truck probably wouldn't be great driving in the snow, and he'd wanted her to get home safely. Not that he cared. But the snow was just starting so it wasn't dangerous yet, and it still looked pretty drifting down in front of the street lights. He'd looked up to fully admire the view, and he remembered the moon, gigantic and full and hazy from the snow clouds drifting in.

A full moon.

How could that be? In his experience, everything had an explanation, every problem had a solution. Every solution could be uncovered with cleverness, determination, focus, elbow grease, or some combination thereof. There were always solutions, and solutions could always be found.

But a curse? How do you fix a curse?

If there even was such a thing.

There must be another explanation. But the more he struggled to find one, the more evidence he found to support what she'd said. Every time her truck was out there, he had noticed. And every time she left, he noticed. Mona's truck appeared outside his office window, the full moon appeared at night.

There was also a solid amount of evidence pointing to the possibility that he was a stalker.

But he didn't follow her; she parked outside his office. Obviously, she was the stalker.

The cursed stalker.

Because he was a prime candidate for a stalking—a small-town accountant who was, he had to face it, generally pretty uptight.

Except when he was with Mona.

She brought out the fun in him.

Curse or no curse, she was worth a gamble.

Mona hoped Dan had fallen back to sleep, because she was about to run the mixer and it was going to be loud. If her night was going to be ruined . . .

No, she didn't really want to ruin his night. He was probably awake, planning his escape from the crazy baker lady. But she couldn't seem to get a handle on her emotions. Not that she was normally buttoned-up—she had a bit of a reputation for her quick temper—but she had never felt such violent shifts in her feelings. One minute she wanted to sock Dan in the jaw, the next she wanted to rip off his clothes.

There was an undercurrent of violence in both, she noticed.

She dropped a chunk of butter into the mixer and pushed it down into the flour with a big wooden spoon. Not violence, she thought. She pushed the button, and the mixer whirred to life, beating the butter and flour together into a creamy dough.

Not violence. Passion.

She felt passionately about him all the time. Sometimes it was passionate annoyance, sometimes it was just plain old red-blooded passion. But no matter what her feelings were for him, she felt them very strongly. More strongly than she was used to. More strongly than she was prepared for.

When the mixture was the right consistency, she stopped the mixer and started to wrestle the beaters out of the bowl.

"It already smells good in here."

She squeaked in surprise and nearly dropped the bowl. She managed to get it onto the counter but lost control of the wooden spoon. She bobbled it a few times, like juggling a hot potato, and finally caught it in her hand. She held on tight and turned to face Dan.

"You're up," she said, noncommittally. She also took in his nearly-naked-but-for-his-boxer-briefs body noncommittally. Totally not committed to finding him attractive. Not at all.

She looked at him for another second, then had to turn back to her dough. Those eyes were too generous, and she was trying to enjoy the last comforting seconds of believing he was an asshole.

"I really do want to help," he said, stepping up closer behind her.

She was suddenly, acutely aware of the thinness of her robe. He was still practically on the other side of the kitchen, but his body heat was distracting her. It was messing up her system. She had a lot to do and not a lot of time, and she was used to doing without help. Frankly, she thought it would be faster if she could do it all herself, the way she was used to.

So she explained it to him.

"No." Not the most loquacious explanation, but it got her point across. Mostly. "But thank you."

He just shrugged. Was this man completely impervious to insult?

"Do you mind if I just watch?"

She did mind, what with the thin robe and those blue eyes and the fact that, even though she had washed up, she could still smell him on her.

But then he sat down on a stool in the corner of the kitchen and pulled the pizza box open. She was about to tell him that she couldn't give him an oven to heat it up when he pulled out a slice and took a big bite.

"I think DiMartini's pizza might be even better when it's cold."

Mona felt exactly the same way about it. God, if they felt the same way about cold pizza, they might as well get married.

"What?"

Had she said that last part out loud? He was annoying and annoyingly handsome, but she didn't want to scare him off.

"Nothing," she said, hoping he would just forget it all.

Because Dan was so good at letting things go.

"People have gotten married for less, you know."

Nope, he wasn't letting it go.

"People have gotten divorced for less, too." Two could play at not letting things go.

"OK, let's see what we've got." He stood up and started pacing the far wall of the kitchen. "We both like cold pizza, that's a plus. We both work downtown, usually. We could save on gas, that's a plus. We both love Delicious, definite plus. We both . . . are intimidated by Mrs. Harris."

Mona laughed. "You're her boss! How can you be intimidated by her?!"

"Have you ever done something she doesn't approve of?"

"I don't think so."

"Oh, you'd know. She's terrifying." He went back to pacing. "What else? I have a stick up my ass and you're more go with the flow. A lot of people would call that a negative, but I think it's really a positive. I think we could balance each other out." She shivered as his voice was a whisper in her ear. She hadn't realized that he had come up behind her. "And you really showed me how to loosen up earlier."

She turned, expecting to melt into his embrace. But he was gone, back to pacing.

"We both think my butt looks really good in these boxer briefs."

She blushed, but when he turned around and wiggled his eyebrows at her, she laughed. His butt did look really good.

"Those are all positives. So, really, I don't see any reason why we shouldn't get married."

Now she really laughed, her breath coming out in a shocked cackle. "Dan!"

"Don't you feel this between us? There's something here." Suddenly he was at the counter again, directly in front of her. "Something powerful and amazing, and I don't want to just walk out of here until you promise you'll see if this can work between us."

So far Dan had always kissed her with his eyes

closed. She knew that, so she closed the short distance between their mouths, welcoming the reprieve from his sharp, tender gaze.

But she pulled back quickly. "There's one negative you didn't mention," she said, stepping back to the counter.

"What?" he said, eyes still closed, leaning in so his arms rested on the counter on either side of her hips.

"I'm cursed, and you don't believe me."

He opened his eyes then, but he didn't straighten. His arms tensed, and his gaze bored into hers, hot and intense.

"That's the thing, Mona. It doesn't make any sense, no rational sense at all. I don't want to believe you." She started to turn away, but he grabbed her chin and she was forced to lock on to his gaze again. "I don't want to believe you, but I do."

Ten

It was ridiculous, of course. But as Dan leaned his forehead on Mona's, he felt very very sure that, even though it was ridiculous, she was telling the truth.

Mona was cursed.

So what could he do about it? He could try to figure out how to fix it. There had to be a way to fix it: every problem had a solution.

He would just approach it the same way he approached every project. Do a little research, get all his ducks in a row, and then . . . attack. Or solve. Attack and solve.

He didn't know where he could find information on curses or how to break them—did they have stuff like that at the library? He could at least observe Mona and see if there was anything in the way she was baking that might give him some clues. So he let her go and watched her get on with her work.

She broke an egg one-handed on the side of a mixing bowl. Pretty impressive. He ate half a slice of pizza in one bite. That was about the extent of his culinary talents. Slightly less impressive.

"So what made you decide to believe me?" she asked as she cracked another egg.

He shrugged as he chewed his mouthful of delicious, cold pizza. Then he realized she couldn't see him while she was facing the counter, so he swallowed as fast as he could without choking. "I didn't decide to believe you. I don't think you can decide to believe anything. You do or you don't. With you, I do."

"Despite your best judgment?"

"Hey, it's not my fault you're the first cursed person I've ever met."

He watched her stir and pour, her forearms flexing with the weight of the bowl.

"Do you think there are other people in this town like you?" he asked.

"What, you mean cursed?"

"Yeah. Or with special abilities. Special and sporadic abilities."

"I don't know. I don't really talk about it much."

"Maybe there are a whole mess of you, and you guys can form a coalition and save the world."

She arched an eyebrow at him. "With muffins?"

"Hey, your apple cake is really, really good. Don't underestimate it."

Mona leaned over and put a pan of something gooey into the oven.

"How much more do you have to do tonight?" he asked.

"A little more. The rest I need to do in the morning."

"It's almost morning now."

She looked up at the clock and frowned. "OK, the rest I need to do in a few hours."

"You need some sleep."

"I don't sleep during the full moon. I'm used to it.

And even if I had time to, I can't. When I sit still for too long, I get kind of itchy to bake."

"Ah, the curse."

"The curse. I'll sleep tomorrow night."

"Well, if there's nothing else to do until tomorrow . . ."

She raised her eyebrows at him.

". . . you could have some pizza."

"Ha! I thought you were going to say we could make out."

"We can absolutely make out if you want to, but aren't you starving? It's always sex with you, young lady. I'm beginning to think you're just using me for my khakis."

Her stomach growled.

"And I got the pizza all nice and cold for you, just like you like it." He inched the box in her general direction.

She smiled, and for the first time since she had left the bed—her bed—it reached her eyes. She took a bite of the slice he held out to her, then went back to work.

He wasn't sure how long he stood like that, watching her move around the kitchen with fluid confidence. It was the same way she moved around Apple of My Pie—quickly, but not rushed. It looked like she knew what she was reaching for before her arm even moved. Sometimes he swore the cabinets opened before her hands reached them. But that, surely, was a trick of his sex-addled mind. She was cursed, not Mary Poppins.

When she looked like she could take a three-second break, Dan stepped in with another slice of pizza. She told him she didn't usually get to eat when she baked, and she thanked him. But he wasn't sure she actually saw him. She was calm and focused, the eye of a baking storm. One minute he saw flour and sugar and butter, and then suddenly he was seeing pie crusts and cookies.

Some of them went into the oven, some she covered in plastic wrap and maneuvered into the already-stuffed industrial-sized refrigerator. He started to offer to help, but she obviously had a system, because she would shift something just a fraction and suddenly there was room for whatever was in her hands.

Eventually, though, Dan had to admit he was not a superhuman like Mona obviously was. He was just an accountant, one who had appointments tomorrow and a business to run. He should go. He should leave her to her baking and talk to her tomorrow, maybe stop by for something sweet on his lunch break, or maybe offer to get Mrs. Harris her morning treat. And then tomorrow night the moon would be decidedly un-full and he could have her all to himself.

But he didn't want to wait until tomorrow. He didn't want to interrupt Mona's flow, either. So he cleaned up the pizza mess, leaving the last two slices on a plate for her, and he headed to bed. As he lay down, he hoped she would wake him up when she got there. As soon as his head hit the pillow, he was asleep.

Mona surveyed the mess in her kitchen and nodded, satisfied. She had plenty to do in the morning—which, as she checked the clock, was in a few hours—but she had gotten enough done tonight that it wouldn't be a crazy rush. Just the usual rush. She was happy. All that done, and with the massive distraction of the Hot Accountant.

She was feeling pretty good about herself, and she wanted to share that feeling. But when she turned, Dan was gone, just a plate with two slices of pizza in his place.

Had he left? His keys were still on the counter, so

maybe he'd been so alarmed by the reality of her moon magic that he'd run out, leaving his car behind. Maybe he'd left his pants, too. Then she saw a shadow move outside her window. Oh, great, now she was going to get murdered, she thought. But then the shadow moved and the moonlight hit it just right, and she realized it was Dan. Dan, basking in the moonlight in her yard, his shirtless form framed by the apple trees. It was a nice picture.

She headed to the door to join him, ignoring the call of the plate of pizza. Her stomach was going through enough right now as the pull to go outside fought in her guts with the pull to stay in and hide. She didn't think she could take pizza, too.

The grass felt soft and dewy under her bare feet as she padded over to Dan. There was a slight breeze that lifted the ends of her hair, tickling it across her forehead and clearing the air so she couldn't smell flour and butter anymore, just trees and summer. The moon was low, but it was bright, and it reflected Dan's pale skin so it looked like he was glowing out here in her little apple orchard. As he watched the sky, she took the chance to appreciate the fine muscles of his arms and shoulders. She stayed in the shadow of the house, ogling her accountant.

No, he wasn't *her* accountant. He said he believed her about her curse, but she wasn't sure if she believed him. And even if he did, there was something about this guy that was too good to be true. This world did not make men who were kind and hot and hard-working and sincere and hot. Or if it did, they were also secretly ax murderers. Oh, God, she was going to get ax-murdered in her yard. She knew it. And her friends knew to leave her alone when she was baking; she wouldn't be discovered for days.

She must have made a sound, because Dan turned. When he faced her, he smiled. It was dark, but light enough that she could see that this was not the smile of an ax murderer. This was the smile of a kind, hot, sincere, hot man who believed her curse was real and was still really into her.

She ignored the knot in her stomach and stepped out of the shadows to meet him.

"Hey," he said, wrapping an arm around her shoulders. So comfortable, as if he'd done it many times before. "I just needed some air after a great nap. You done?"

"For now." She rested her head on his shoulder, relaxing into his warmth. She never slept during her cursed-baking extravaganzas, but she felt close to it now. Standing in her backyard, with Dan's arm around her shoulders, she felt closer to sleep than she had in days.

She wasn't sure if that was good or bad. Usually she just went on a baking binge, and then slept for about twenty-four hours. It wasn't the most healthy cycle, but her body had more or less gotten used to it. Not that she had a choice—she couldn't sleep if she wanted to. Once right out of high school, she threw all of the flour and butter and baking powder in the dumpster behind the diner, hoping that some distance between her addled brain and baking ingredients would let her sleep. But, no. At four a.m. she was driving miles and miles to the nearest all-night grocery store, and even with stale ingredients she baked masterpieces. That was the first time she had made apple cheese tarts, and now they were one of her best sellers.

"Hey," Dan said, tilting her chin up. "You still here?"

"Barely." She was tired, sure, but the possibility that she might be able to actually sleep tonight had her too wired to sleep. Stupid irony, she thought.

"You must be exhausted."

"You have no idea."

He stroked his fingers over her forehead, down her cheeks. "You want to go inside and lie down?"

Yeah, right, lie down. But the thought of lying down with Dan got her excited too, and she watched the dream of even a bad night's sleep fly away on the summer breeze.

Then Dan leaned down and kissed her, and suddenly she didn't give a shit about sleep.

She felt him part her robe, and his hands were warm against her skin. She wrapped her arms around his neck and let him lay her down on the grass. The moon shone bright through his hair, and she held on while he unwrapped her, and then he was all around her, and inside her, and the wind carried her gasps and her sighs up to the moon.

Eleven

Dan was dimly aware of Mona running her fingers up and down his side. She couldn't seem to stop moving. After they made love, he collapsed on top of her robe, and she collapsed on top of him. But as soon as he settled her next to him, her head on his chest, her arms around his waist, she started moving. Not that he minded. Her hands felt good. The gentle tickle of her fingers combined with the summer breeze blowing through the orchard, the crickets, the owls, it was all putting him to sleep.

He didn't want to sleep. He wanted to look at Mona and watch her work and help her out if she needed it. She didn't need it, and even if she did, she probably wouldn't accept it. She was stubborn and prickly. But she was also passionate and generous and warm and loving and, honestly, the most amazing baker. But just sometimes, because she was also cursed. Life with Mona would not be easy.

But it would be so worth it.

The thought startled him, but not enough to let go of Mona. He had always gathered the evidence and made the sensible decision. Planning a life together when their first meaningful conversation had happened less than twenty-four hours ago was not, on the surface, a sensible decision. But it was like her curse—it didn't make any sense at all, but at the same time there was no other possible explanation. She had opened that up in him—the possibility of . . . possibilities. Of seeing beyond what he expected to see, and really looking to see what there could be. And there could be Mona and Dan. He was sure of it.

He turned and shifted so he was facing her on the grass, his arms going around her waist just as hers did the same. Her head still rested on his chest and her eyes were closed, but she wasn't asleep. Her fingers were running up and down his back, making him shiver. She couldn't make him shiver like that if she was asleep.

So he knew she heard him when he whispered, "I love you, Mona."

Outside of the kitchen, Mona was not known for her speed or coordination, but as soon as she heard Dan whisper to her, she was up like her house was on fire.

He loved her? Was he crazy?

Because she was crazy. She was moody and prickly and cursed. Cursed! There was no way that a man so straitlaced could love someone like her. She worked once a month; he worked nine to five, Monday through Friday. He ate the same thing for lunch every day; she ate whatever was in front of her. He wore khakis; she wore pink tank tops. He drove a sensible sedan; she drove a pink food truck. Well, she had a car, but for the purposes of this freak-out, she drove a pink food truck. He was sensible; she was full of nonsense. He probably wore a pocket protector!

OK, maybe not the pocket protector. But in another life, he probably would have worn a pocket protector.

Who was she kidding? He was so sensible, he probably didn't even have a past life. He just came whole into this one fully formed and making perfect sense.

He made so much sense that he made no sense at all.

Before she was fully aware of it, she was in the kitchen, the screen door slamming behind her, leaving Dan outside in the wet grass.

She should go back out and talk to him. A man doesn't like to declare his feelings and have the screen door slam in his face. At least, she assumed that. Men didn't declare their feelings to her very often.

Further evidence that there was something wrong with Dan.

She should go out there. They had shared some really special moments. Who was she kidding? she thought. They were friggin' magical. Khaki Dan *was* a Secret Love God.

So why did the thought that he loved her fill her with gut-churning panic?

The screen door opened and Dan walked in, carrying her robe. She looked down. Yup, she was naked. He had put his clothes back on, like a normal, practical person. She just paraded around the kitchen, where she was preparing food, completely naked.

"Thanks," she muttered when he handed her the robe. She slipped it on, the silky fabric cold against her skin.

"So . . ." Dan started, then stopped. He stood there, in her kitchen, and stared at her. Those blue eyes, those damn eyes, they always gave him away. In them, she could see his earnestness and his desire, but also his uncertainty. They were too expressive for his own good.

She looked down at her toes.

"So," she muttered. She couldn't even bring herself to use her whole voice. She was ashamed of her reaction. But what was she supposed to do? Panic this strong—that had to be her gut telling her something, right? Surely, if she wasn't naturally and giddily falling into his arms, that was it, right? Not meant to be at all. Right?

"I love you, Mona."

Oh, no. Not again. Her stomach flipped and her hands started to sweat. This was panic, right?

"Did you hear me?"

"Yes," she whispered.

"I know it's fast."

She heard his feet shuffling, but she was too cowardly to look up and watch him come toward her.

"Believe me, I never would have expected something like this to happen. I thought that if I ever fell in love, it would be after dating for a while, getting to know each other slowly, finding out if we were compatible."

She saw his feet now, right in front of hers.

"I thought it would follow a predictable pattern, like everything in my life. I never even imagined it would be like this, that I would know you for so long, but not know you at all. Then when I get to know you—"

"Stop." Without looking up, she put a hand on his chest. She felt his heart beating, hard, under her palm. He was giving her that heart. It was hers for the taking. And she wanted it. She wanted it so badly, but then her gut and the panic got into the act and she couldn't.

He put his hand over hers, and she closed her eyes. Tears dripped down, right to her feet, bypassing her cheeks entirely.

"Look at me," he said. She wouldn't. But then he

tilted her chin up and she kept her eyes closed, the tears running down her cheeks now.

"Please don't be sad," he whispered, wiping her tears with his thumb.

"I'm not sad."

"You're not?" She heard the hint of laughter in his voice, and she laughed too, a sad, wet sound from the back of her throat. Sort of like a sob.

"I'm . . . I don't know what I am." She opened her eyes now and looked at him. "Dan, how can that be? How can you love me?"

"I don't know. I know that I like you, a lot, because we've spent this time together, and you're clever and smart and even though you snapped at me a few times, I like that too, because you're not afraid to be yourself around me. I don't know how I know it's love. I just know what I feel." He pressed her hand closer to his heart. "And when I say I love you, it feels right. Doesn't it feel right to you?"

It felt right. It felt so right she didn't trust it. Nothing was ever this good for her without being too good to be true. Her gift for baking? It was a curse. It came with conditions that made her life, not unbearable, but it made her life necessarily separate. Because how could she share the kind of life she had to lead with someone else? Only working sometimes, and when she did, being so completely consumed that she had to ignore everyone around her? It had never worked before; now Dan was telling her it could work with him?

She couldn't. The look in those eyes was too raw, too real to be real. She had her life. She would bake, and when she couldn't bake she would do what she always did, whatever she wanted. And she would have fond memories of a perfect night under the moonlight with an anally retentive, pushy, perfect man.

She couldn't afford to believe in happily ever after. Nothing good ever came to her without a price.

"You should go." She couldn't look at him when she said it, so she looked over his shoulder at the open curtains above the sink where the moon shone and laughed at her.

She felt him tense, as if she had struck him, and then she felt him go. She didn't watch him leave, but she heard the door close behind him. Then, as she stood there staring at that vicious moon, she heard his car start, saw his headlights make a wave over her windows, and he was gone.

She took a shaky breath. She had work to do.

Twelve

"You're wearing jeans," Mrs. Harris said to Dan as he entered the office, her eyes flitting between his wardrobe and the clock. He was late. He was never late.

"Yes."

"And a T-shirt."

"I'm depressed."

"Oh, honey," she clucked, coming over to take his briefcase. She never took his briefcase. "Bad date?"

"It was amazing," he said as he followed her into his office. When she pointed to his chair, he sat.

"But you're depressed?"

"I don't understand. We had such a—" He waved his hands in front of his face helplessly. Connection didn't feel like the right word. What they had went much deeper than that. But obviously he had been imagining it. "And then, boom, she kicks me out."

"A love 'em and leave 'em kind of girl, huh? I wouldn't have pegged Mona for the type."

"What is that supposed to mean?" he said, standing up. Was she calling Mona a slut? Sure, she'd trampled on his heart, but that was taking it a little far. Mrs. Harris had never been so . . . priggish before.

She always left that crap up to him.

"Calm down, cowboy," she said, putting a hand on his shoulder and sitting him back in his chair. "I just mean maybe there wasn't as much between you as you thought there was. Maybe she wants to keep it casual. Maybe she wants to get to know you a little. You haven't exactly been rolling out the welcome wagon for her."

Dan dropped his head onto his desk. He was an idiot. He had been a total asshole to her before yesterday; hell, he had been an asshole for a lot of yesterday, too. Why should she believe in his change of heart?

He believed in her curse, dammit. Why couldn't she believe that crazy things were possible with him, too?

"I told her I loved her," he told his desk.

"What? Oh, Dan." Mrs. Harris patted his back, then reached over and turned on his computer. "Oh, Dan, what were you thinking?"

"I was thinking I loved her!"

Mrs. Harris leaned on the corner of his desk, smoothing back his ruffled hair. "Well, sweetheart, sometimes . . . sometimes people don't do what we want them to. You can't control everything, you know."

"I know! I don't try to control—"

He stopped as soon as she raised her eyebrow.

"Fine, I try to control a lot of things. But not this. I mean, I wasn't expecting her to say anything back. I just had this feeling, and it was so strong. I've never felt anything like it before. It was so clear, right here—" He pointed to his chest. "How could it be anything but love?"

"Maybe it was the sex."

He sighed. "Yeah, the sex was . . . never mind."

"Dan," Mrs. Harris said, helpfully ignoring his comment about sex, "you can't control what other people do, or how they feel. You are a nice guy, and people like you."

"She doesn't."

"Most people like you. You don't have a lot of practice with rejection. But in time, this will pass."

"So I need to just forget about her?"

"This is a small town, so that's probably not going to work. But when she shows up today, just talk to her. Don't interrogate her. Just say hello, and if she wants to talk about feelings, she'll talk about feelings."

"Fine. But I'm not buying anything. That apple cake is what started all of this."

"OK, you don't have to buy anything. Now quit pouting and get to work. She'll be here soon." She looked over at the clock. "She should have been here by now, actually."

Dan had been really, really late. But Mrs. Harris was right, as usual. He would lose himself in his work and then, when he was feeling calm and in control of himself, he would go say hello.

But he still wasn't buying anything.

Even if his mouth was already watering thinking about apple cake. His stupid, traitorous mouth.

And that made him think of Mona's mouth, and how soft and sweet she was, and how she had arched and gasped underneath him, and how the moon had made her skin glow.

He put his head back on the desk.

"You've got it bad, haven't you?"

He nodded, but he didn't lift his head. He was never going to lift his head.

"I have to say, I'm surprised. I thought once you two finally stopped dancing around each other, you would really hit it off. You really seemed like you would balance each other out. Two sides of a coin." She shook her head and headed toward the window. "Well, I guess I was wrong."

Mrs. Harris was never wrong.

"She really should be here by now," she muttered. "I wonder if something's happened?"

Something was happening.

Mona pulled another tray of tarts out of the oven. She fanned her cow-shaped oven mitt over them, as if that would really cool them off faster. But she had to taste them.

The last batch had tasted like liver and raspberries.

They were supposed to taste like peaches and ginger.

She hadn't tasted the crust before she baked that first batch. It was barely sunrise, and she was exhausted and she had made this crust millions of times before. And she wasn't really thinking—not about run-of-the-mill pie crusts, anyway.

No matter how hard she tried, she couldn't get Dan out of her head. He'd just . . . left. She'd told him to go, and he'd gone, because, even though he was not always smooth or subtle about it, in the end he had always respected her wishes. He'd stopped talking about work when she'd asked him to, he'd left her alone in the kitchen when she'd needed it. He got her, and he respected her.

And now he was gone, and it was all her fault. The squeeze of panic that took up residence in her innards when he'd said that he loved her had not eased at all. In fact since he had gone, it had gotten worse.

What had she done?

But she had a business to run. Dan, if anyone, would understand that. She had decided she would track him down after work—there was no way he was going to approach her—and . . . well, she wasn't sure what, yet. But the idea that she would see him in a little over twelve hours made her feel better.

And then the tarts happened.

She didn't think she had ever cooked liver in this kitchen, so there was no chance of a postcoital haze mix-up. And yet, somehow, the ginger peach tart tasted like liver.

The real tell, though, was the aftertaste. The stuff she baked when her curse was off-duty always tasted really terrible, but the aftertaste was even worse. It was usually just sort of a general disgustingness, like the taste of bad breath. This, though, was stronger. It was an aggressive aftertaste that got up in her business and told her she was a coward.

Fear, with notes of liver.

That was hours ago. She had tasted the raw crust and it didn't taste like anything, which was not right, either. It should have been buttery, even before she baked it. But it tasted like . . . nothing. So she whipped up a new batch and let it rest in the refrigerator while she tasted all the other stuff she had made. It was an explosion of new flavor profiles, each one more disgusting than the last. Garlic and blueberry. Burnt popcorn. Briny marshmallows.

Horrible. Ruined. She looked at the clock. She should be out there by now. People would be waiting for their morning coffee-break treat. Darla James always stopped by before she opened the salon. Dylan Gunderson always sent someone to get a box of whatever was good for the guys. Mrs. Harris would pick a treat, then stick around to speculate about what her boss would choose if he wasn't such a stick in the mud.

Mrs. Harris's boss. Dan.

This had to be all Dan's fault. The moon was completely full last night. It was a blue moon, the fourth full moon in three months. It didn't happen often, but it happened every few years, and Mona knew what to expect—her curse lasted a little longer, and it was so powerful on the night of the blue moon, she barely had to do the baking. Pies and tarts and coffee cakes seemed to bake themselves.

That was the constant. Dan was the variable. Dan came over, made amazing sweet love to her, then told her he loved her and threw off her game. It had to be him. His love was somehow poisonous to her culinary arts. She was right to reject him, then. Imagine if she had given in to the instinct to fall into his arms, to say, yes, yes, this is crazy but I feel it, too.

Did she feel it? She knew she felt anxiety and dread, and now her pie fillings tasted like anchovies.

She pulled open the fridge and took out the oversized mixing bowl that held her pie crust. She steeled herself against Dan's love. She rejected him over again in her head. She didn't feel the kind of relief she had imagined she would feel, but she was sure her crust would taste right and would roll out into perfectly even, perfectly sellable pies. She took a deep breath and held it. No, she told the Dan in her head. Go away, I don't need you. She peeled back the plastic wrap from the bowl and pinched off a small bite. She rested the bowl on her hip and brought the crust to her mouth, open and ready for whatever flavor came her way.

Thirteen

"Mona? Mona!" Dan banged on Mona's kitchen door. At first, he had knocked hesitantly. He wasn't sure if she wanted to see him—well, he was pretty sure she didn't, but he had to make sure she was OK.

Then he heard a blood-curdling scream and a crash, and now he heard what sounded sort of like a donkey getting its tail pulled. But unless the nature of her curse had really changed, it was Mona crying. She must be hurt. What if her hand was caught in the blender? She had gorgeous hands; she had talented hands. He had to save her.

He pounded on the door, louder this time. "Mona! Are you dead?" Her responding wail told him she was still alive, but she definitely wasn't answering the door. He panicked. Something was really, really wrong and he had to get in there to see what he could do. He had never felt this surge of protective adrenaline before. He had always imagined that if he ever saw a burning building, he would call the fire department and stand politely away from the danger. But hearing Mona wail like that made the hairs on his neck stand up and made his blood run faster through his veins. It gave him power and physical confidence. He pushed his shoulder into the door; it didn't budge. There was silence in the kitchen, and then a less loud but no less painful moan. He backed up, then went at the door with all his might. There was a *crack* and the door flew open, and he landed on his knees on the kitchen floor.

"Dan?" The voice was wobbly, but it was Mona, standing over him with one of the biggest knives he'd ever seen.

He held his hands up.

"What are you doing here?"

He stood, took in her messy clothes, her red, puffy eyes, the streaks that her tears had left on her flour-strewn face, but didn't go any closer. She was still brandishing that knife.

"I thought something was wrong. Your truck wasn't downtown, and it's always there by nine-thirty."

"So you broke down my door?" She put the knife on the counter and wiped her nose with a paper towel.

"I called first."

Her chin wobbled and she shook her head. He didn't know what she meant by that, but she was crying again. He went toward her, and when she didn't back up, he pulled her into his arms and absorbed her shudders with his body.

"You ruined everything," she said into his chest.

"What?" He loosened his hold so she could look up at him.

"Everything tastes terrible and it's all your fault. It must be."

He couldn't imagine anything that she baked ever tasting terrible. She moved with such confidence and grace and besides, he'd tasted her apple cake. It was perfect.

"You don't believe me," she said, a wary look on her face.

"No, it's just that . . ." But he didn't believe her. Maybe it just wasn't as good as some other things she had made, and maybe that was because she was tired because he had been making love to her instead of letting her do her job.

"Here." She thrust a bowl of what looked like dough into his hands. "Taste."

He peeled back the plastic wrap, pinched off a piece, and confidently popped it into his mouth.

If Mona wasn't so depressed, she would be laughing her head off.

"It tastes fine," Dan said around a mouthful of raw pie crust.

But his face told her a different story. He smiled at her while he still chewed. He looked like he didn't want to swallow it.

She handed him a paper towel.

"It's not fine, Dan," she sniffed.

He spit the crust into the towel, then wadded it up and tossed it in the trash. "How is it supposed to taste?"

"It's supposed to taste buttery and a little sweet."

"It's not supposed to taste like burnt coffee?"

"It's not funny!" she said when she saw him smile.

"You're right, it's not. OK, let's whip up another batch. I'll help." He started rolling up his sleeves.

"That's just it! It's your fault it's ruined in the first place!"

"What? I didn't touch it, I swear!"

"But you're the only thing that's different. Everything else was exactly as I've done every other full moon. No new ingredients, no new recipes, same schedule. The only difference is that I slept with you. It must be your fault!"

"But I thought everything was going so well last night," he said. "I thought that on many levels."

"Yes! Last night it was fine, then I woke up this

morning and everything tastes like something died in it!"

"It's not that bad."

She gave him an eyebrow.

"I mean, it's inedible, but it doesn't taste like something died."

She threw up her hands. "It doesn't matter what it tastes like. Like you said, it's inedible. I can't sell this. I can't bring this to my customers. It's all completely unusable. If you hadn't come over and been so nice and sweet and sexy and then said that stupid stuff to me in the morning—"

"What stupid stuff? That I love you?"

She stopped. That was it. That was where it all went bad. "Yes. If you hadn't said that, I would be in the center of town right now having one of my best days of the summer!"

"Fine, I shouldn't have said it, since it clearly freaked you out. But I still feel it, Mona. I fell in love with you last night."

"Well, stop it!"

He laughed, but it wasn't the kind of laugh that sounded like he thought she was being funny.

"Believe me, if I could, I would, since you obviously don't feel the same way!"

No, she thought. That's not true.

"Listen," he said, taking a deep breath. "Let's just try another batch. What have you got to lose, right?"

"Dan, there's no way that can work."

"Come on, just one more. What do we need? Eggs? Butter." He started to gather up ingredients from the refrigerator.

"No, I'm not wasting perfectly good butter on a pie crust that's not going to taste right."

He ignored her and continued to pile stuff on the

counter. "What else goes in here? Flour?" He grabbed the bag of sugar and plopped it next to the flour.

"Dan . . ."

"Is there sugar in pie crust? I've never made it before, so you've got to help me here. What else? What's this?" He held up a bottle of vanilla extract. "Does this go in there?"

"Dan."

He opened it and sniffed it. "Whoa. OK, probably some of that, right?" He picked up the baking powder, brown sugar, honey, all kinds of things that didn't belong in a pie crust, and started piling them on the counter.

"Dan!"

"What?" He leaned into the bottom cabinet and pulled out a mixing bowl.

"I'm afraid!"

He came up quickly, knocking his head on the shelf.

"Are you OK?" she asked when he didn't say anything.

"No. My head hurts and the woman I love just told me she's afraid of baking."

The knot in her stomach twisted and clenched, and then eased a little. It wasn't panic. It wasn't anxiety that Dan would be too good to be true. It was fear. Fear that he was perfect for her, and that her life was about to change.

"Oh, my God," she said, and she flopped onto the kitchen floor.

"Mona?" He got on his knees next to her, a small circle of flour marring the jeans she'd just noticed.

She threw her head into her hands. "It's not your fault," she said.

He pulled her hands away and held on to them until she looked up at him.

"It's my fault," she said, finally meeting his eyes. And she saw it there, the confusion, the concern, and, most of all, the love. "It's my fault this got all messed up. It's my fault, because I love you, too."

A zing went through her, like a tiny lightning bolt, and Dan flinched a little, but he didn't let go of her hands.

"What was that?" he asked.

"It's back," she said.

He just looked at her, confused and in love. She loved looking at that face. How blind she was not to realize that before. Her fear had blinded her to the truth. Dan believed her about her curse, he stayed out of her way when he had to, and he was there when she needed him, even after she completely rejected him. He was addicted to routine and a little uptight, but he was steady, and he was willing to miss a morning of work to come kneel in the flour with her while she got her head out of her butt and realized that she loved him back.

She was cursed, but, it turned out, she wasn't stupid.

"I think you just said that you love me," Dan said, squeezing her fingers. "And then I think you electrocuted me."

"I feel better now," she said, and she stood up and pulled him with her. "I think I'm back. And I really want to kiss you right now, but I have a ton of baking to do."

"OK," he said, finishing the job of rolling up his sleeves. "Baking now, kissing later."

She grabbed the neck of his shirt and pulled him to her. "Just one kiss first."

"Just to seal the deal," he said, and then he didn't say anything else because her mouth was covering his and her arms were around his neck, and he lifted her and spun her around. Then he put her down, and they got to work.

Fourteen

Dan had really wanted to drive. Mona said she thought if his clients saw him driving a pink food truck, they might rethink his reliability and it would be bad for business. He could tell she just really wanted to drive the truck herself. That was OK; he would wait for his chance.

It was just after five, and what little rush hour Delicious had was basically over. But Dan watched the side mirror, and it seemed like every other car they passed turned on its blinker and made some dangerous traffic maneuver, and now they had a line of cars following them back downtown. A pink pied piper. Of pie.

He held on to the dashboard as Mona swerved into her spot, right across the street from his office. He glanced into the food part of the food truck, but it looked like the bakery was pretty secure. Of course; Mona knew what she was doing. He took a quick look over at her, her tongue pushing into her lip in concentration. He smiled. He loved this woman.

When they were in the spot, she unstrapped her seat belt and looked over at him. "Ready?" she asked.

"Just tell me what to do," he said, unbuckling himself and following her to the back of the truck.

They had baked all afternoon. Well, she did most of it, but she coached him on kneading and filling, and he put himself in charge of pulling hot things out of the oven after the third time she reached in without an oven mitt. And they tasted. Everything, from the apple pie to the apple cheese tarts to the top-secret pie (which was really just a mixture of leftover fillings from other desserts) tasted perfect. Light and homey and sweet. They probably looked a mess. Mona's hair was tied back in a kerchief, although she did have on a clean apron. Dan's shirt had long ago bitten the dust, and he was wearing the pink Apple of My Pie shirt she had given him the night before. He never went out without being polished and pressed, but now his jeans were covered in flour and bits of fruit. He didn't care. They had done it. He was proud of her, and proud that he'd helped.

And now they were going to sell some pie.

Mona swung the side window out, her arms strong and sure as she hooked the latch. There was already a small crowd gathered outside, their faces anxious.

"Mona! Where have you been?"

He wasn't sure who said it, but that was the general chorus from the crowd.

"Sorry," she said, shrugging. "Kitchen snafu. But better late than never, right?"

"Do you have any of those little tart things?"

"My mother-in-law is in town! I need pie!"

"What have you got that will go with roasted chicken?"

"Don't be mad, but I'm going to say that I baked it."

Mona laughed and worked. No, she didn't work. She was a whirlwind, boxing up orders and slinging them out to people, taking money and stuffing it into her apron. All the while, she kept up a steady banter, greeting customers by name, carrying on whole conversations that Dan didn't think he could do even if he wasn't also trying to slice a cake.

She was amazing.

And he was in the way.

But he didn't want to leave. He wanted to watch her, watch the power that coursed through her as she worked. It was similar to the power he felt rolling off of her in the kitchen, that controlled mania that produced meltingly tender pie crusts, but this was a little less intense, a little more familiar. So he just plastered himself to the inside wall of her pink food truck and soaked in some of her energy.

He could stand there, watching her make people happy, making herself happy, for the rest of his life.

Forever.

Mona turned. She thought Dan might have snuck out. She wouldn't have blamed him—she had kept him from his office all day, and he was wearing a pink shirt. But there he was, leaning against the only counter space he could have leaned on that would keep him out of her way. He smiled at her, and some of the manic energy she felt when she'd first opened the hatch dissipated. So she smiled back.

"Dan! There you are, I thought you'd died!" Mrs. Harris was leaning over the counter, her eyes on the inside corner of the truck.

"Hi, Mrs. Harris," he said, giving her a weak wave. "I'm fine."

"Well, you could have answered your phone!"

Mona saw him pat his pockets. "I don't have my phone."

"I know! You left it on your desk! Hi, Mona," she said, turning to Mona with a sweet smile. "What have you got tonight?"

"Are you the one who sent him over to me?" she asked

"Well, I may have suggested . . ."

Ha, suggested. Mrs. Harris knew exactly what she was doing. And for that, Mona would be forever grateful.

"OK, I forgive you," she said, handing her a white baker box. "Classic apple pie. Last one."

"Last one?" said Dan, coming forward to stand next to her. "We made a dozen of them!"

"It's a hot item."

"We've only been out here for ten minutes!"

She looked at her watch. It was more like half an hour, but she wasn't going to argue. He looked too shocked and impressed for her to argue.

"Gotta move fast to get what you want," said Mrs. Harris, winking at them.

"Weird," said Dan, just quietly enough that only Mona heard.

Mona leaned into him; she didn't know why. She just needed a little reassurance that he was real.

"She's right, though," he said, putting his arm around her.

"Mrs. Harris is always right," Mona said. Mrs. Harris waved on her way back across the street, her pie clutched firmly in one hand. Mona squeezed Dan's hand, then moved away to help the next customer in line.

"No," he said. "This time she's really right."

"Right about what?"

"About moving fast to get what you want."

"Well, I may have lied. There's still one apple pie back there—" Mona turned to show Dan her secret pie stash, where she had been saving one pie for them to share later, a reward for all of his hard work. But she stopped, because Dan wasn't standing where she had left him. Instead, he was down on the ground in front of her. On one knee.

"Dan," she whispered. "What are you—"

"I want you," he said, reaching for her hand. "I love you. I know it's fast, and I know it's crazy, but it feels so right, why shouldn't we?"

"Why shouldn't we what?" she said, glancing at her now-curious customers.

"Marry me."

"What?"

"Yes!" said the crowd.

"Marry me. I don't want to waste another minute being too uptight to see what's in front of me. I don't want to let my dumb preconceived notions deprive me of the biggest gift I have ever been given. That's you, Mona. You're not cursed, you're gifted, and I want to spend the rest of my life appreciating how wonderful and talented you are."

"Do it!" someone from the crowd shouted.

"Dan! This is crazy! We can't—"

"Why not?" Another shout from the crowd.

"Because," she said. Because every gift she had ever been given was a curse in disguise. But . . . maybe she had it all wrong. Maybe Dan was right, and her baking was a gift, and the conditions that came with it just meant she should treasure it, treat it preciously. And he was a gift, too. God, it was so cheesy, and she couldn't believe those words had even come out of his mouth. But he wasn't wrong. He had come to her rescue when she didn't even think being rescued was a possibility. He was a mild-mannered, orderly superhero. In khakis.

They were good together; they could only get better.

"Answer him, would ya?"

"OK," she whispered.

"OK, you'll answer him, or OK, you'll marry him?"

Dan stood up and punched the latch out of the window. It slammed shut in the face of the crowd.

"Sorry about that," he said. "I didn't mean for this to be so . . . public."

"Did you mean for this to happen at all?"

"No. I never in a million years could have imagined someone as perfect for me as you are," he said. "I don't think I have that kind of creative capacity."

"But here I am."

"Here you are," he said, taking her hands. "And here I am. What do you think?"

She looked at him, his eyes clear as the summer sky, and she knew she would always have this from him. Openness. Honesty. Love.

"OK," she whispered.

"As in, OK, you'll marry me?"

She nodded. "OK, I'll marry you."

He whooped, a distinctly un-accountant-like sound, and wrapped her in a tight, joyful hug. She laughed and threw her arms around his neck.

"So did she say yes?" came muffled voices from outside.

"Yes!" shouted Dan, and she laughed again, and kissed him.

When they finally came up for air, Dan reached over and opened the side window. They were greeted with cheers and whoops, and she laughed and cheered with everyone. This was magic. A car drove by, honking, and Mrs. Harris waved out the window and drove off into the sunset.

Read on for a sneak peek at *Jamie* by Lori Foster, coming next month.

When she lay naked in front of him, the proof of her perfect body there for him to see, Jamie took only a moment to absorb the sight of her before hefting her into his arms. She wasn't a petite woman, but then, he wasn't a slouch. He could, *would,* carry her—as far as necessary.

With his right hand, he snatched up her torn pile of clothing. It had been so long since he'd held anyone, since he'd allowed himself the comfort of physical contact, that his heart felt full to bursting, pounding hard and fast. Never mind the mud and rain and whatever ailed her, she still smelled like a woman: soft and feminine and ripe with sex appeal.

He'd missed that smell so much.

First things first. Rather than climb back up to his cabin, Jamie made his way to the west, toward the plunging edge of a cliff. He looked over to a deep ravine cut through the mountain by a fast-moving stream, now swollen from the heavy rains. Tightening his hold on the woman, he reared back and slung her clothes over the side. The ruined garments soared, sank, and hit the creek with a dull splash, separating, dragged along by the current to get dumped a good distance away from him.

Just getting rid of the clothes made Jamie feel better.

She could still have a surveillance device on her body somewhere, and he'd check for that as soon as he got her out of the foul weather. She might not like his thorough inspection—what woman would? But then, he didn't like being hunted, either. Given the howling wind and stinging rain, it looked like they both had to tolerate a few things.

Even burdened with the woman's weight, the climb to his cabin didn't tax him. Whenever he went anywhere, he walked, so his legs were strong and he had an abundance of stamina.

The woman didn't make a peep, didn't open her eyes again, but she must not have been entirely out of it, because her arms went around his neck and she tucked her face in near his chest to avoid the rain. Prodded by a strange yearning, Jamie curled her closer still, even bent over her a bit to afford her more protection. He could feel the rapping of her heartbeat on his chest, her gentle breath on his throat.

Cravings he hadn't suffered in far too long awoke within him. He didn't like it. Or maybe he liked it too much.

He knew the moment Clint spotted them. He felt the sheriff's shock and curiosity slapping against his already heightened senses. Eyes narrowed against the rain, Jamie forged onward, refusing to look back.

Clint called to him, but his words blew away on the storm. Knowing the woods better than even the bears, Jamie easily lost Clint by moving between trees and boulders and across narrow streams.

By the time he reached his cabin, he knew Clint had turned back. What tales he'd tell to the others, Jamie could only guess. But when the rain stopped and the mud dried—tomorrow or the next day—they'd come for him.

He knew it as sure as he knew the woman in his arms would be trouble.

And still, he carried her over the threshold and into his cabin.

When he nudged the door shut with his shoulder, she shifted, making a small, purely feminine sound of discomfort. Charmed, Jamie watched and waited for her to become fully aware.

She lifted her head slightly. Her gaze shied away from his, and she took in her surroundings, then, blinked twice. No smile. No fear. But she had nervousness in spades, almost equal to her tenacity. While Jamie continued to hold her, she licked her lips, hesitated, and finally turned her face up to his.

His awareness on a razor's edge, Jamie assessed her. Mud streaked her pale cheeks. Her long, wet hair tangled around his shoulder. Her lips shivered with the cold.

Taking him off guard, she lifted one small, woman-soft hand to touch the side of his face. "Thank you."